Greater Good

Steve Wash

Brothers, sisters, where are you now?

ACKNOWLEDGMENTS

I would like to thank my family. You have supported me through my dark days and you have stood by me. Thank you to my friends who helped me by proof reading this work, Carl, Nick, Chris, Mark and my dad Jim.

Of all people that have supported me and given me the self-belief to write the most important is my wife Jo.

Introduction

I needed to set this book somewhere. It could have been set anywhere. Any of the Northern Towns would have worked. I know Scunthorpe, I know the town. That geographical knowledge was important to the plot. The journey between the everyday life, in which we live, and the fiction in this book is not so great. Behind the facades of the towns and cities of England. Behind our communities and cultures is a different world. Not some farfetched alternative dimension or some parallel universe but the seedy, and all too real, world where sex, violence and innocence are a commodity. At what price that commodity? Is the value of innocence higher than the value of loyalty when the scales are loaded?

The current scandal taking place in Rotherham has made this work all too topical. It provides a backdrop of sordid credibility to the story. The tragedy of fourteen hundred victims lost youth bear silent, or at least unheard, witness to that credibility.

Thank you for reading.

Chapter 1

Tanjoc, Guatemala.

May 6, 1994.

The jungle was alive with movement. Movement all around. The only still things in the jungle were the soldiers. They had been still since before first light, it was now ten thirty, just gone. They were British soldiers but they wore American clothes. No standard issue British army combat kit. Their kit was made in the USA but it was made for hunters in the Southern states. There were only two of them. Not a standard eight man section or four man fire team. Just two of them. They carried Remington shotguns. No British issue rifles or machine guns.

The problem was simple. They were operating in Guatemala, Central America; a country hostile to Britain. In fact if any of their kit was examined there would be no way to identify who they were or where they had come from. Deniability.

Their mission was to watch a junction north of the jungle hamlet of Tanjoc. The American intelligence agents said that they believed that workers from Tanjoc were transporting coca leaves up to the junction where they passed it over to others who would take the raw leaves into the jungle factories and refine it into the cocaine that was swamping the streets of America and Western Europe.

The Two soldiers were to watch the junction all day and then at night extract and return to Belize where, the next day, they could get heli-lifted out of the jungle and returned for a full debrief to Airport Camp, Belize City. It would be a long and boring day. Both of the men had done this mission dozens of times over the past months. They had been in the field now for two weeks, today was their last day on the observation point. They occasionally saw a kid walking by or maybe a rough four wheel drive pick-up truck pass if it dare brave the terrible 'roads'. Whilst laying in the brush Bombardier Pol Winchester passed the time by allowing his mind to wander. It is a trick at which he had become expert. His body could lay there in the weeds in the forty two degree heat and humidity whilst his mind was at home with his wife or in the bar enjoying a nice cool beer. Any movement on the track only thirty meters away from him would snap his attention firmly back to the here and now.

Pol's right ankle was crossed over the ankle of Lance Corporal Stuart Hicks. Hicks was from a different regiment to Winchester, but since they had been in Central America they had worked together regularly. It was almost accidental, Hicks' normal partner had been bitten by a coral snake and was evacuated straight out. It was fortunate that Winchester had been in the camp at the time. He was the only radio operator with the required experience available for the senior ranks to use. Hicks' unit was the Special Boat Squadron. There had been some resistance when it was suggested that the Artillery unit supply the signaller to the observation team amongst those senior officers. But Winchester was a tough veteran of Northern Ireland and Operation Desert Storm. Since his move over he had become a fully integrated team member. He had fitted in very well.

The man appeared on the track in front of the soldiers. He was coming from Tanjoc. He was carrying a large cotton pack on his back. The pack was huge, it seemed to bury the man and give him a top heavy appearance. The man had a pair of dirty beige bloused trousers on and pink flip flops. He wore the ubiquitous Manchester United football shirt. He wasn't a young man, maybe fifty years old but it was difficult to tell with these people. His Hispanic features like old leather.

The pack on his back would have been harvested from the small fields in the jungle. Cut out with his machete, dug by hand with a spade. The product of a year's hard work. He would have a family to support and the coca crop would be the thing that fed them throughout the year. The only cash crop that was available to these subsistence farmers. The Anglo American Narcotics Intervention Team searched for the fields and sprayed them with weed killer. The farmer would lose a year's crop and income. He was a victim of the war on drugs.

The soldiers watched him. Prior to stepping out into the jungle the soldiers had looked over albums of photographs of the local people suspected of being involved in the coca trade. They knew this man. They had never spoken to Jesus Vinales, or his wife Gabi, but they knew him by face, they knew where he lived. They had studied him, amongst the folders and files that the analysts had prepared. Seeing him in person gave him identity and took him from the realms of theory and into physical existence. Pol knew that Jesus scratched a living on a patch of dirt near his one room shack in Tanjoc. As Pol watched him walk slowly along the track underneath the heavy load of the coca leaves he was overwhelmed with a feeling of empathy for this man. He was forty five years old, younger than the fifty plus that he looked. He was unlikely to make fifty. He would be broken down and worn out before that.

The soldiers brief was to simply watch and report back. The track was close, in the jungle everything was close. Thirty meters away from the soldiers the mud at the edge of the rutted track started. Winchester and Hicks lay concealed in the spreading shadows of a large leaved palm. Their faces painted in green and black stripes. The hollows around the eyes pale green, the raised areas of the cheeks dark to give them shadow. The shapes of the faces hidden and disguised by the black camouflage paint. Sweat beaded on Winchesters brow, ran and joined in rivulets on his eyebrows and ran down his nose and dripped onto the jungle floor. One drip at a time. A small pool of salt rich sweat formed on a leaf below Winchester's head. Insects, smelling the salts, came in to drink in this small oasis. Winchester lay still and watched as Jesus walked in front of him as a small jungle fly left the pool and flew up and landed on the cheek of the stationary soldier. The soldier had controlled his breathing. His breaths were shallow and controlled to be minimize movement. The fly, on the soldiers black painted cheek, bit and drank the soldier's blood. The pain was sharp and hot as the fly feasted on him. The soldier lay still, his breathing calm his attention trained on the man in the red tee shirt.

Hicks and Winchester were part of the jungle. Fully

committed to the brief. Weapons in their hands with safety catches off. In the chamber of the Remington shotguns were loaded commercial buck shot. Each cartridge contained only nine lead balls. Each one of these balls weighed the same as an individual nine millimetre bullet and travelled a third faster. The impact of one shot from one of these soldiers' guns was more than the impact of nine pistol bullets at one time. But, using the weapons was a last resort. Any shot would compromise their position and potentially prejudice the operation. Emerging onto the track behind Jesus came a small mongrel dog. This was an unexpected complication. The dog could cost the operation's integrity. He could scent the soldiers and bark. The jungle was not good for tracking and scent. The heavy humidity and profusion of wildlife hampered the spread of scent. Not many people could afford to keep a dog in the desperately poor existences they suffered. There was no record of Jesus owning a dog. He turned round and looked behind him at the dog.

"Hola Chico" the dog wagged its tail and approached Jesus. Clearly the dog knew the old Guatemalan farmer. Pol watched carefully as the drama started to unfold in front of him. The intelligence section had not mentioned that Vinales had a dog. It was possible they didn't know, but they knew of other farmers with dogs; that was always in the profile.

The dog was a small mongrel, uniform brown in colour with erect pointed ears and a long high tail. Not much bigger than a spaniel. He fussed around Jesus' legs and the as the farmer continued under his burden the small dog ran along with him.

It seemed as though the dog and farmer might walk along the track and out of sight with no further incident. Pol hoped so, the pain of the insect that was on his face was becoming really quite distracting and he really wanted to brush it away. The dog stopped in its tracks and pricked its ears. Pol saw the change, he could feel Sticks tense up through their touching ankles. Jesus continued to walk.

"Just keeping walking, Jesus" Pol willed silently.

The dog's hackles rose and they could see, although not hear, the dog was growling. Its lip pulled back in a snarl exposing his white canine teeth.

"Aqui Chico" They both heard Vinales say to the dog. They had very little Spanish but enough to know that Vinales was calling his dog to him.

The dog barked.

Jesus turned round and looked at the dog, he looked at the edge of the jungle. He looked directly at where the two British soldiers lay concealed in the shadow.

"Lo que pasa, muchacho? bandidos?" Vinales spoke to the dog.

The word "bandidos" was all that Pol could get from the sentence. Occasionally the farmers would get robbed by desperate bandits on the forest tracks.

The old farmer looked scared as he stood rooted to the spot and surveying the impenetrable wall of jungle foliage in front of him. He let the big bale of leaves fall from his back and on to the ground beside the track.

He stood for a second as if caught in two minds of what to do. Both soldiers willed him to pick up the bale of leaves and head into the jungle.

The dog started to bark continuously and advance on the soldiers. This was not going according to the plan and pattern that the two soldiers, hidden in the jungle, were used to.

Jesus stood looking towards the dog and took a step forward.

"Buen perro, ¿dónde está"

The British soldiers could not understand that Vinales was praising his dog, but the tone of his voice was clear. He stepped towards them. As he stepped off of the track, within twenty meters of the men, he reached with his right hand behind his head and between his shoulder blades.

With a deepening sense of despair the soldiers watched him pull a large parang from behind him. The parang was a heavy bladed jungle machete, originating in South East Asia but had now become accepted as the best machete and in universal use. The blade was over a foot in length with a deep cutting edge. The type of weapon that would kill easily with one blow.

Jesus stepped off the track and closer to the soldiers, the little dog in front of him, the barking continuous and only interspersed with snarls and growls.

"You take the dog" Hicks breathed to Winchester. The words were so quiet and gentle they could be no indication of what was to follow.

Pol slowly moved his right hand down to his waist belt and from his belt pulled a knife from its sheath. Not the big heavy survival knife of Rambo fame but a long narrow bladed dagger called a Fairbairn-Sykes. The razor sharp blade was nearly twenty centimetres long. Finished in a gunmetal black it remained invisible in the shadow. There could be no discharge of guns in the forest, the crash of the report would be heard all around.

Jesus was now slowly walking toward the soldiers through the scrub between them. He weighed the parang in his right hand and held it close in front, blade vertical. As he looked to one side and then the other the soldiers moved their legs forward and got in a position to get to their feet quickly.

The dog had stopped barking, he was just growling and advancing with his head held low now. He knew how close the soldiers were.

Jesus was now only a meter from the soldiers who remained concealed in the bush. He turned and looked in the direction he had come from and both soldiers knew this was the moment. Without any speaking or communication they exploded from the cover. The hours of inactivity had been overcome by the constant exercises they had performed keeping the circulation moving. Clenching of the toes and calves whilst lying motionless.

Jesus and the dog were startled both leaped back a step to be confronted by the two big and heavily armed men with black painted faces.

Pol took one step forward and as he dropped down towards his knee he was able to plunge his knife in between the dogs front legs, he knew the point would penetrate deep into the heart of the animal and that his death would be almost instant and painless. Withdrawing his blade he turned to his right to assist Hicks. He did not need any help. Hicks was highly skilled with a knife and as Jesus had swung the parang down in a sweeping vertical arc Hicks neatly stepped to the left of the swing and transferring the knife to his left hand he grabbed the farmers right forearm isolating the parang and with his left hand struck between the collar bone and the side of Jesus' neck. The point of the dagger swept through the aorta inside of the old farmers chest and within a second the degree of blood loss made him unconscious and death followed seconds later. There was little blood, the narrow blade of the dagger left a small puncture wound. The bleeding was all internal.

Pol swatted the fly from his cheek.

"I'll search him" said Hicks.

Meticulously Hicks checked over the dead Guatemalan every pocket checked and turned out, he had nothing. Not a single Guatemalan Quetzal, nothing. They searched him for evidence or intelligence that might be of use to the agency. But the man carried nothing of any use to the soldiers.

"We can make it look like bandits have done this" Said Hicks.

"For sure, but your job looks a bit neat for a bandit job"

"If we hack him about a bit and chuck the dog in the bush then it will be ok" Hicks replied.

"What, chop his corpse about?" Winchester asked, looking directly at Hicks.

"Yeah, not many bandit murders are done with a technique practiced in Poole," Replied Hicks bending down and taking the parang jungle knife out of the hand of the still warm Jesus. Vinales.

Pol was incredulous, he understood clearly why this had to happen. The killing of Jesus had been unavoidable and necessary to keep the operational security intact. But this was the mutilation of a human.

Hicks said "Just stand back a bit, Pol, don't want you to get blood all over."

"Ok mate", Pol took a few steps back but he was fascinated by the ghoulish spectacle unfolding in front of them. Hicks raised the parang high above his head and struck Vinales across the top of the head, he grunted with exertion as the dark steel smashed through the dead man's skull and into the brain. The blood, brain and bone fragments splashed up Hicks arms and in to his face. The SBS man wiped them away and carried on with his work.

The bright sunshine shone off the exposed white skull, the man's head had split open and gaped open three centimetres. His scalp shrunk away from the bone and his brain was exposed below. Both of his eyes were open and as

Pol moved away he felt like they were following him. Big, dark brown Hispanic eyes, still clear. They had not yet fogged up with death.

"Just hold his arm up for me, Pol" asked Hicks.

"Yeah, no problem, why?"

"They need to look like defensive wounds, like he has had his hands up to protect himself" replied Hicks.

"I see," Said Pol as he lifted Jesus' arm up and across his face.

"Venir aquí, buen perro, ¿dónde estás?" The voice carried clearly through the jungle. It reached the soldiers and they stopped their macabre work.

Both looked directly at the source of the voice. They both saw the boy at the same time. He was watching the soldiers, he saw what they were doing.

"Abuelo, es lo que," He said.

As he finished his sentence he turned and ran back down the track. He was running back towards Tanjoc. If he got there he would tell the people what he has seen. How he had seen the two soldiers chopping up his grandfather.

Pol had no choice. He needed to stop him getting there. Pol set off in pursuit. As he ran down the rough, rutted, muddy track he closed on the boy. As he did he realized how small the boy was. He was less than one hundred and fifty centimetres tall. He overhauled him quickly and grabbed him round the throat. The boy was only about twelve years old.

"No me hagan daño, por favour" The soldiers would never know that Jorge Vinales was his name. He was ten years old. He was helping his grandfather in the fields during a school holiday. They would never know that he loved his little mongrel, Chico, and his old grandfather. They would never know how his mum, Maria, worked as a prostitute three nights a week so that young Jorge could go to school and she hoped that her nameless sacrifices could pay for him to have a different life away from the coca leaves.

Pol knew that he had no choice; that the little boy must die to preserve their mission. At what cost their mission? Was this little Guatemalan boy a cheaper price than an American boy from the Midwest heart land of the republican electorate?

The soldier spun the boy round so that the boy was held tightly against the left hand side of his chest. His right arm went around the boys head, he could feel the sweat of the boy's brow on his wrist. His fingertips touched the soft top of Jorge's ear. His right hand crossed the boy's face lower. His fingertips hooked behind the jawbone of the boy.

With a sudden explosive application of power he broke the boy's neck. There was no loud Hollywood style crack or snap.

Pol felt the dislocation as the resistance in the neck gave. He knew that the two vertebrae would shear against each other and he knew that the boy's spinal cord would be severed the second he felt that. The dislocation was high in the neck, at the atlas joint. The pathway for the impulses that made the boy's heartbeat was cut. He was dead.

Pol held the dead boy close to his chest as he felt the boy twitch involuntary. He could feel the warmth of the Jorge's body. Jorge felt so small and light in his arms. A warmth spread onto Pol's thigh as the boy's bladder voided. The boy was still.

Pol stood in the middle of the track with mud on his boots. The track stretched before him towards Tanjoc. Behind him towards the junction of the tracks. The track cut through the solid wall of the jungle like a river gorge. The walls of the gorge were made of large leaves and jungle vines and creepers. Jungle birds flew backwards and forwards across the gorge. The screech of the parakeet just another noise in the cacophony that is the normality of the rainforest wildlife. The vista continued around the motionless soldier now holding the boy he had killed. For Pol the world stood still. This had not been a hot contact between fighting men with weapons, this had not even been a planned strike on a target that was engaged in terrorism. This had been a murder to Pol. An innocent had been murdered to allow a report to be sent to a faceless suit in an office. Pol didn't even know which country the suit's office sat in.

Waves of sorrow built up and gathered momentum, they swamped Pol with black hopelessness. He lifted the body of the boy and took it into the jungle just a few yards away from the edge of the track. He threw the body into the bush. The animals of the jungle will strip him to bones within days. He swallowed down the power of the raw emotion that had threatened to overwhelm him and turned back to the track. He would see Jorge Vinales in his dreams. In the longest darkest watches of his night, Jorge would be with him always.

He broke into a trot and made his way back up the track where he soon came upon Hicks who had finished his macabre work and was washing his hands in a muddy puddle in one of the ruts along the track.

"All done mate?"

"Yeah, sorted." Pol replied.

"Ok mate, let's get the fuck out of here"

The soldiers took a drink from their water bottles and looked at each other for a few seconds. The bond between them was sealed in this moment.

They put their water bottles in their webbing pouches and unslung their shotguns. Pol worked the pump on his gun and chambered a cartridge.

"You, better believe it, let's fuck off, I need a shower". Said Pol.

They turned and headed through the green wall and back into the primary jungle. Under the canopy the light was muted and dull. The soldiers slid soundlessly through the half light of the jungle. The moved with silent, smooth fluidity. Became part of the fabric of the jungle. Each footfall was placed and rolled out. This prevented any sticks being broken underfoot. The men patrolled back through the jungle towards the Belizean border.

The border was not far from the track near Tanjoc. As per their orders the soldiers performed a snap ambush. This was purely a routine to be sure that they had not been followed by the Guatemalan army. Both men knew that they had not been followed. It was not arrogance it was a realistic evaluation of their skill set when compared to any opposition that they might find within this theatre. They would soon be at their admin area, an area where they had left their large ruck sacks.

Two hours passed as again they lay in the sweltering jungle mid-day heat. The humidity was very high and both men were sweating very heavily, they lay still. Pol's eyes fixed on the game trail through the forest that they had used as their route. In his left hand he held the claymore clacker. The device, correctly known as an M57 detonator is a small pulse generator that would fire the claymore mine. The claymore was concealed just off the game trail in a small depression. The tactic was simple. Should any enemy personnel come along the track Pol would engage them with the shotgun. The following men would seek cover from the fire in the small depression. When they did the claymore would be detonated raking the whole depression with a deadly spray of steel balls, there could be no survivors in a contact like this. As soon as the claymore was detonated the two British soldiers would deploy a smoke grenade and extract back down the track. Back towards the border, although out here borders didn't stand for much. The line on the map was a long way from the sweaty heat of the close jungle contact. Here the contacts were close, visibility was short and ten meters was quite typical. Sometimes Pol could actually smell the men, sometimes after the contact he could smell the blood and the stench of the smashed intestines and stomachs. This type of fighting was personal and close.

This time there was no contact, no patrol of Guatemalans winding their way after the British soldiers. After the two hours had passed the men rolled over, sat up and drank deeply from their canteens. They each took two salt tablets to make up for the electrolytes they had lost and sat quietly for a moment. Without saying a word they got back to their feet and made their way east. They recovered their back packs from their concealment under a large spiky bush.

They hefted them on to their backs and continued through the jungle. They moved less cautiously now whilst under the huge weight of the packs. The area they had planned to spend the night was only three and a half kilometres away. Three and a half kilometres was a long way on foot in the jungle heat.

The men were now well inside Belize and prepared to spend the night in the jungle. The helicopter extraction was due at first light. They quietly sorted out their camp. Hammocks and mosquito nets were essential. The rain started to fall heavily on the men as they put their hammocks and ponchos up.

The rain washed the remaining morale clean out of Pol's spirit. The poncho was up and held tight between trees with elasticated cords. Pulled taut over the hammock and sloping steeply to drain the rain away. His back pack suspended on a cord beneath the poncho to keep the rain off and the snakes out.

Pol lay in his hammock listening to the rain on the poncho. The jungle animals and insects imposed their own wall of noise over the descending night.

"Oi, Winnie, you ok?" Stu's voice ventured from the dark.

"Yeah mate" Pol replied, he actually felt very far from ok.

"Was he the first for you?" asked Stu.

"No, but before it was not like that. It felt like I murdered him" Pol confessed.

"Think about it, mate. You know the score, you had no choice it has to be that way"

"I know this. Have you got any antihistamines in the first aid kit? This fucking bite is going to shut my eye if we are not careful." Pol said.

"Yeah, no problem"

A moment later a hand appeared from the darkness at Pol's hammock and passed two tablets in.

"Here you are, sweat. They should help take it down."

"Cheers bro, it is fucking killing me" said Pol.

"So, your others weren't like that?"

"No mate, only two before"

"Oh right, where were they?" asked Stu.

"One in Belfast and one about five miles north of here."

Pol did not expand on it any further. He knew that talking about the day's operation would help him deal with it but he did not feel like talking about it. He wanted the shelter that sleep would give him.

In most theatres the men would have posted sentries and would have shared the night watching the tracks. When darkness fell in the jungle its inky blackness was impenetrable and prevented any sort of military operation. There was no need for sentries here.

"Mate, I am fucked, I need some sleep. Let's have a beer

tomorrow night"

"Alright, Pol, now cock off" Sticks replied. It had become a standing joke between the men.

Sleep came quickly for Pol. Jungle operations are extremely demanding and tough on the body. The next day they would return to camp, get cleaned up and embark on a recuperative feeding regime to try to replace the weight they had lost in the jungle.

It was late in the night when Pol awoke, the darkness of the jungle made him ache to hear. His vision was null and void, hearing the only sense he could rely on. The jungle animal night shift had commenced and unseen animals screeched and called through the darkness. The rain had stopped. He lay still, not sure what had disturbed his sleep. The bite on his face was swollen, his skin felt stretched and hot. His mind wandered towards home. He tried to remember how his wife's body felt in his arms. He tried to remember the taste of her kiss, the shape of her breast. She was very far away. She felt very far away.

Through the dark the image of the dead boy burned itself into his consciousness. Try as he might he could not get the image out of his head. Pol slipped back into the realms of sleep, Jorge Vinales went with him and stayed with him in his dreams until first light bought him some welcome respite.

"Come on Stu, let's get down to the pick-up point."

"Fuck me Merrick boy, seen your mush?"

"No. Is it bad mate?"

"Yeah, sure is, you need to get to the med centre when we get back in, I reckon it has got infected", said Hicks.

The soldiers packed up their equipment in a few minutes and stowed it in their packs. The small jungle clearing was only two hundred meters from their overnight spot and soon they were in position.

Pol opened his back pack and took out the radio set. The Clansman PRC 320 was a heavy and bulky piece of kit to carry. The radio set was eleven kilograms and the batteries a further four. Normally this radio was carried as a full back pack on its own. But in this case it was just another piece of kit in Pols back pack. The radio used an end feed trailing wire antenna which was defined by the frequency of operation. In this case pol had to wind out fourteen meters of the green cable. The angle and direction of slope was important to the propagation of the signal and with his compass he located the correct direction. He tied some normal green string to the end of the antenna and a stick on the end of the string. Throwing the stick over a low branch he was able to pull the string down and establish the correct angle and direction on the antenna. With the radio attached at the end he knelt bent over the big high frequency set and adjusted the tuning. High Frequency radio was the only method to get reasonable range of communication in 1995.

He plugged in the telephone shaped hand set.

"Hello zero this is November four two, over"

HF whine and feedback. Pol cleared his throat as if that

would make the signal clearer.

"Zero, send over" the voice from the radio responded.

"November four two, we are at point charlie zulu, awaiting alpha whisky over" replied Pol, alpha whisky was the helicopter unit's call sign.

"Zero, roger figures ten, out"

Ten minutes until the helicopter arrived and lifted them to civilization.

The radio was dissembled and packed away. The men waited and strained their ears for the sound of the aircraft. Pol's face was sore now, very swollen and hot. His eye was not closed, but it was close to being so.

The sound of the aircraft built slowly into their consciousness from a low and distant thump building all of the time until it became clear. The two bladed Bell Iroquois seemed like a throwback to Vietnam and the jungle war in that theatre. Pol mused on this as he waited the last couple of seconds and he thought about how the lessons had been learned there by the Americans and the SAS had been translated into the new tactics they had employed in the jungle. The British SAS has rotated its soldiers through the operation under the guise of the Australian SAS. The combat effectiveness of the Aussies had been legendary. Together with the British they were able to carry forward the skills learned in Malaya and Borneo and had taken to the jungle in small and flexible units under the command of non-commissioned officers to hunt down the Viet Cong in their own environment.

Low to the canopy the helicopter appeared up the valley. The American captain piloting the old bird looking for the clearing, he knew the landing would be tight, normally only with a couple of feet to spare around the rotor disc. Sure enough this pick up point was cut in dense jungle.

"This is a tight one, Zak" he spoke to his co-pilot.

"Yes sir, this will be close, I can't see them or any smoke" Lieutenant Zak Cohen was a recent arrival in the Anglo American team, a fine pilot just learning his way round the jungle.

"You won't see them, they will appear and get in"

The captain spoke as he gently put the helicopter into the centre of the clearing with inch perfect precision. As the skids touched the ground the load master opened the doors.

Cohen saw two figures appear from the tree line and run to the helicopter. Both were so dirty the pattern on their fatigues was indiscernible. Both men bearded and one of them had an injury to his face. The two men they were collecting had been in the bush for over two weeks on hard routine. Their skin was orange tinged with the anti-malarial quinine tablets they had taken and the effects of the sun under the canopy.

The load master pulled their heavy packs on board and the men climbed into the cabin, sat in the orange nylon webbing benches and strapped themselves in. They unloaded their shotguns as the helicopter left the ground and very quickly they were both sound asleep. The pilot flew low out of the jungle, the rollercoaster ride did not disturb the exhausted sleep that had overwhelmed them both.

Twenty minutes later skids were down at Airport Camp, Belize City. The soldiers climbed out of the helicopter and dragging their back packs with them they walked in slow motion towards the Nissan hut. They handed their shotguns in at the armoury.

"Winny, get yourself to the med centre mate, your face looks bad"

"Yeah, will do Sticks, just going for a shower and to get changed and I will. What about debrief?"

"It has been set for 10.00 tomorrow morning." Replied Hicks.

"Ok mate, let's have a beer later"

They would not go for a beer, Winchester's insect bite had become infected and he spent the next five days in the military hospital on intravenous antibiotics. Hicks gave the debrief in the morning and when he disclosed the killings that had taken place in the field it was decided that they could no longer operate in the theatre. Hicks was flown to Fort Bragg in Carolina where he temporarily joined a training team. When Winchester had recovered sufficiently from the infection he was returned to his normal artillery unit. It was as if Tanjoc had never happened.

Chapter 2

Scunthorpe 2011

The house was not what Stu Hicks had in mind. He had
gone from being one of the elite warriors of the British forces
and found himself unable to hold down a job. Twenty years
of elite soldiering had not prepared him for this. He had
been out for over two years now. There had been a series of
menial jobs. Security man at a shopping precinct, the
economic collapse had seen the town centre collapse in its
turn. There had been no need for a security guard in a
precinct with boarded up shops. They let him go.

There was always mercenary work. Offers had been
forthcoming regularly. He was very good at what he had
done. He was one of the most skilled people in his field. He
had established a reputation for solid professionalism. The
thought hurt now, a skilled professional, a professional at
what? A professional at killing. He was not sure anymore.
The tide of his certainty seemed to have ebbed away from
him. He handed it in when he handed back his uniform. The
direction and order that at one time had governed every
aspect of his life was removed from him. No, he would not
re-enter the sphere of combat soldiering. He knew his
dreams were filled with the faces of the dead already. There
was no more room in there to add more.

All the time in the Royal Marines and then in the Boat
Service he dreamed of living a life free of the fetters of
military discipline. He was trying to live that life now. He
grew his hair for the first few months and stopped training.
But he looked at himself in the mirror, saw the man he had

been fading away behind the blood shot eyes and belly. He looked for his soul and realised the more he abandoned it the more it abandoned him. He saw behind him his wife Dianna. He saw the sorrow in her eyes. The more of him that he lost, the more of her he lost in turn. He looked at the decay before him in the mirror and knew that this was a deciding point in his life. If he failed to deal with what he saw he would lose all he ever was and all he ever could be. He turned from the mirror and kissed Dianna as he walked past her into the kitchen. He walked to the fridge and opened it. There was a case of Kestrel super strength lager. With no hesitation he reached for a can.

Dianna cried inside. The silent sob of a person watching the man she loved destroy himself certain in the knowledge that she would not be able to curb this streak. She heard the ring pull open, the hiss of the beer froth. A minute later she heard another. It would be one of those long nights of picking up the pieces of her broken man as he sat crying on the floor like a child scared of the monsters in the wardrobe. She decided to make herself a coffee, it would be a long night. She got up from the sofa and as she walked through she heard another can open. She stepped into the light of the kitchen and picked up the kettle. It was empty. She walked the two steps to the sink and as she filled the kettle Stu stood beside her. He popped another can, that was four now. She looked him in the eyes, he didn't smell of beer. He poured the beer into the sink. It ran down the plug hole and away into the drains. He placed the empty can with the other three on the work top. He crossed to the fridge and picked up the remainder of the case of beer. He said nothing as he emptied all of the beers down the sink. She knew he was not a man to make false promises. This might be a corner that he was turning.

Silently he walked through to the bathroom and she heard the buzz of the hair clippers start. He knew if he looked better he would feel better. In the bathroom mirror a different face looked out at him now, older, greyer, a little heavier. He could get the weight off, the years would stay.

The iron industry had built the town into what it was, in the industrial revolution the town hammered out huge quantities of iron and steel for the new locomotives, ships and trains. The exploding economy's thirst for the iron town's products was matched only by the works' appetite for labour. The Crosby area of the town housed the majority of these workers in the newly built, red brick terraces. The housing built in linear streets backed onto each other with gardens and alleyways between. Early in their life, when the iron industry was healthy, they were smart and well maintained with gardens turning out vegetables to nourish the families.

A hundred years later and the area was very different. The steel industry had reduced and employed only twenty percent of the amount of men. The houses had been bought up, cheap, by investors and landlords. Many had been split into bedsits or flats. They now provided cheap housing, with all that goes with that. The pristine gardens were gone. The alleyways now a jumble of rubbish, burned out cars and filth. Rats ran in these alleyways, pursued by feral cats and dogs. Waves of immigration had given the area colour and life. The smells of Asian cooking enriched the area. The area had housed many of these immigrants within the cheaper housing. Many had come from Pakistan then Somalia after World War Two to work in the furnaces, in the steel mills. Prospects were now sparse for the children and grandchildren of that pioneering generation. They gathered

on the street and hung around in gangs. The latest waves of
migrants moved into the area from the former Warsaw Pact
countries of Poland, Latvia, and Lithuania. Like the previous
waves of immigrants they sought out opportunities to work
hard and make a little. Some sent their money home to
family. Others spent it on vodka.

When Hicks retired from the service he had invested his
savings in a nice house in the village of Kirton Lindsey, in
Lincolnshire, ten miles away from the town of Scunthorpe.
He had a small mortgage to pay and a steady job as a
security man in a shopping centre. The job was not a big
earner, but on top of his pensions it would be ok, they would
be able to afford the small mortgage that was outstanding on
the house. This was until he was made redundant. With only
his pensions and no wages coming in it was a matter of time.
Dianna had found a cleaning job in the big new medical
centre on West Street in the town centre. But it was not
enough to stop the rot. Sure enough the HSBC foreclosed on
the mortgage and the house was repossessed. Stu had gone
into the local branch to talk to the manager, to try and work
something out with him. It had not gone well. The young
manager was governed by what the computer told him and
could not make any other decision. Stu had asked him for
some sort of discretion and just a couple of months whilst he
got back on his feet. The lad had made the mistake of telling
Stu that he was not in the army anymore and people didn't
do what he told them. Stu's reply of "It was the fucking
Navy, you jumped up little fuck. Go and get a fucking
grown up to sort this out, cunt", ensured he could only do
his banking on the phone or the internet from then on.

So Stu and Dianna found themselves tenants of a house on Acheron Street. They wanted to keep themselves to themselves and just get on with their life. They could shut the world out behind the curtains and be together. They had visited the rescue kennels and rehomed a German shepherd dog that Stu had insisted on calling Winston. He liked to take Winston down to the memorial gardens and throw a ball for him. Dianna watched their bond grow and she knew that Winston was a major part of Stu now.

Later in the night Stu lay awake and thought whilst beside him Dianna snored quietly. Winston was down stairs, he had the run of the ground floor at night, if anyone was foolish enough to break in then he would be waiting to greet them. Periodically the flashing blue lights of a police car or ambulance would illuminate the room through the light curtains. Stu thought about how he could make his way forward and how he could start working again. He decided he would have to get fit and take up one of the adverts for "interesting work abroad". He could no longer run from who he was. He has a very specific skill set that Her Majesty's forces had given him and he needed to work to his strengths.

He felt desire starting to rise in him again. He knew that he had been very down and this had really damaged his libido. He could see the hurt in Dianna's eyes when he had rejected her advances. It was time to put things right and start to get a grip of himself, and her.

She was softly snoring laying on her side facing away from him. She slept in a dark blue vest top and a pair of briefs. He could smell her body as he moved closer to her and reached his hand onto her hip. The smooth skin of her body felt warm and soft to his touch. He moved closer again and wrapped his arms around her.

He held her tightly to his chest and felt her breathing through her skin. She was so close and she turned him on so much. The feelings flooded back to him. He slid his hand into the front of her panties, he felt her start to wake.

The response was not what he expected, she grabbed his wrist and pulled his hand away from her and moved away from him.

"Don't touch me" she said.

"What's wrong?" He was confused and hurt by this rejection. But then he had rejected her enough times over the past couple of months.

"I don't want your hands all over me. I am not just some kind of piece of meat for you to maul when you want to."

"What are you talking about?" he asked in a small voice.

"Look, just get away from me" she sat up on the edge of the bed and turned on her bedside lamp. She turned and sat on her pillows, pulled her knees up to her chest and hugged them tight. She buried her face between her knees and cried.

He could see her shoulders shake as she sobbed deeply and he saw the tears on her naked thigh. Her long chestnut hair was becoming wet as she cried more and more tears.

"What's wrong?" He asked simply.

She made no reply and just carried on crying, weeping.

He sat on his side of the bed with his back to her. "Is it me, Di?" he was scared that his problems and all of the rejections that she had suffered at his hands had now caused her not to want him.

"It's not always about you, for fuck sake" she replied in a sobbing voice.

He was in turmoil now. He knew he had not been the best husband of late but he had always loved her and wanted her. He was a different man to the one that he was when she married him. Maybe she was fed up of working and living in this place when she had been used to a nice house and plenty of money in the bank. The days of driving a two year old car were now passed for them. Indeed they could not afford to drive at all now.

He got up, pulled his jeans and fleece on and slipped his trainers on. "I know I have not been up to much lately, but I love you and I only wanted to love you tonight to let you know that you are still everything to me. I am going for a walk." She had wounded him deeply.

"Winston, wake up, time for a walk" the dog was fast asleep stretched out on the sofa. He was nearly as big as the full three cushions of the old three seater. The dog lifted his head and opened his big brown eyes. It was just after half past two in the morning. He looked as if he would say "What, at this time?" Once Stu had picked up the lead and tennis ball from the worktop Winston was at the door wagging his tail and ready to go on this late night excursion.

They stepped out of the back door and walked down to the alley way that ran between Acheron Street and Percival Street. It was a mild May night. The air was heavy with the smell of sulphur from the remaining steel works. A slight mist filled the air. Stu was convinced that the steam of the cooling towers would decent on high air pressure and make the town always damp and misty. The sky was illuminated by the deep orange glow of the blast furnaces. It seemed to reflect down upon the mist and low clouds above the works. The rumble of the machinery of industry echoed across the town. As the man and his dog walked down the path towards the alleyway Winston curled his lip back and started to growl. Stu secretly hoped there would be some local thug wanting to chance his arm in a mugging or an attack. He was in the mood for some of that.

They stepped into the alley way. Stu saw what Winston was growling at. In the dim sodium street light there was a black rubbish sack spewing its contents across the alleyway. The bag had been torn open by the feral dogs that now stood over it. One of the dogs was eating the contents of a disposable nappy whilst another held a can with its front feet and had its muzzle inside trying to reach in. The alley was littered with bin bags, and carrier bags, there were beer cans and plastic two litre cider cans randomly distributed along its length. A dark shape ran from a pizza box and into the shadow of the garage across the alley. The garage was a wreck now, the door hung off. Inside was dark. Old Mr Karnas had kept his little Honda 90 in the garage for years. He used it for work. Every morning he would kick it over and ride it to the poultry processing factory. Until the kids from the Acheron crew broke in and took it. They rode it up and down the street, round the alley way. Mr Karnas was scared to go out and challenge them. They burned it in the alley.

Now the garage was a haven for rats and for junkies and street drinkers. Mr Karnas had quietly moved away.

Stu bent and picked up a piece of broken brick that lay in the alleyway. He threw it in the direction of the mutts at the end of the street. The brick bounced into the bin bag near to one. They looked up and saw the man and his dog and ran from the alleyway and around towards the memorial gardens.

"Heel boy" The big dog did not really need to be told to heel. He was immaculately well trained and well behaved. He walked close to Stu's left calf. Both Stu and the dog were alert and aware as they made their way through the alleyway amongst the waste from the houses and the dog shit that littered the old street.

As they got down to Teal Street they turned to the right towards the patch of green space that had been left when the old houses of West Street had been pulled down. Piece at a time the old Victorian houses were being swallowed up and removed. Compulsory purchase orders seemed to be issued freely for people's homes to be torn down and wild flowers planted in the space where the community had been once, long ago.

On the other side of the green space was West Street. Late night traffic continued to move up and down the street. Pedestrians walked up and down, drunks from the town centre, young men in their tracksuits and their pseudo hard man swagger looking for trouble and then there were the working girls. Stu had imagined that Central America and the third world had a monopoly on this type of squalor. But it was alive and well here in Northern England. He felt such sorrow when he looked at the girls, they weren't dressed up in glamorous mini dresses and big boots. The customary dress for the working girl in Scunthorpe was tight jeans and

a hoodie. They plied their trade for just a few pounds. Most
of them had terrible drug habits and used heroin or crack
cocaine every day. They were shadows of people, the real
world zombies of the underclass. The sorrow he felt for them
seeped into him. Di couldn't have kids, these whores had
once been someone's little girl. He wondered what sort of
upbringing had lead them to this. He wondered if, when
they were little, they had been transplanted to somewhere
else and to some other parents would the same destiny await
them. They paced the street under the false lights. Trying to
make eye contact with the occasional passing car. They
continued to work and ply their trade whilst a police van
drove down the road past them. The van didn't stop or slow
down when it passed them. The cop, sat in the passenger
seat turned his fluorescent back to the window and the pain
as it passed the girl.

Further up the street he saw a young couple in the shadows
at the full extent of the streetlight's reach. He recognised the
lad. It was Kharon Khan he lived just across the street from
Stu and Di. He lived with his mum and younger brother.
Sometimes an older man would visit the house, maybe an
uncle. The mum and the older man dressed in traditional
Muslim clothing and the man wore a large full beard.
Kharon had changed a lot in the couple of years since Stu
had known him. He was no longer the polite Asian boy that
always said good morning. He was now strutting around
the street at all hours with a group of other boys in tow. He
wore designer jeans low on his back side, that style just
irritated Stu. Whenever Stu saw him he said hello to the lad.
Kharon had stopped saying hello to him. With Kharon

tonight was a skinny white girl. With a mop of died black hair. Stu walked towards them with Winston. He could see the girl more clearly as he got closer. She looked young, maybe only fourteen or fifteen years old. It was difficult to tell with these girls they all looked so skinny and dressed so alike. Kharon was quite a lot older than she was. Stu thought he was approaching twenty years old now.

He could hear the conversation with between them as he got within about ten feet of them.

"You know I love you, if you loved me you would" Kharon said to her.

"I don't know, I am going to be in trouble anyway" The girl replied.

"They don't love you back there at the home, I love you, I care" He continued.

"I know you do Kazzy" she kissed him on the lips.

Stu was level with them. "Hi, Kharon, how are you?" He asked civilly.

Kharon turned to him with a look of savage malevolence in his eyes. "If you have to talk to me you can call me Kazzy Mad Man" and gave a loud hissing exhalation.

Stu was taken aback by this boy's arrogance but did not rise to it.

"Yeah ok, Kazzy Madam" he replied with a chuckle in his voice. He walked on. He heard Kharon say to the girl how he would kick Stu's white arse. Stu laughed a bit to himself.

That boy was losing his grip on reality now he was running with the Acheron Crew. He would have a word with the boy's mum or that man he thought was the uncle. The Pakistani community were respectful and decent people, he knew they would deal with this.

He turned into the park and stood in the dark. He liked the dark. Darkness was his friend. He could see out but no one would be able to see him. He did some of his most savage soldiering in the darkness of the jungle or under the impossibly inky desert night skies. He allowed his eyes to adjust to the night and watched the dog. Winston's ears and nose were better in the dark than Stu's eyes. He could hear grunts and shuffles in the bushes near the gate. Probably one of the whores and a punter doing their 'business'. There was drunk laughing coming from the far corner interspersed with loud voices swearing in an eastern European language, maybe Polish maybe Lithuanian. He guessed a group of about five or six drunks, not a threat to him.

"Shall we play ball?" He said to his dog.

And he threw the ball out for the big black dog. As the dog ran out for it across the grass Stu stood and thought about what had happened at home. He wondered if this was it for Di and him. He wouldn't blame her if it was. He was not the man that he had been. He had not been near her for ages. He had it coming. It was just sad that this had happened today when he had decided to turn the corner in his life. He might have to go on alone. Di and the dog were the only people that he had in his life now.

Winston sat in front of him and presented him the ball.

"Good lad, let's go again". He took the ball from the dog and threw it again. He continued to muse over his current life. He threw the ball again and sent the dog. He would go home and settle himself down on the sofa. Then in the morning would have a chat to Di and sort this all out. He felt a lump rising in his throat. Emotion was not a new thing to Hicks but he tried to keep it in check and control its effects on him.

"Ok," he said to himself, let's go and sort this out. He turned and walked from the Memorial gardens and headed back towards his house. Kharon had left Teal street, the girls still worked on West Street. No matter what time of day it was there were always girls working on West Street. As he walked up the filthy alleyway he could see the lights in his house were on, the bathroom at the rear of the house and the kitchen lights spilt white light into the alleyway. He was a little worried about what he might find when he arrived at home. Would his bag be packed for him or would it be Di waiting to go.

He unlocked the back door and stepped into the bright and clean kitchen. Di was sat at the table. She was wearing her white towelling robe and a white towel on her head like a turban. Her skin was red and scrubbed from the shower. She had put the filter coffee machine on and there was a jug of strong dark coffee filling the air with its wonderful aroma. Stu, not for the first time that night, felt confused.

"Stuart, let's have a talk, there are some things we need to sort out". Di said as she poured him a coffee.

"Right" he replied, he felt nervous and a little shaky. He sat down at the table with his coffee in his hands, he looked down at it. He averted his eyes from her.

"The first thing that you need to know is that I love you, Stuart Hicks" Began Di.

"I love you too, Di."

"You are the only man in my life and the only man that will ever be in my life. But there are a few things that you need to know about me", she continued.

"Ok", he replied.

"I have never told anyone the things I am going to tell you now, please don't say anything until I have finished, this will be really tough for me to do."

"Ok, I won't say a thing" he replied.

"You know that Michelle and I were in care when we were kids?"

"Yeah for sure," he said. Michelle was Di's sister, they were pretty close although Stu didn't like Michelle much. He thought that she was a shallow and workshy skiver that had never worked a day in her life.

"Well it all happened then"

"Yeah, ok, what did?"

"Well we were in a children's home in the town at that time, I was about thirteen and Shelly would be about fourteen. We depended on each other and looked after each other. The children's home was a rough place to be. The carers didn't care. For sure, they were professional enough, but that's not the same as caring. I started to come across town and hang about on Frodingham Road."

Di had never spoken to Stu about her upbringing before, he knew nothing of this.

She continued, "I started to knock about with an Asian lad in the town. Back then he worked in one of the kebab shops" Stu was watching her eyes now as she spoke to him, they were filled with a great sadness. "He treated me well, showed me some affection, or so I thought at the time. He used to give me cigarettes and beer, I thought it was great to start with. I was only a kid and I fell in love with him. It was an escape from the care home life and a little bit of something that was mine. Shelly used to come along with us and soon this lad's mate started to go out with Shell, we double dated. The lad was a couple of years older than me and used to work in one of the restaurants as a waiter. I don't know where he is now." Stu saw the lie on her face as soon as she had said it. She knew where he was but didn't want to tell Stu.

"Ok", Stu said.

"Well I had been going out with him for a week or so, he used to encourage me to stay out all night and not go back to the children's home. The staff would report me missing and the police would come and look for me. He would tell me that the police would take me away from him if they found me. He said that they would lock me up so that we couldn't be together. I believed him and did what he said. I viewed the police and the carers as my enemies. He would get me drunk and then have sex with me. I had only just started my periods and wasn't ready for it. It hurt and made me bleed. But he used to tell me that he loved me and that I would do it for him if I loved him too. So I did." She looked back to his face.

Stu reached forward and over the table he clasped her hands in his. "It's ok, sweetie" he said to her. She was crying.

"Why haven't you told me before?" He asked her.

"I am so ashamed of it and worse happened to me. I just never wanted you to know. One day he said that if I loved him he would take me to see his friends in Sheffield. I was excited. He had kept me separate from his friends and family because I wasn't a Muslim. So I thought this must be quite an honour."

Stu had no idea about this part of his wives life. This was a journey into the unknown for him.

"When we got to Sheffield he took me to a house, like ours, and we went in there for a drink. I had a couple of drinks with him but he had spiked mine. I only had a beer or two and I was so drunk I could hardly stand. He led me through to a room… Oh Stu … I am sorry" she sobbed and put her head down on the table. A second later she had recomposed herself and was sat back up, tears ran down her cheeks. Her eyes blood shot and red rimmed. She continued. "In that room there were lots of older men. All Asian, all of them laughing and joking. In the middle of the room was a table. He said to me "If you want me you get undressed now." So I stood there in front of all of them leering and letching men and stripped down to my bra and panties, I didn't know what they were saying, they didn't speak in English. The men all watched me as I took the last bits of clothing off. He got hold of me and pushed me down on the table. The men all raped me, there were fourteen of them. They raped my mouth and the raped my bum. They all hurt me so bad. Some of them took me several times over." She had stopped crying and looked angry and tough. "When I left there I was bleeding and hurt. He threw me in the back of his car and drove me back to Scunthorpe. He didn't speak to me at all. When we got to town he said he had something to take away the pain and injected me with heroin. It washed away the pain, but left me numb. I felt numb without the heroin. When we got on Frodingham road he told me to fuck off and called me a 'Kafir bitch.'"

Stu reached across to her and stroked her face.

"That's why I can't have kids. My cervix was torn and I got infected. I kept it quiet and went back to the home. By the time I got really ill the infection had spread and I was sterile."

"Oh my God, You should have told me."

"I know, but I am so ashamed of it, I was used and soiled and broken by them."

She wiped her running nose on the sleeve of her dressing gown and reached over and held his hand.

"Stuart Hicks, I love you more than anything you can imagine. Tonight when you touched me I was dreaming of it. It made it flood back and I am sorry. It wasn't you Stu."

"That's ok my sweetie. I am so glad you told me I thought it was me, you know that we can overcome everything together"

She went on, "they never got to Shelly. I am scared for Rhianna, I love her, she is like our daughter. Shelly isn't like me and she doesn't keep a close enough eye on her."

"No, Di, she is not like you. There is only one of you!" They both smiled a welcome smile in this most intense of conversations. He continued, "She will be ok, she is doing well at college and will be fine"

"Yeah, I hope so."

They talked until the morning. They talked about how Stu felt they had turned a corner and that it was time for them to move on together. Time for him to get another job, maybe some security contracting. In the morning Di went to work, Stu went running and then looked online for work.

Chapter 3

Scunthorpe 2011

Police work was tough. Police work in the North of Scunthorpe could be very tough indeed. Sgt Pol Winchester drove the marked police van down Frodingham road at, what he termed, patrol speed. This translated into a steady crawl of about fifteen miles an hour. It meant that should something happen he could stop the van and get out to deal with it. It also meant that he could be seen by the community for the maximum amount of time. He knew that he had very little actual time to patrol so he had to maximise the exposure. Frodingham Road was a tough beat to have. The old part of town with its tough Victorian side streets, social housing and slum lords had attracted the cheapest people to the cheapest houses. Crime was rife in the area. With the cheap housing came the unemployed of the town and the welfare state dependants. Drug use was endemic in this community. Heroin and crack cocaine the drugs of choice for the residents of this end of town. As Pol slowly drove past the chapel on the Frodingham road he saw the group of street drinkers. He pulled the van up and climbed down. Suddenly forty years old didn't feel quite as young as once it did. His ankle hurt as soon as he put any weight on it. It was twenty years previously on a rainy Belfast day when the Provo explosion had bowled him off his feet and broken his ankle. Three operations later and he knew he was going to need another before too long. There was a cycle of recovery, a period of stability then it would deteriorate. The conclusion to this cycle would be the next operation. He was due a bigger one this time, a graft. This period of deterioration was the part of the cycle he was now experiencing again. The weight of the stab resistant vest and the equipment belt aggravated it. Each time he took a step the fluid in his ankle joint was forced down into the fissures at the top of his ankle bone. The hydraulic effect of this caused the bone to fragment. The fragments were loose in his ankle and had an abrasive effect in the joint compounding the injury and preventing movement.

This group of drinkers had started to cause a nuisance to the local people. They met up before ten in the morning, every morning, and sat on the benches. The drinking started early and the super strength lager and cider was drunk by the gallon. So by mid-afternoon the gathering had become drunk and raucous. Drunken arguments spilled across the pavement and often erupted into clumsy fights. They would relieve themselves in the street and as Pol walked towards them he was hit by the strong scent of urine. It was approaching mid-afternoon in late May. The sun was shining and the drunks were in fine form.

One of the regulars stood up when the lone police officer approached, he staggered towards the officer. "Do you want a can sergeant?"

"No thank you, I am on duty" The sergeant replied professionally.

He spoke to all of the gathered drunks, there were ten of them sat on the wall around the church. "Listen up guys, I came round yesterday and moved you all on, you are all back today. What happens is every time we come round I record who is here. In a week or so we will get ASBOs for you. Then we will arrest you."

The group murmured and one lone voice shouted out "Fuck off, black bastard"

The cop was not fazed by this sort of thing. The medal ribbons on his chest represented some really tough challenges not the slurred insults of drunks.

He continued "You all know that I am a reasonable man and that I always show you guys respect".

Some murmurs of ascent.

"Now, later on I am going to come past here again and I am going to get the constables to come along here. We are going to start to enforce the alcohol exclusion zone now. This is the last warning before we go down that line"

The drunk that initially greeted the sergeant with the offer of a beer spoke up, "Ok Sergeant Winchester, we have got it, but we have nowhere else to go"

"Yeah I know that, Robin, but the thing is people around here are getting a bit fed up of this mess and the bother that you guys are causing them"

Robin Chamberlain had been a problem to the police in Scunthorpe for ten years. Pol Winchester had arrested him many times and they had cultivated quite a rapport.

"Alright then, Sarge" Chamberlain replied. It always amused Pol when he was addressed as 'Sarge' by the people he had arrested and dealt with in the charge room when he was custody sergeant.

He knew that later in the afternoon Chamberlain would be the worst of the drunks, he would be shouting abuse at passers-by and publicly pissing in the street in clear view of the main street.

"Right everyone, I have to be off, remember we will come later and look to lock up if you are drinking in the street"

He turned and walked back to the marked police van. As he climbed up into the vehicle he sat in the driver's seat and watched the group of drunks drift away and evaporate into the alley ways and side streets. They would be back soon and his team would be trying to make an arrest or two tonight to keep the council happy. He wrote in his notebook as he sat there, he had to get it up to date for the day and he might as well do it whilst he was there in the van in the street where he could be seen. On the other side of Frodingham road was a small youth club. It had been converted from a shop and it was now called the Acheron Multi-Cultural youth centre. It had been claimed by the Acheron Street Crew as part of their territory now and as he sat watching the door he saw the self-styled leader of the teenage gang walk out. Kharon Khan was a smartly dressed Asian lad. He was nineteen years old but not working. Pol had done some homework about the lad. He called himself Kazzy Mad Man. It made Pol chuckle to himself when he heard that. Walking behind Khan was his sidekick, a lad called Nuelleh. He was part of the large Somali community and ran with the Acheron Street Crew. Pol was not sure of what part he had to play in their organisation but he was always there, he seemed to be a trusted lieutenant of Khan. They liked to wear some signature piece of clothing. Khan wore a tight knitted black beanie hat with a picture of a revolver embroidered on it. The rest of his clothing was always black except for a red lace in his right shoe. Nuelleh wore a red lace in his right trainer, his signature clothing was a thick leather belt with a heavy oval belt buckle.

Pol was just looking down to his notebook to continue his work when he caught sight of a young white girl following the two boys from the youth centre. He recognised her instantly as Jasmin Peters. The shock of died black hair made her very conspicuous. She was dressed in clothes he thought inappropriate for a girl of her age. The mini skirt and loose low cut t-shirt hung off her slight frame.

Jasmin's face had appeared on the briefing today. She was missing from the council children's home in Ashby and had been away for two nights. She was just fourteen years old and had been in care since she was a small girl. Pol remembered the case when her mother was sent to prison together with Jasmin's step dad. It had been very difficult for Pol to believe that Jasmin's own mother had been there when the offences had been committed and allowed her husband to do those things to the little girl. There had been some suggestion at the time that she had known from the very beginning that he wanted her only for the little girl and she had encouraged the acts.

Now the girl was starting to fall through the cracks of society and would soon be one of the many statistics. He could already see it starting, the regular missing person reports then it would be minor crime and shop theft. Before long she would be another user and would be on the streets 'grafting' for her heroin and crack cocaine. Just another statistic. Wasted.

Pol sprang out of the van and ran across the busy road and into the alleyway behind Acheron Street. Nuelleh was there but Jasmin and Khan were nowhere to be seen.

"Where did they go, Mohammed?"

"I ain't seen no one, five-O" Nuelleh spoke in his most gangster drawl.

"Don't be an arse, Mo. Where did they go?" Pol repeated the question.

"I aint helping you, dog. You don't show me no respect you don't get none" Nuelleh said, again in his best gangster voice.

"She is just a little girl"

"Not to us, she is nothing" Nuelleh replied.

Anger welled inside Pol. He would like to grab hold of this boy.

"Ok, Mo. We will get you, you know" Pol said to the boy as he walked out of the alleyway and back to Frodingham road. He turned and walked into the youth centre. As he walked in the few remaining lads in there became quiet. There were a couple of pool tables and a large flat screen TV on the wall. The screen showed an Arabic language channel. Abdul Mohammed, the youth leader, was also in the room. He held court. As the policeman walked in the lads all looked towards Abdul. He was a tall, Asian man. Abdul once told Pol that his family had originated from the Kashmir region of Pakistan. But that was his grandfather's generation. Pol guessed he was towards thirty five years old. Slim build and sporting a beard around his jaw line with a shaved moustache. He wore jeans and a t shirt but a small and neat embroidered kufi hat.

"Good morning, Pol" Abdul greeted the sergeant.

"Morning Abdul, how are you?"

"I am well, and how are you?"

"Thank you for asking, I am also well. Abdul, a few minutes ago Mo Nuelleh, Kharon Khan and a girl were in here. Had they been here long?" Pol asked.

"They were not in here today, Pol" Abdul replied.

One of the boys sniggered.
"I just saw them leave here a few minutes ago" Pol added.

"I think you must be mistaken, Sergeant Winchester"

Pol looked at the man, he had just seen the girl leave the premises. How could he lie so blatantly?

Abdul continued, "I am at a meeting with the divisional commander later this afternoon, should I tell him that you called by or is this unofficial business"

This instantly aroused disdain in Pol, There was no need for him to say this. This was simply a pulling of rank and a posturing manoeuvre by Mohammed. Pol knew he was part of the Divisional Equality Council.

"Mr Mohammed, you can say as you wish to the divisional commander, my business with you is always official"

Pol looked him straight in the eye and said his goodbyes. As he turned to leave he heard one of the lads round the pool table call him a "Kafir", Pol knew this was an Islamic insult for unbelievers.

He stepped back onto the pavement and the sunlight. Crossing the road he got back into the patrol van and headed back to the station for a cup of tea and a meeting with his inspector. He liked the Inspector and it was a chance to chat about how the team was developing and progressing. He knew that this meeting would be about target setting and the direction that he wanted Pol to take with his work. Pol would have to mention the problems with his ankle. As much as he would like to think that there was no problem it was clear there was. Pol was not able to do foot patrol anymore. Generally this was no problem, as a sergeant he had very little time to foot patrol anyway. He spent the majority of his time in meetings and at his computer terminal. But the annual fitness testing had just about as much as he could manage now. Running on the bleep test had been really impactive on his ankle and he suspected this would be the last time he would be able to pass the test.

"Afternoon, Inspector" Pol walked into the inspectors office and placed two cups of tea on the desk and a packet of chocolate Hobnobs.

"Sergeant, how are you doing?" Inspector Philip Robinson was ten years younger and had ten years less service than the sergeant. He was being groomed to go places, that was clear. But things had suddenly taken an unexpected move for him when he was moved from being the youngest ever Detective Inspector to a Neighbourhood Policing Inspector. Pol suspected that something had clearly happened, he must have really upset someone.

"How is the world of inspecting today, sir?"

"Very well thank you, how is the world of tough police supervision, Sergeant?"

The formality of the banter was very tongue in cheek. Both men had real respect for each other and had become great friends.

The conversation covered the increasing productivity of the team and general management issues then moved to the difficult question of Pol's fitness.

"Pol, Graham from officer safety training has called me. He says you struggled on Tuesday's fitness test."

"Yes sir, it was tough, I am not sure if I can do many more before I have the next foot operation".

The use of 'sir' did not escape the inspector's attention. They had been chatting on first name terms immediately before this topic had arisen.

"You know, Pol, I will support you through this and I would rather have you as my sergeant than anyone else"

"Thanks, Guv'nor, it is appreciated."

"Pol, we need to look at the policing plan targets for the next three months"

"Ok, there are a few things starting to brew up that I would like to try to get a grip on" Pol said.

"They are pretty prescriptive I am afraid mate. Burglary dwelling, shop theft and burglary non-dwelling" The inspector read from the email directing him.

"Ok, we have made significant improvements within that and we will continue to see that over the next couple of months. The offender profile for the majority of this volume crime is the same. The group of people we are already targeting are the most prolific offenders in those fields. We will continue to see that."

They discussed how the drug intervention processes that they put in place had worked. Both men knew that few very active criminals really pushed their statistics high. So they had worked to get the most prolific offenders on methadone programs and watched as their drug fuelled offending tumbled.

"Boss, what do you think about the Acheron Street Crew?"

"We have had direction from the DCI that we are not to get too involved with them"

"I think they are up to all sorts of stuff" Pol said.

"Give me some sort of evidence that I can take back to the DCI" the inspector asked his sergeant.

"What about all of the intel forms that we have been

submitting about them?"

"I am going to need more than that, have you got a snout in there?"

"No, Guv, we can't get a snout in there. They are either juveniles or they are Asians. We find it really tough to recruit from that group"

"Are you sure Pol? You can normally talk them round to our way of thinking."

The sergeant was coming up against the same brick wall. He understood that the inspector would not yield on this. He tried a different tack.

"What do you think about Abdul Mohammed, from the youth centre?" Pol asked.

"Why Pol?"

"Well I saw that misper from Ashby side coming out of there with Kharon Khan and Nuelleh. I swung in there for a chat with Mohammed and he said that he hadn't seen them. I know damn well he was lying to me"

"He is a pretty big fish in the community and is a big hitter with the chief super, I hope you have got something solid to run with because if you piss them off you open a whole big can of fuck worms for yourself."

Pol admired the inspector's pragmatism. The boss had not ordered him not to go near him and he knew for sure that the sergeant did not have a 'too difficult' tray on his desk.

The Inspector looked at pol in the eye. He suspected that the youth centre was, at best, part of the Acheron Street Crew's 'turf' and at worst but most likely that the pillar of the community that is Abdul Mohammed was part of something bigger, darker. The inspector had suspected for a while that the area's drug supply and prostitution was being looked after by the Acheron Crew. The prostitutes working twenty four hours a day on West Street used to talk to the police. They were victims of the sex and drugs trade as much as anyone. They used to be pimped by their junky boyfriends. Their boyfriends seemed to have faded away from the street and now whilst the girls worked there was a group of boys in the background watching from the memorial gardens.

The vulnerable girls from the children's homes were turning up at this side of town more and more often. The Inspector watched them as they slowly faded away from society. The first time that the kid went missing the police would give it a big response. But when they had been missing every day for three months that response had started to slip to nothing. The girls' identity to the police as an organisation had changed from the victim to the pain in the arse regular misper. And so the view of the police as the enemy to the girl was reinforced and the conflict between authority and the 'glamour' of running with the Acheron crew was already lost.

The Inspector wanted his sergeant to go after this crew and put them away one at a time, where they belong. The email from the DCI directed him to leave them alone. Directed him to focus his efforts on the commercial burglaries and the massively decreased house burglaries. He knew that he needed to tread a fine line with Pol. Pol was savagely loyal to him but if Pol felt he had been betrayed by the inspector he would have no compunction about letting him take the flak. So whilst he did not personally order Pol to leave the Acheron crew alone he informed Pol that the DCI wanted them left alone and the potential consequences for crossing the line and kicking over the equality hornets' nest. He knew that Pol understood what was going on and would go about his business in a professional manner.

"Ok, Guv. I suppose we will have to see how things pan out for the time being" Pol said. That simple sentence confirmed both of their understanding.

The meeting then followed the normal course of a personnel briefing by the sergeant and a general chat about the performance of the team. This was interspersed with the odd anecdote. As Pol got up to leave the room the inspector said, "Be careful Pol". This struck Pol as being unusual. He replied with "Thanks, boss. I will do, you keep safe too".

Pol returned to his office via the station kitchen with a fresh mug of tea in his hand. He sat at his computer and continued to wade through his daily email list. The station was empty, his constables and community support officers were out on patrol. He could not help thinking about the girl Jasmin Peters. He was quite sure that the Acheron Street Crew had taken to recruiting these young and vulnerable girls for moving of drugs and also, he suspected, they were procured for sexual exploitation. Although this would be a very tough one to evidence. Girls that had been victims of this were not often willing to talk to the police. Often they had been so well conditioned by the shadowy figures that orchestrated the abuse that they didn't even know that they were being exploited. Sipping his brew slowly pol thought about how he could bring the problem into the spotlight so that he could sell it to the inspector and so that he could sell it to the DCI. He knew how carefully he had to tread. Only two months previously he had been in front of the inspector explaining why the stop search submissions had shown a higher proportion of non-white people had been stopped and searched than the data showed that North Lincolnshire had as population. Pol had later been able to show that within his beat areas the groups that had been searched were in proportion with the population. The meeting had been uncomfortable and there was the insinuation from the senior management that he had acted in a racist manner and his team had been targeting the ethnic minority groups. Pol had totally refuted this and now felt suspicious of the reticence in dealing with the issues he saw.

He opened a new email:

To: Scunthorpe North all staff

Cc:

Bcc: Robinson. Phil

From: Pol Winchester.

Subject: Vulnerable Mispers

Dear all,

It has recently seemed that more than our fair share of vulnerable mispers are turning up on our beats. Please can you all make sure that when you parade that you check the briefing for the day's mispers and keep observations out whilst on your duties. Please submit any sightings on an intelligence report and copy me into it. Please make sure you get a full description of any person they are seen associating with.

Thanks team

Pol

He would wait and see what that produced. Nothing in that the DCI could criticise and nothing to suggest the Inspector was party to the request.

He collected up his coat and helmet. Closed his pocket book and headed out onto the streets. He thought he would have a quick scout round the alleyways and see if he could find Jasmin. He walked from the station and dropped straight into the alleyways behind Frodingham road. He chose the side that Acheron Street was on. The alleyway was a highway for those who wanted to escape the CCTV system that covered Frodingham road and those who wanted to cross town without drawing attention to themselves.

Pol felt comfortable in the alleyways. In Belfast they used to say "there's death in the alleys". But this wasn't true there. There was more danger in the streets and in the open spaces. In the alleys there was a chance of coming across a terrorist and engaging them. Scunthorpe's alleys did not hold that level of excitement but Pol had always found them to be a rich hunting ground for criminals.

He walked silently near the side of the alleyway, he had picked up his black coat and left the big high visibility coat hung on the back of his office door, where it belonged. Behind Teal Street and not far from the memorial park he saw what he first took for a bin bag laying in the alleyway. As he got closer he saw and recognised the hair. It was Jasmin. He ran over to her and crouched over her.

She was breathing, but not strongly. Her eyes were open and

she was making murmuring sounds. It was the first time he had seen her this close. Her bright blue eyes did not focus. She stunk of alcohol. Her black hair was plastered to her scalp with vomit and a trail of vomit trickled from her nostril. He could see she had the smooth white skin of a child with a few light freckles across her nose.

He called for an ambulance using his personal radio. As he gave his location he looked for the best route in to the alley for the ambulance. He saw West Street, with its working girls and traffic close by and he suggested that that was the best route in and out for the paramedics. He started to perform first aid on the girl. He opened her mouth and removed the vomit with his fingers and then started to check her over for more injury as he ran his fingers over her head feeling for injury her body began to shudder as she retched. He feared she would choke on her own vomit and decided to roll her into the recovery position. To make it easier he bent her knee up and put his hand on it to pull her towards him. With his other hand he cradled her head and gently he rolled her over towards him. He arranged her head to keep her airway open. As he moved his hand from her jawline he saw blood on her face. The blood was on his hand. He had not seen any. As he looked over her to try and discover where it had come from he saw it was on the knee and thigh he had turned her with. There was no wound visible. He checked further up her leg having to lift her mini skirt. He found she was not wearing any pants and the blood was coming from her vagina or anus. The bleeding was not of a life threatening nature. He pulled her skirt back down and covered her with his coat. She deserved some dignity. The policeman stroked her hair back from her face and held her hand whilst he waited for the ambulance. All of the time he talked to her in a gentle reassuring voice.

Chapter 4

2011 Unit 21 Kings Cliffe Industrial Estate, Peterborough.

The pleasant early summer morning sunshine washed over the industrial estate. The small unit was in an ideal spot, tucked away in the back of a fairly innocuous industrial estate. Peterborough was ideal equidistant for both of the men.

The plain black Ford Mondeo pulled into the car park and stopped adjacent to the silver Vauxhall insignia. The car only carried the driver.

The driver got out of the car and picked up his brief case from the passenger seat. The car was sterile. It contained nothing but the driver and his case. No CDs or even an empty coffee cup. There were no receipts for diesel nothing to identify the driver of the car. Even in the sunlight and warmth the driver wore a pair of light kid leather gloves. He strode across the car park towards the unit door. As he got to the door he punched the combination into the pad and entered. He was white, slightly under six feet tall. He had short, dark side parted hair. He was clean shaven and had no distinguishing features. It was difficult to tell his age but he looked like he was in his mid-forties. He wore a decent quality but not tailored pinstripe grey suit, a pale grey shirt and a blue narrow tie. His plain lace up black shoes could be bought at any larger branch of Tesco. He was instantly forgettable. The brief case was plain black leather, the same as so many thousand other brief cases in the hand of so many other grey men.

He knew that the Vauxhall would be the same; sterile, empty. The unit had a small lobby area and another key pad into a small meeting room. The room contained a pale wood table and six chairs around it. There wasn't room for anything more in the room. The walls were magnolia and the carpet a neutral beige. There were no pictures.

Sat at the table was another man. He was dressed very similarly. He was a little older, and he carried more weight. The younger man was athletic and proportionate. The older man stood up and spoke.

"The sun is warm for June", he said coolly.

"Not so wet as last June", the younger man replied.

This greeting was a prearranged code with a built in duress indicator. Had either men mentioned May then the other would know that their security had been compromised. The younger man spoke next. "I am Mr Green."

"Yes, I know, I am Mr White"

Mr Green opened his brief case and removed a Dell laptop. From his inside pocket he took a Kingston DT6000 BlockMaster flash drive.

"We are starting to have a problem in Scunthorpe." He said as he started the computer and plugged in the drive. He tapped in the first, then second password to enable him to open the securely encrypted data.

"What's happening up there, surely not much?" Replied Mr White.

"This man," Mr Green indicated at a face on the screen, "is going to cause us problems."

"Ok, let's break it down and see what we can do about it". Mr White, the senior man, seemed to be very calm.

Mr Green explained that in Scunthorpe some leading members of the Asian community were involved in the procurement of vulnerable young girls for sexual exploitation.

Mr White nodded and said "Like many other places,"

Mr Green continued, "The real issue is that several of these men are involved with the Humberside Police equality board. One of them is the Mayor. This can't come out."

Mr White asked, "Well, why should it?"

Mr Green moved to the next slide. This slide showed an unconscious girl laying in an alleyway with a police officer squatting beside her. Mr Green touched the play icon. The image showed the officer take his jacket off, cover the girl and wait with her for the ambulance to arrive. Whilst he waited he stroked the girl's hair".

"How touching," Mr White said.

"That officer is going to become an issue. His name is Pol Winchester, I've done my homework on the man and he is not going to just go away"

"What sort of a name is Pol? Can we just have the policing priorities for the area changed?" Asked Mr White.

"I have already done that but his line manager does not think he will stick to it." Replied Mr Green.

"Ok, can he be neutralized?"

"That is an option, I can look into it. I don't know the origins of Pol. Maybe some foreign way of saying Paul"

"So for now, Mr Green, I would like you to monitor the situation. I would like you to develop the intelligence on both Winchester and on this exploitation thing. Please look to employ any assets that we might have in the area."

"Thanks for the direction on this, would you like a weekly report?" Asked Mr Green.

"No thank you, I would like a weekly meeting."

Mr Green was a little surprised by this. Normally his work was delivered electronically and he had not met anyone else at his or a more senior level within the department.

Mr Green removed the flash drive from the computer. As he did so a small program, invisible to most users, that was concealed within the system files cleansed away any electronic footprint that the data might have left.

They stood up and said goodbye. Mr Green headed north to his area. Mr White headed south towards London.

Pol sat at his terminal. It was a hot and sticky afternoon. The new stations had metal roofs double glazing and no air conditioning. Since he had sent out his email about the vulnerable girls turning up on Frodingham Road he had been overwhelmed by the response of the team. In front of him was a pile of intelligence reports. His officers had clearly been touched by the plight of these kids. He knew his contemporaries on other areas did not read all of these reports, they just sent them in to the great paper eating monster that was the Divisional Intel Bureau. Pol read them, all of them. He wanted to know everything about his area. He wanted to know who was doing what to whom. When he had worked his way through the reports he entered the numbers per officer onto the database he was required to maintain. This would enable him to monitor the performance of the officers. Some thought they could outsmart the system by submitting stacks of poor quality reports when Pol first used the data in supervision checks. Those days had passed now and the quality of the reports were now good. The team had shaped well under his leadership and the management of Inspector Robinson.

The reports made grim reading. The Acheron Crew were busy. It seemed that they were involved in the supply of heroin and cocaine on the streets. They had a constant stream of young girls running with them and they held themselves to be some kind of gangster group. Pol knew that if that was what they aspired to be then that's how they would act. Once they started to act in the way of the American gangster then that is what they would become.

Then the town would start to feel the consequences of the police inaction. Surely with this weight of intelligence the DCI could not help but be swayed and seek to take them down. The sergeant gathered the sheaf of yellow papers up in his hand and took them upstairs. He wanted to show the inspector what the staff had produced.

"Hey, Guv, how are you doing?" Pol tapped on the inspector's open door.

"Come in mate" the Phil replied.

"Look at all these int reps. Pol put them down on the desk in front of his boss.

"Fuck me, the guys have been busy."

"You better believe it, boss. Do you know what the majority are about?"

"I reckon I can guess."

The inspector leafed through the first few. His face was worried. He looked Pol straight in the eye. Pol saw a he was uncomfortable.

"Pol, shut the door". The sergeant got up from his chair and shut the inspector's office door. He did not sit back down. He stood beside the chair.

"Sit down, you tough old fucker" Pol respected the Phil and knew he meant no offence. This banter kept them together in their unique positions of huge pressure and stress.

Pol sat down.

"Last week how many int reps did our team submit?" Phil asked.

"It was about eighty, Phil."

"How many were about the Acheron mob?"

"I can't remember off hand maybe thirty or forty" the sergeant looked at the young inspector quizzically.

"My guess is it was about forty four." As he spoke the inspector slid a piece of paper across the table showing all of the teams and their relative performance. Against the int rep column the figure thirty six was printed.

"I have had an email from the DCI." He read from the screen:

"Dear Inspector Robinson, It has come to my attention that your team is not following the policing plan as developed in accordance with the National Intelligence Model. Please ensure that all of your staff follow this direction. The divisional policy is to follow this direction. Should any of your staff fail to follow divisional policy disciplinary action may be instigated"

The inspector looked up at his sergeant.

"Pol, that's about you. He wants to fuck you up"

"He wants me to leave Acheron Crew alone, that's for sure" Pol replied.

Both men sat and looked at each other.

"Sergeant, let's have a brew and think about it then."

"Boss, now you are talking sense"

They sat quietly and enjoyed their tea.

"You know I am not going to stop, don't you?"

"Yeah, I know Pol. Be careful though, they will take you down"

Pol walked back downstairs to his office in a daze. He was being directed to turn a blind eye to crime. Not just any crime but, he suspected crimes where children were being exploited and abused. He couldn't understand it. He was not a cynical politician. He was just a cop who liked to help people and put crooks in gaol, where they belonged.

He walked across the big open plan constables' office. The office was stiflingly hot. The civilian office manager, George sat on the terminal nearest to the open fire door. He had removed the fire extinguisher from its wall bracket and held the door open with it.

"George, remember to bring that in when you go home mate"

"You think just because I am old enough to be your dad I have gone senile." The retired inspector had retained his sharp wit and sense of humour.

"That's right, old timer." Pol replied.

Pol smiled on the outside but he felt very uneasy, the conversation he had just had with the boss had left him quite shaken. He went into his office and closed the door behind him. He would rather cook in the stifling heat of the office than talk to the team right now. Standing for his principles had always been a source of great pride for Pol. Now he was as good as being told to make a choice between pursuing the criminals or his career. He had never been in this situation before.

There was a tap on his office door and George stepped in. "There is someone here to see you Pol."

"Who?"

"He gave his name as Charlie Jackman, says you don't know him. But he wants to talk to you about the Acheron Gang". George replied.

"Ok mate let him in" Pol's interest was immediately sparked

The sergeant put two dirty coffee cups in his desk drawer and turned over the yellow int reps that covered the desk. The information on the reports was sensitive. The door opened and George showed the man in.

Pol stood up and extended his hand "Mr Jackman, come in, do take a seat"

Pol indicated to a chair opposite his desk. Jackman shook Pol's hand.

"Thank you," he said.

Jackman sat down in the chair opposite Pol and Pol said to him, "How can I help you today?"

George left the office and shut the door behind him on his way out.

"I am a lecturer at North Lindsey College. I am having some problems with some lads there"

Charlie was not how Pol imagined a lecturer to be. He did not wear a nice dog tooth check jacket. He was in his late forties. He had short but spiked iron grey hair a goatee beard and a profusion of facial piercings. His nose was pierced, his lip, eyebrow and he had a large stretcher through each ear lobe. He wore a motorhead t shirt and jeans.

"What do you lecture in Mr Jackman?"

"Motor vehicle engineering and also engineering. Please, call me Charlie"

"Thanks, I am Pol."

"Yeah, I know who you are, that's why I have come to see you, I know the college is not on your patch but I think you might do something about the problem"

There was a gentle tap on the door and George brought in two cups of tea and some chocolate biscuits. "Sarge, get them biscuits quick, they are just out of the fridge" he said.

"Thanks, George, be sure I will" Pol replied.

"So what's happening, Charlie?"

"I take this one group and in the group is this Girl called Rhianna. Now this girl is pretty bright but she has quite a difficult family life"

"Ok, please go on." Pol encouraged.

"Over the past couple of weeks we have had trouble with the Acheron gang coming into the college. They just strut about the place like they own it. They are trying to get to this

Rhianna."

"How do you know they are the Acheron street gang?"

"Last year I taught a kid called Kharon Khan, he left before the course finished. He talked all the time about how he was the top boy in the Acheron Street crew. When I first started to teach him when he first left school he was a nice lad. He would show respect, complete work and be punctual. But, I don't know, something changed"

"Grab a biscuit, Charlie, if you don't I will eat them all. What happened?"

"Well it just came apart. He started to turn up late all of the time. He would seek out confrontation, initially with other students, but then with me as well".

The experienced sergeant looked at him and said nothing. He knew that if he kept quiet the lecturer would fill the space in the conversation.

The experienced lecturer smiled as he filled the space in the conversation that he knew the sergeant had left for him. Both men recognised the others' skill and intellect.

"He started to hang around with a Somali lad called New Mo, I don't know what his real name is and they would spent time in the games room surrounded by a group of other lads. The word was that he was selling drugs in the college."

"Do you think he was?" Asked Pol simply.

"Yeah, I reckon so".

"One morning he was dropped off by a bloke in a bullshitted up beamer and his entourage seemed to expand. I don't know who that bloke in the beamer was but it certainly increased his credibility."

"What was it, the car?" asked Pol.

"It was a red 3 series probably about a 2003. With big wheels body kit and tinted windows. I have seen it a few times here"

Pol recognised the description of the car. One of the int reps that he had read related to a car like this. When he had checked the police national computer it had come back as belonging to a Tariq Hasni. Hasni had been seen with Khan and the girl Peters had been seen to get into the BMW by one of the community support officers on the area.

"Alright so he left?"

"Yeah, as a part of the contract with the college there is a clause that allows the college to request a piss test for drugs. One morning he came to college particularly anti and I thought that he was on something. I gave the testing agency a call and low and behold after lunch they agency decided that it would be a good time to do a random test on my group"

"Gosh, really? You do surprise me". Both men had a laugh.

"So when the students finally turned up after lunch break the testers came in and Khan made a big scene. Saying that the test was only going to be done on him because he was an Asian and that the college hated Asians. He stormed out of the room. He didn't come to another lecture. To be honest, I couldn't care less about him. He was just a toerag trying to big himself up."

"Hmmm", the policeman sipped his mug of tea and thought to himself. There was no more 'pause for effect'.

"What's the story with this girl, then?"

"I don't know, the lads from the gang have been coming onto college premises and trying to get her to go with them. She seems to possess a special fascination for Kharon. When he was in the course she would not faun around him as the others would. She is a bit of a loner, I guess she may have learned to depend on her own company."

"Right, why?" Asked Pol.

"There is a government initiative called Pupil Premium where some kids are identified at being at risk of under achieving and additional resources are put into them to try to get them to do well."
"Yeah, we call it the troubled families' initiative."

"Don't get me wrong, Pol, I think it is a really great thing. For years we could watch the kids of certain families follow the script that had been written for them over the generations before them".

Pol nodded in agreement. He had the same thoughts about

the troubled families' initiative, he had seen three generations of some families come and go. Seen them start into crime, seen them start drugs young, have their kids when they were fourteen and fifteen. He watched them get into more serious crime and the kids go to the same care homes as their parents before them as their parents went to the same gaol as their parents before them. He saw them die in stinking bedsits as drug addicts; over dosed on heroin, wasted with AIDS or hepatitis. Anything was worth a shot. The cycle could not go on any more.

"So Rhianna came to us on a pupil premium, she would have made it onto this course anyway. I had a look at the files on her. Her mum came from a terrible upbringing and statistically Rhianna was likely to end in the same circles."

"Ok, is it looking like she is going that way?"

"Not really" Charlie continued, "she has some pretty good support from her auntie and her husband or it didn't look that way until she started to get wrapped up in the Acheron street crew, her work has gone to pot. Her attitude has changed. She has started to wear a few bits of nice jewellery, I think that Kharon is getting them for her".

"Ok, but hardly really a police thing", the extensive notes he had made tended to show that it really was a police thing.

"I was lecturing today when Khan came into the building. He came into my workshop. I asked him to leave. He said 'I have come for my bitch' he called over to Rhianna and tried to get her to leave the lecture".

"What did you do?"

"I told him to clear off, which after a bit of posturing and shouting he did. He threatened to slash my face".

"Ok, will you give a statement about that?"

"Well I can, but I then told him to fuck off or I would smash his face in, so maybe I better not"

"I would say that is pretty reasonable considering what he threatened you with." Pol said.

"Yeah, the college governors wouldn't see it that way and I would rather not make myself an easy target in their regime of cutbacks"

"No I guess not."

"Something has to be done about them, they need sorting out"

Pol had to agree with that.

When Jackman had left Pol sat in his chair. The door of his small office was closed. George had gone home. Pol should have gone home by now. His mind was buzzing. He had previously resigned himself to follow the DCI's instructions and leave the Acheron street crew alone. He did think he might try to slowly influence the decision of the senior managers by the weight of intelligence that was being generated by the staff. The conversation with Jackman had changed that for him. He had made his decision. There could only be one outcome. He would put them in gaol, he would build a case and get them all one at a time. If the DCI didn't like it he would go to the divisional commander and show him what he had.

He stood undid his boots, took them off and put them under his desk. He put his epaulettes in the top drawer of his desk. Locked his papers away. He pulled on the leathers and his biking boots. Walking out of his office and into the main constables' office he said goodnight to the two community support officers that were sharing a pizza.

"Good night, Sarge, ride safely" one of them said, he didn't know which one because his helmet blurred the voice a little.

The Suzuki Bandit was his counselling at the end of the day. It was an old bike now, over ten years. He loved it. He didn't polish it much, but he rode it a lot. Twelve hundred cc, about a hundred horse power and with the exhausts he had fitted he could hear every one of those horses roar.

Pol was soon home.

His wife, Fleur had just got home from work and when he went upstairs to get changed she was in the bedroom getting changed after her shift. He walked in whilst she was in her bra and panties.

"Hey sexy, nice arse". He greeted her.

"Hey horny, nice lunch". She laughed as he changed out of his police trousers.

"How was your day?" She asked.

"You know, pretty steady away really." Pol didn't want to tell her about the decision he had made to go against the DCI.

"Fleur, can I take you out for tea tonight?"

"Yes, Pol, that would be rather nice", she replied laughing.

As Pol walked past her to his dressing table he slapped her playfully across the buttocks.

"Cheeky!" She said.

It didn't take Pol very long to get ready to go out to for tea. He only wanted to go to the local pub for a steak. Fleur had a different plan. She wanted to go to the very nice Italian restaurant in Barton.

Whilst she got ready to go out he sat at the kitchen table and enjoyed a strong filter coffee and opened his laptop. He checked the spam emails he had received through the day. He opened Facebook and looked at his notifications.

He had a friend request.

He checked it. It was from Stu Hicks.

He stared at the screen. He almost forgot to breathe. He had last seen or heard from Sticks the day they came out of the jungle.

He was rocked to the core.

Time stopped.

His stomach lurched and he felt cold.

He accepted the request.

"Ready Pol?" Fleur said.

He turned and faced her. "Are you ok, Pol, you look like you have seen a ghost".

"Oh yeah, I am ready to go. Sorry I was miles away, years ago."

In the car on the way to the restaurant there was no conversation. Over the fifteen years since it happened he had almost put it to the back of his mind. It still visited him in the night. Now it was back in front of his eyes.

Elios was the couples' favourite restaurant. The food at the restaurant was really outstanding. The Winchesters did not eat out often, even as a police sergeant the money was a little tight. So a meal out at their favourite restaurant was not a weekly event. They would be expecting to spend three times what they might in the local Chinese restaurant.

"What will you have, Pol?"

"I don't know really, last time I really enjoyed my steak"

"You always have a steak you are so boring!" Fleur gently teased Pol.

"Yeah, that's right just a boring old git". It was really unlike Pol to react like this. Fleur was upset by his moody outburst.

"What's wrong, Pol?" She asked.

They were at the restaurant, they were tense as they walked into the bar area. The maître d was a seasoned professional and saw the atmosphere between the couple. He had seen them in the restaurant many times. Normally they laughed and drank. Not tonight, they were frosty towards each other.

"Mr and Mrs Winchester, a table for two?" He gently asked.

"Yes please, somewhere tucked away, if you can", he turned to Fleur, "we need to talk"

Fleur felt very nervous. Pol was not a great communicator and she did not know what was coming here. He got himself a beer and a glass of tempranillo for Fleur.

The maître d showed the couple through to a table for two tucked away to the rear of the restaurant.

"Come on then, Pol" she spoke nervously. "Whatever it is let's get it out", she thought the problem was between them.

"When I went to Belize I did something very bad. I put it in a box at the back of my memory and left it there."

"Right, go on".

"Sometimes, in the night, it comes back to me in dreams. I have never told you about it before. I can tell you about it but it is a real secret..." He was nervous. He looked deeply into her eyes. She saw pain etched into his soul through his eyes. She knew that this was not about them.

"It's alright Pol, start at the beginning", she reached across the table and held his hands in hers. He felt vulnerable in her hands. He had never felt vulnerable to her before this.

"We were on an operation, it was me and a bloke called Stu Hicks, we were in Guatemala working on a secret operation and things went tits up". Emotion rose in his voice and he wavered.

"Come on Winny, it's all ok", Fleur reassured him.

"No Fleur, it's not ok. I killed someone. He was a boy."

"Pol, you are proud of your service, proud of killing the IRA man."

"When I say he was a boy, he was a kid, maybe ten years old. I broke his neck. It was a murder." He wept quietly to himself as he looked at her and held her hands.

"What happened, Pol?"

Pol went on to explain what had happened in the jungle in 1994. He talked about the operation and how he had no choice but to kill the boy to prevent the mission being compromised. His words sounded hollow in his head, like some sort of echo of an excuse.

This secret was out and there was no putting it back in the box now. Fleur knew what sort of a man she was married to. She knew that Pol would kill a child just to keep a mission intact. She spoke quietly, "Pol, this is what you had to do. There wasn't a choice for you." She gripped his hands over the table and held them tight in hers.

The meal was good. Pol had his steak, Fleur had her halibut. They talked and were happy to have taken the hidden skeleton out of the cupboard so that they could both see it and deal with it.

When they got home from the restaurant Pol started up his computer and opened Facebook. He had not seen Stu for a long time. He was worried about whether he would still get on with Stu. The friendship that they had forged in the firefights of the jungle was a long time in the past now.

As he opened Facebook he saw that Sticks was online, he contacted him.

Pol: "Hello"

Stu: "Hello. It's been a long, long time."

Pol: "It has mate, it's seventeen years since…"

Stu: "Yeah, I know."

Pol: "Where do you live mate?"

Stu: "Scunthorpe, it's in North Lincolnshire."

Pol: "I fucking know where it is, I work there."

Stu: "No way."

The two men chatted online for what seemed like just a few minutes. Fleur came through, "Pol, It's one in the morning, you are on days tomorrow"

"Fucking hell, time has got on a bit". He said good night to his old mate and turned the computer off.

"We are going out to the pub with Sticks and his wife Di."

"That sounds good, I like to meet up with your old mates".

They went to bed and Pol slept. He did not have any dreams that night. The boy stayed away from him. The Belfast nightmare didn't come to him as it did most nights. He awoke with his alarm. Normally he was relieved when the alarm went off in the morning because he would be able to get up and stop struggling to sleep.

Pulling his bike boots on he thought about the night at the pub he had planned with Stu.

Chapter 5

Scunthorpe, June 2011.

The ring tone that Tariq Hasni used was slap my bitch up by
the prodigy. His i-phone rang as he sat at home watching the
music channels on his sky TV and enjoying a beer. He had
furnished his house very nicely. He looked around and saw
what he had earned. A really nice Technics mp3 and Bose
speakers, fifty four inch flat screen television with a full sky
package, the sound was channelled through the Bose
speakers and gave him really good surround sound on the
music channels he liked to watch. The keys to his BMW lay
on the smoked glass coffee table in front of him. He was
starting to think that he might upgrade the car. He had
moved on and up in the world. He felt he needed something
with a bit more style about it. Maybe an Audi Q7, yeah for
sure, they were nice cars and right for a guy of his status to
drive. Tariq picked up his phone and looked at the display.

It was his friend Abdul Mohammed.

"Asalaam Alaykum" he spoke with a traditional greeting.

"Wa 'Alaykum Asalaam", replied Abdul.

"How is business, Abs?"

"It is good, thank you my brother. How is yours?"

"Alright, I am thinking that I might have a new car more
befitting to me, I really like the look of the Q7." Tariq said.

"Very nice, business must be good"

"It is, the boys are doing us proud, they have a really good thing going now. They have started to get their names known and started to run the streets around there. I will tell them to give one of the piss heads a good kicking to up their cred a little bit more."

"Are they making much with the dealing, Tariq?"

"They are making a killing. They have just about taken over the brown and rock business in this part of town." Tariq replied.

"Good, they are so much more reliable than the Kafir junkies we used to use."

"Yeah, they won't rip us off for our profits and shoot it up their arms."

"Tariq, I have had a call from randy old Ranji, He wants another white girl to be taken to Sheffield to give to his brothers over there."

"I wondered how long it would be until they wanted another one, I have got the boys working on one now. They will like her, she has yellow hair and blue eyes."

"What happened to the black haired whore that I saw Kharon with the other day? She would be ok." Asked Abdul, referring to Jasmin, he didn't know her name, he didn't care if she had a name.

"The boys used her to make a film with, when it has been edited, formatted and burned onto the DVD it will be seen by Randi's friends and they won't be happy that before she went there after she was used in the film with all of the boys."

"No, we cannot show them that disrespect", agreed Abdul. "Not if we want to continue to do well"

Tariq laughed at this. "Mate if the money keeps rolling into the pockets of the old goats they couldn't give a fuck where it comes from"

"I guess not. Is there much to be made from the DVD market?" asked Abdul.

"Mmm, it's not quite as profitable as the drugs but, you know, it's pretty good. And if it is going to happen in Scunthorpe then I want to be the one doing it. I don't want anyone else starting to get their fingers in." replied Tariq.

Tariq continued, "Once she is out I will have her on the street and I will let Kharon run her, see how he does. He has to learn to do business as we all did in our turn"

Abdul exhaled loudly, "Do you think he is smart enough? He seems to like to throw his weight about and use violence, when we need him to but do you think he has the acumen to actually make money?"

"Abdul, you worry too much, I will keep a close eye on him and we will keep him straight. If he starts to cause us to lose money then I will rein him back in." Tariq reassured him.

"I had that copper in the youth centre the other day, will you have a word with Ranji see if we can get him sent somewhere else to fuck someone else's business up?" Abdul asked Tariq.

"Yes for sure I will. I don't think he is smart enough to bother us. If he starts we will just get him on his own and cook up a story about how he racially abused one of us. That will take care of him".

"Tariq, I want in to this video gig, I have got a lock up in Bradford, it's full of fags at the minute but they are going this week. I can venue the films there. My cousin, Rashid, has a scrap business in the city with a crusher and incinerator, if we need to get rid of anything we can take it to him".

"Ok Abs, that sounds good, it is a better investment to keep hold of them and put them on the street. Once they have a good enough habit they will do what I want. I get the cu from their heroin requirement and also from the punters. It is a win, win scenario for me. What do you want for the use of the lock up?"

"I reckon twenty percent of the net profits from the DVD?" Abdul asked.

"Fuck off, you are living in a dream world my brother. After Ranji's percentages and the cost of production it will leave me with fuck all, the best I can do is ten percent?"

"Let's meet in the middle and agree on fifteen?" Abdul knew this was the deal that Tariq was looking for.

"Ok my man, but can you also point Kharon in the right direction when the whores come into your place on Frod road?" Tariq knew that this part of the deal would be far more important than a small cut from the lucrative video market. This was about sustainable business growth.

"Of course I will, anyway brother, it is time for me to get on with shifting these fags from my lock up. Do you want in on that?" Asked Abdul.

"No thanks, I already have them sorted out on my patch. The boys are taking care of that for me too and they come in from a man who would be less than happy if I went with a different supplier for fags." Replied Tariq.

"Fi Amanullah" said Abdul.

"Fi Amanullah" replied Tariq as he switched his phone off.

Tariq reached for another beer and flicked through the channels of the TV. He found nothing that he liked so he opened the MP4 file of the boys taking that black haired, skinny, white whore. It was ok, but she was too pissed or high, she was hardly fighting. Next time he wanted to see about more physicality from the boys.

He picked up his phone from the table. He scrolled down the numbers until he reached Kharon. As he opened the contact he looked up at the huge flat screen and saw a close up of Jasmine's face as she pitifully cried, the video panned down her body and zoomed in on her violation. Tariq opened an SMS to Kharon.

Tariq: "I want you round here now."

Kazzy: "On my way."

Tariq: "I want a whore - bring one."

Tariq got up and went through to the stairs and up to his room. He slipped off his casual track suit and put on a silk robe. He walked through to the second bedroom of the house. The room was no longer as described by the agent when he bought it. The window was now covered in thick black curtains. There was a single divan bed centrally in the room. It was covered with a red plastic sheet. He pushed it to one side and from the drawer in the base of the divan he removed a box around sixty centimetres square and only about 10 centimetres deep. The box was of black cardboard. He turned the lights out and returned down stairs.

He switched the TV off and pulled the memory stick from the back and placed it in his robe pocket.

Kharon arrived within just a few minutes and knocked gently at the back door of the house.

Tariq took his phone from the table and text.

Tariq: "come in"

Kazzy: "Yes uncle"

Tariq was not his uncle, but it was a term of respect that Kharon would always use when speaking to Tariq.

Kharon came into the lounge, he had left his trainers near the back door. Behind him was a woman that Tariq had never seen before. She looked nervous. Her bleached blonde hair was starting to show dark roots, her blue eyes looked scared.

"Uncle, this is Nadia." Said Kharon.

"Take this upstairs. Turn right at the top of the stairs and go into the room up there. Open the box and put on what is inside, do not come down, wait until I come up". Tariq said to the woman.

"Ok," she said in a strong eastern European accent.

"You call me master, bitch." Tariq growled at the woman.

"I am sorry master," She replied, looking at the floor. She was confused, she didn't know what was going on.

He passed her the black box and she turned and went out and upstairs. When Tariq heard the doors shutting he said to Kharon, "How long has she been working for you?"

"Just a few weeks, she does not inject drugs. She is illegal and I have her to stop her being sent home."

"Mmm, that's fine then." Tariq said.

"Uncle, how is it I can help you tonight?" Kharon asked with respect.

"How close are you to getting another Kafir whore for Sheffield?"

"I am working on one at the moment but it is quite difficult with her, she has no respect for men, she has no respect at all." The young man spoke quietly.

"She sounds ideal for what we want, in the video you boys made the girl was too doped up. I want to take one to Sheffield that will struggle a bit whilst she is being used, this is business and we both know that to make the most money we must provide the right service to meet the demand." Tariq spoke quietly to his young protégé.

"Yes uncle, give me a couple of weeks and I will have her eating from my hand then she will be ready to go to Sheffield."

"That's fine. Make sure you do. There is something else I need you to do."

"Yes uncle what is that?"

"I want you and your boys to move the stinking alcoholics away. I want you and your boys to go and give them a hammering. I want people to see you do it. I want the people to see that we are more powerful than the pigs".

"I don't understand." Kharon replied. Tariq wondered if he was bright enough to progress within the community.

"Ok," Tariq explained, "the police go there twice a day and try to move them on. The drunks don't move, they stay there smelling like piss. If we go there and move them away you have shown that you have more power than the police so that we are then the top dogs in the street."

Kharon understood how important that could be, he knew he would hand out a kicking in broad daylight and in front of the whole street. He was quite excited by the thought of it. He had figured out the extent of the CCTV coverage along the street and knew that there would be room for him to operate quite easily if he stayed close to the wall of the church. The road was well covered but the pavement, on that side, was not.

"I understand this now, uncle."

"If you do this right for me I will give you the girl to run on the streets and I will only take a reasonable slice". Tariq waved the carrot of added responsibility in front of him.

Tariq had actually hoped that he would be able to take more of a back seat and let Kharon take more on and just take a healthy slice of his profits. More of a senior manager rather than a supervisor.

"Thank you Uncle. I will not disappoint you." Kharon replied.

"Kharon, fuck off back out there and start selling drugs to the junky scum".

"Yes Uncle, I will." Both laughed as he left the room and soon afterwards Tariq heard the door shut quietly.

Kharon walked into the dark alleyway. He took his Blackberry from his tracksuit pocket.

He sent a message.

Kazzy: "I have been thinking about you all day sexy"

A reply came back in just a few seconds.

Rhianna: "I have been thinking of you too, top boy"

Kazzy: "You wanna hang out just me and you?"

Rhianna: "Yeah, I want you bad. I will sneak out when the

old bitch is asleep"

Kazzy: "Do it baby x"

Rhianna: "I will."

Kazzy: "Bet you don't"

Rhianna: "I will show you how serious I am".

Kazzy: "Yeah right".

Rhianna sat in her room on her own. Her mum was drunk down stairs with the latest boyfriend. John, Pete, Wayne or Kev; she didn't know and she couldn't care less. She stripped off her t shirt and bra, stood in front of the mirror and sent Kazzy a selfie of her tits.

Kazzy: "Baby, they are fantastic".

Rhianna: "Told you I meant it".

Kazzy: "Can't wait to see them for myself"

Rhianna: "Tonight might be your night".

Kharon knew that he had her now. The picture on his phone was what he needed to ensure that she would always do what he said. It was leverage.

Tariq went upstairs to his 'play room.' As he walked in he saw that Nadia was sitting on the bed against the wall.

"I did not tell you to sit down, did I?"

"No master."

Nadia was now dressed in a tightly fitting PVC basque with low cut cups. Her still ample breasts bulged from the top of the cups.

Tariq opened a small wardrobe and from inside took a length of chain. The chain was just over a meter long. On each end was a separate locking cuff. Like those from a set of normal handcuffs. In the centre of the chain was a clip.

"Come to me, bitch" Tariq commanded Nadia.

She took slow and faltering steps towards him. She averted her eyes from him. She understood the BDSM rules and new her place in this game.

"Yes master, what can I do for you?" She asked him.

"Hold out your hands, bitch".

She did as she was instructed straight away. He put the cuffs on her wrists. He put them on tight.

"Master, is there a word?" She asked. It was normal that there would be a safe word that could be used if either felt uncomfortable.

Tariq reached up and clipped the chain to a ring on the

ceiling. Nadia stood in front of him. He thought she was a good looking woman for a white whore. Her arms were unmarked by needles. They looked strong and trim. She maybe did some sort of manual labour when she wasn't selling herself for silver. Her hands long and graceful tipped with red nails. Her blonde hair flowed onto her smooth white back and on to the back of her basque. He looked and studied the contrast of the blonde hair and the black shiny garment. The basque was tight around her waist. He didn't care if it fitted her or not. Comfort was not on his list of priorities when it came to selection.

He moved behind her. Her full and rounded buttocks, so smooth and rounded. There was a small gap at the top of her thighs. He liked that. He raised his right hand and slapped her hard across the buttocks. She let out a sharp cry of surprise and pain.

"The word is America." He looked down at her white buttocks and he could see the red hand print start to rise above the surrounding skin.

He moved round in front of her and stood back to look at her. He examined her face, her blue, tired eyes. He looked at her blood red lips and at her gracefully long neck. Her collar bones stood clearly and her breasts swelled amply from beneath them and into the cups of the basque. Below the basque her hips curved down and onto her thighs. Between her thighs was her shaved pussy, freshly shaved and smooth. Tariq liked what he saw. He turned his back on her and walked to the wall mounted TV. He took the memory stick from the pocket of his robe and plugged it into the back of the TV set. He started the unedited footage of that he had been watching downstairs. He saw Nadia's eyes open widely as she struggled to take in what she saw on the screen. The volume was set low so that she could hear, but the sound would not travel far. She would be able to hear the slaps of hands on her skin. She would be able to hear the sobs and moans. She would be able to hear the boys laughing as the girl was hurt so bad.

Tariq turned away and walked out of the room. He made his way downstairs and turned on the lounge TV again. He switched it back to the music channels and sat down with another beer.

He text Abdul to let him know that he should be able to supply the girl they wanted in a couple of weeks. He knew that Kharon would not let him down. If he did he would tell Kharon's uncle Abdi. Abdi was an old time friend of both Tariq's and Abdul's. They did business together. Abdi brought the heroin into the area. He was a big player in the north of England supply network. He didn't get his hands dirty anymore. This was where Tariq wanted to be. But Tariq new better than to try to displace Abdi. He had too much respect for that and he also knew what a tough customer Abdi was. Abdi need only make a phone call to his associates in Manchester and anyone could just disappear. So Tariq treated him with the utmost courtesy and respect.

Only ten minutes later he received a text from Abdul saying that Ranji was very happy with what he had done and would speak to him at the Mosque about the arrangements on Friday, after prayers. Tariq knew that the arrangements in question would be the payment.

Nadia could see into the wardrobe that the man had got the chain from. The back panel of the wardrobe had hooks and pegs attached to it. On the hooks were all manner of BDSM implements. She could see small and light leather straps and cuffs. She could see more heavy duty things in the wardrobe. There was a real cat-o'-nine tails with heavy plaited leather straps. A heavy strong leather bound handle. She saw a cruelly and heavily studded leather paddle for spanking. She saw a variety of phallus shaped dildos and vibrators in the cupboard. Masks and gags. She saw on the floor of the cupboard a large blue roll of industrial tissue paper. She could not help but keep watching the terrible images on the screen in front of her. She recognised the girl, she had seen her in the area before. She knew the boys, the film occasionally showed their faces. She knew that in its final draft the video would be edited and the boys' faces would not appear. She saw one of the boys in the street regularly. He thought he was a big tough guy. He was nothing just a little small town thug. Back home in Bulgaria these boys would be sorted out by the real criminals that ran the towns. They were lucky that the British police protected them from the people who were sick of them.

She watched on the video as one of the boys took a broom handle. He forced it into the girl. She was crying out in pain. The boy pulled it back out from her. It was streaked in blood. Nadia thought the girl might have some nasty injuries because of this violation. The boy on the video laughed. It was the boy that had bought her to this place tonight. She thought "If I make it out of this place alive I will find a way to get that shit".

She heard the volume of the television down stairs increase. Then she heard the door way at the bottom of the stairs shut. She knew why the TV had been turned up. It was to drown out her screams.

The door behind her opened and the young man that had tied her in the room walked in. He circled around her. He was naked now. His body was trim, he was not fat. He had the physique of a boxer or a rugby player. He had no hair on his body. His body shone with oil and accentuated his well-defined musculature. As he walked in front of Nadia she was surprised to see that he was flaccid. She thought he would be aroused but he showed no signs.

"How can I be of service to you, Master?" She asked him. She had done this BDSM role on a number of occasions and new how this worked.

With no warning and with extreme force the man punched her hard in the kidney. The impact was crushing on her right side. She stifled her cry, but still it escaped her lips.

"You don't talk to me you Kafir whore." He growled.

He walked in front of her to the wardrobe and took out the heavy studied paddle. She wept as she saw him walk back to her. The pain from her bruised kidney rolled in waves up and down her injured side. She could not roll up and shield herself from him. He still remained flaccid.

He walked to her side, she tried to watch him and prepare herself for what was to follow.

The pain of the impact on her buttock was sharp, hot and immediate. There was no escape from pain. It was all around her now. Pain radiated from her side, from her bum. She felt sick and her breathing came in ragged bursts. She was light headed.

"America, please stop, America". She begged him for a release from the torment.

"Fuck you," was his response. He walked round in front of her so that she could see him. She tried to look away from him and look at the floor. He had become semi excited now. As she looked down to the floor she saw small trickles of blood on her inner thighs and running down her ankle bones and pooling under the arches of her feet. For just a second she was fascinated by the way the two small puddles began to grow and expand. They joined and merged together. The next impact on her other buttock rendered her unconscious. The faint provided her with some respite from the waves of pain. The respite was short lived and soon she regained consciousness to find herself looking down as her head hung to her chest. Her wrists hurt as she hung by them. The pool of blood near her feet had been diluted by her urine. When she was unconscious her bladder had voided.

He kept her there and used her for a while, she had no idea how long it was.

He left her on the floor in her urine and in her blood.

"Clean up." He said to her as he threw her the blue roll from the wardrobe. She did not cry. She did as she was told.

The boy that had taken her to the house came in and helped

her get back in her clothes. She could not do it on her own now. When she was taken into the alleyway she turned round and looked at the house. She wanted to remember.

"This is how we are gonna do it", said Kharon to the assembled Acheron Crew. It was early for them to get together. But Kharon knew that on a Friday the police all came on duty after lunch time.

The two young Skuja boys were there, Mo Nuelleh and a couple of other boys that were trying to gain acceptance into the gang. Rhianna didn't want to come and be a part of it. That was ok, Kazzy didn't mind that. He had spent the night with her and she had crept off home in the early hours. She said it was her first time. He hoped it was.

"Skujas, One of you go to West Street, the other one to Ferry road. If either of you see the pigs coming then you ring New Mo straight away. Ok?" Kazzy asked.

The two boys were eager to please and they did as they were told straight away.

"Ok, Kazzy, we can do that."

"Ring Mo when you are in position."

"Yes Kazzy."

Mo and Kazzy, went into one of the newsagents on the street and helped themselves to a can of redbull each. They didn't pay. Old Mr Singh would not challenge them. They walked back onto the street and waited for a few minutes.

"Mo, you have to start to step up your business." Kazzy spoke quietly.

"Yeah, I am looking at taking the trade for the West street whores".

"Yeah good idea, some of them have junky boyfriends as well, they could be ideal." Kazzy approved of Mo's idea. Kazzy thought that he would be able to sell the whores on the street so they could feed their habit and then deal to them and their boyfriends to maximise their profits. It seemed like excellent business.

Mo's phone rang.

"Yo, it's Mo". He said into the blackberry.

"Ok". He ended the call.

"West Street is covered", he turned to Kazzy.

The phone rang again. He turned and nodded to Kazzy.

"You are on Kazzy Mad Man, time to show your thing". Mo understood what this was all about.

Kazzy put a bandana over his lower face and pulled his hood up. He walked over Frod road and went over to the drunks.

"You are a load of fucking filthy bastards!" Kazzy stood amongst the drunks shouting at them.

People walking along the street either hurried on or stood still and watched. Kazzy continued to shout. "Why don't you all just fuck off somewhere else so you don't bother decent people?"

Robin Chamberlain stepped forward and said. "Who the

fuck do you think you are?"

Kazzy took a couple of steps forward to make sure he was out of the view of the CCTV cameras. He pulled down his hood and took off his mask.

"You know who we are, you know who I am. You scum can fuck off this street. This is our manor. We look after it."

He looked around himself and saw that there was a crowd of shoppers and passers by watching from across the street. He walked up to Rob and stood just inches from him. They stood face to face.

"You are a waste of humanity". Whispered Kazzy.

This tipped the old drunk over the edge. Rob's face flashed red with anger and he prodded Kazzy in the chest once with his right forefinger.

No one saw the knuckle duster in Kazzy's tracksuit pocket. This was what he wanted. He slipped the duster onto his right hand and launched a savage uppercut into the jaw of Chamberlain. The old man shook as the bone in his jaw was smashed. Kazzy put the duster back into his pocket and stepped to his left. As he did he swung a short left hook into the temple of the semi-conscious man. The old man slumped forward now and as he dropped down. Kazzy met him with another uppercut into the nose. Rob Chamberlain fell to the floor, his face a bloodied mask. There was nothing more coming from Chamberlain. He was unconscious. As he lay on the ground the younger man kicked him brutally in the back. He didn't know but the kick ruptured his already inflamed kidney.

This had taken only two or three seconds. The other drunks in the group realised what was happening and one of the women lurched forwards towards Kazzy. She held her vodka bottle by the neck. Kazzy knew that this could be a disaster.

She raised her bottle above the head to hit him. He knew with this amount of people watching it would be counterproductive to hit her. Her clumsy swing was easy for Kazzy to deal with. He grasped her wrist as the bottle came down with his left hand and took the bottle with his right hand. He pushed her away. She staggered back but did not fall.

"Now, the rest of you go away. The next time you are here someone else will get what that old fuck did." The young man pulled his blackberry out of his pocket and called for an ambulance for the old man. He made the call loudly so all of the watchers could hear.

"Time to go." Shouted Mo. He had received a call from one of the boys, the police were on their way.

Mo and Kazzy ran into the alleyway behind Acheron Street. As they did they were met by Abdul Mohamed. Kazzy stripped off and passed his clothes to Abdul. Abdul passed him fresh clothes. "I will wash the others and you can pick them up from the youth centre tomorrow."

Said Abdul.

"Ok, thanks. Where now?" said Kazzy

"Go to Uncle Abdi's he will give you an alibi and let you

shower".

Stu Hicks stood in his back bedroom window and watched this unfold below him.

Chapter 6

Scunthorpe, June 2011.

Friday.

SMS Conversation.

Kazzy: Hey gorgeous.

Jasmine: Fuck off

Kazzy: I miss you

Jasmine: Fuck off.

Kazzy: I really want you.

Jasmine: you and your mates had me and you hurt me.

Kazzy: I needed to see if you were serious about us.

Jasmine: I loved you.

Kazzy: I am sorry, but now I know that you love me and I want you for me.

Jasmine: I had stitches in my bum. It hurt me so bad.

Kazzy: that's how much I hurt not seeing you or having you in my world.

Jasmine: You said you respected me.

Kazzy: I do you showed me that the other day.

Jasmine: What do you want?

Kazzy: I just want you.

Jasmine: Really?

Kazzy: I miss you. It was just a test to see if you respected me.

Jasmine: Do you want to see me?

Kazzy: Just me and you?

Jasmine: That would be nice.

Kazzy: I won't let you down.

Kharon turned to Tariq, "I reckon we are on, Uncle".

"I know this was short notice and not the girl that you had wanted to send, but she will be ok." Tariq had received the call at quite short notice. He knew how important it was not to let the customer down. If he did they would simply go somewhere else.

"I have had a word with Mr Quereshi, you can take her to his restaurant, his guys will treat you well and there will be no bill." Tariq wanted to increase Kharon's credibility amongst the Asian community and also instil some confidence in him to perform a little higher.

"Thank you, Uncle, I will take her out tonight and then tomorrow we will take her across".

"Will you need to have her knocked out to take her?" Tariq didn't like the idea of having to drive across the country with an unconscious teenage girl in his car.

"No, Uncle, I will tell her we are running an important delivery for you. She will think it will be something to do with your other business and keep her mouth shut. She will do anything to belong to something".

"When she comes back give her crack to smoke, tell her it will numb the pain. Let her have it for free for a couple of days, then offer her the streets."

"Yes Uncle, of course I will." Kharon wanted to assure his uncle he would follow his directions and his normal was of doing business.

SMS Conversation

Kazzy: I want to take you to dinner.

Jasmine: Really?

Kazzy: Have you got a nice dress?

Jasmine: No, I don't have many clothes.

Kazzy: It's ok I can get you something that I will like.

Jasmine: Thank you.

Kazzy: What size are you?

Jasmine: size 8

Kazzy: shoes?

Jasmine: size 4

Jasmine: are you getting me shoes too?

Kazzy: Nothing is too much for you.

(As he typed this he showed the phone to Tariq, the men

both laughed.)

Jasmine: Where shall we meet?

Kazzy: come to the youth centre, we can get ready in the rooms upstairs. I will get you everything. Come at seven I want to spend some time with you.

Jasmine: I can't wait xxx.

Kharon spoke to the older man, "Ok, sorted. I will send out some grafters to pick up the gear for her to wear."

"Well done Kazzy, you are learning well." Tariq's use of Kharon's nickname was intentional and planned. It would give the lad a feeling that he was starting to achieve some recognition in the eyes of the older man.

It would be a shame the video couldn't be released yet. But in a week or so no one would remember her face.

Just before seven that evening Jasmine arrived in the alleyway behind the youth centre. She had never been taken out to dinner before and she was excited. No one had ever bought her a dress before. She didn't own any feminine shoes. She opened the gate from the alleyway and went to the bottom of the steel steps that led up to the flat above the youth centre. As she stood at the base of the stairs nervous about what to do the door at the top of the stairs opened. Kazzy's uncle Abdul was at the top of the stairs. She didn't know whether he was actually an uncle or not. Kazzy respected all of the elder men in his community and referred to them all as uncle. She was a little nervous of Abdul. He dressed traditionally most of the time and he had a long beard. She thought it looked a little funny as he had shaved his moustache away.

"Hello," she said nervously and stuttering.

"Come up, Jasmine. Kharon is waiting here for you". He made his way down the stairs and left the door open for her.

As he passed her she said "Thank you, Uncle."

He looked at her and laughed as he turned towards West Street and the town centre.

Jasmine walked up the stairs and into the flat. Kazzy was waiting for her in the kitchen. As she walked in he kissed her on the lips. "Hello, my princess." He said.

"Hello," she was still nervous, "are we on our own today?"

"Yes we are. Just you and me."

He was wearing a silk robe. She had seen him in his street clothes and naked before but not like this. He seemed self-assured and confident to her.

"I don't have anything to wear". She was embarrassed by her tracksuit and trainers.

"I have everything for you, nothing is too much." He said to her.

"Can I look?" She could not contain the excitement.

"Let's shower together first shall we?"

He took her by the hand and led her through the flat to the bathroom. The shower in the bathroom was already running. The large double sized cubicle was full of steam.

"I have done my hair and make-up." She said.

"It's ok, some of my people have brought makeup and hair things"

"I don't want to use someone else's stuff on my face"

"No, it is all new. It is all yours now."

He turned to her and as he kissed her he pulled her shirt over her head. They took a long and slow shower together.

Kazzy gave her the clothes that had been stolen for her to his order. The black mini dress didn't quite hang properly on her boyish frame. Her hips had not really widened to fill the shape. The stockings he had given her would not stay up on her too skinny legs. Fortunately a pair of tights had also been collected and they would stay up. Kazzy told her he preferred her in stockings but tights were just as nice, she blushed at the compliment. Whilst she dressed he stood behind her and watched. "You look lovely", he said to her, "All you need is some shoes," From behind his back he produced a pair of very high stiletto healed ladies shoes. "How about these?" He asked.

"OMG!" She exclaimed, "They are lovely!" He passed the shoes to her and she put them on. She stood in front of the mirror and she thought she looked glamorous and

sophisticated. Whilst she put on her make-up he went into
the other room and got dressed. He wore a pair of smart
black leather shoes, black slack trousers and a traditional
kurta top. The kurta was a long shirt with embroidered front
and a three buttons on the chest. The kurta was black. He
combed and spiked his short black hair and he looked at
himself. He looked smart, he knew he did, but this was not a
look he would normally go for.

When he walked back into the bedroom Jasmin was ready.

"Let's go" he said.

Together they left the flat and made their way to the Bengal
Raj restaurant on Frodingham road. When they entered the
restaurant they were immediately greeted and treated with
respect and deference by the waiters. The waiters called
Jasmin "Madam" and Kazzy "Sir". She thought then that she
really loved him.

Di walked through from the kitchen with two coffees. She liked it much better when she carried two coffees and not a beer and a coffee. "I liked your mate, Stu, he seemed like a nice bloke".

"Yeah, he is a good guy. Like his Mrs as well. Bloody funny French name though. Fleur. What the fuck sort of name is that for a woman?" Stu Hicks replied.

"I don't really know, anyway, why haven't you ever told me about being called Sticks?"

"I hated it at the time. I quite like it now. It reminds me of the old days and the things we used to get up to." Stu replied laughing.

"I am not sure I really want to know".

"I can't believe that he works here. I can't believe we haven't seen him before." Stu picked up his coffee and sat quiet for a moment.

Winston, lying flat on his side on the floor stirred. He would often look up at the window if someone was passing by or if any stray dogs were in the garden. He lifted his head and cocked his ears towards the back garden.

"What's up boy?" Asked Stu.

The dog let out a low rumbling growl and got to his feet. He held his head low and his hackles were erect. Slowly he made his way towards the back of the house.

"Let me see what daft lad here wants." Stu said to Di as he made his way to the back door. Through the window he could see a group of lads stood in the back garden. He recognised them as local lads that hung around with young Kharon from the street. Stu had not invited them into the garden and was not too pleased that they had decided to congregate there. He was sure he had closed and bolted the gate. He opened the back door and stepped out into the garden in his slippers, T-shirt and shorts. He made sure that Winston was kept in the house. He didn't want the dog to get out and go into the road.

"Alright guys", he spoke to the lads.

Kharon was not with the boys but there was his mate Mohammed and the two younger Latvian or Lithuanian boys, he wasn't sure which, and another tall lad. The tall lad looked like Mohammed, maybe Somali or another North African race. They were sitting down on the planters in which Stu grew herbs in. They were drinking from plastic bottles of cider and Mohammed was smoking a joint.

"Do me a favour guys, would you get off the plants please?" Stu was calm and relaxed with the boys. Everyone needed somewhere to be and he really didn't mind them being there so long as they cleaned up after themselves and didn't damage anything. The younger of the two Eastern European lads said something to his brother which Stu could not understand. The boys ignored Stu and just carried on sitting in his plant pots and drinking.

"Come on guys, be reasonable, I don't mind you being here so long as you get out of my plants".

The tall lad said to the others. "I think I just farted, did anyone hear anything?"

"Maybe it was a fart, maybe it was a white shit." Mohammed said. He looked directly at Stu as he said it as he finished saying it he spat at Stu and the spittle landed on his leg.

"Ok boys, there is no need to be disrespectful. It is time for you to leave now". Hicks had remained quiet and calm throughout this provocation.

"Fuck you, white trash". Said the older of the Eastern Europeans.

"Look in the mirror some time, daft lad, you will see that you are white too". Hicks replied. The hilarity of what the boy said made him laugh. As he did he noticed that the boys had got up and as Mohammed approached him the other black lad was starting to move round him. The two smaller boys knew what was going on. They had also spread out. He instantly knew they were looking for some trouble.

"Boys, please don't do anything too stupid." The tall lad mistook this for weakness. From his sleeve he pulled a knife. It was a small dagger shaped knife with a four inch blade.

"It's not too late for you, just leave." Said Hicks, quietly.

The boy lunged towards Hicks with the knife in his right hand. He was to Hicks' right hand side. Hicks used his own right hand and parried the knife away. He hoped that he would not have to do anymore as the lad gathered himself and held the knife low and close to his stomach. Mohammed closed the gap to the left side of Hicks and aimed a punch to the back of Hicks' head. The punch arced round in a hook. Hicks moved smoothly on his feet and deflected the blow upwards and grasped the boy's wrist with his own left hand. He used the boys own momentum and twisted the arm into a straight arm lock and pushed Mohammed away.

"I haven't hurt anyone yet but if you do not go now I am going to hurt you really bad". Hicks said to the boys.

Ishan, the taller of the boys didn't believe Hicks. He wanted to slash him. He needed to keep his reputation. If there was a problem in the Acheron Street Crew Ishan was the enforcer. Who did this old man think he was calling the odds and disrespecting them in their own street? He was going to pay, big time. He came forward again, no thrust this time. A short horizontal sweep towards the old white man's gut. Before the knife really got moving he felt the crushing impact to his upper arm and the upward thrust into his outer thigh. Hicks had struck his brachial pressure point with his clenched fist and at the same time hit the femoral pressure point with a powerful knee strike. The knife dropped from his grip and landed on the ground. The boy remained standing but the leg and arm that Hicks had struck felt like jelly now. Mohammed came onto Hicks swinging both arms wildly. Hicks stepped forward and as he did so Mohammed passed him. Hicks jabbed him once in the side near the bottom of his rib cage. The connection was solid and winded Mohammed with impact and the pain of the broken rib.

The two Eastern boys were rooted to the spot with fear. They watched, transfixed, as Ishan now pulled a screwdriver from his trouser waistband with his left hand. He lunged wildly at Hicks. Hicks stepped towards Ishan and trapped his left arm, with the screwdriver between his right hip and elbow. He transferred the grip to hold the boys forearm with his own and struck with the heal of his left palm. The breaking of the elbow joint was audible. Ishan screamed. He clutched his arm and held it to himself. He shook and his face became ashen with the start of shock.

"Sit down, there." Hicks sat him back on one of the tall planters.

"I am going to call an ambulance for you and give you first aid. If I don't you might lose the use of your arm". Hicks reassured the boy.

He untucked Ishan's T-shirt and turned the bottom of it up over his forearm to make a sling.

The back door of the house opened and Di stood there she was aghast. She had never seen her husband in this light before.

"Di, please could you get the first aid box?"

"Yes Stu, no problem"

Mohammed lay curled up on the floor he was clutching his side. Hicks checked his breathing for any traces of blood and satisfied that there were none he reached into his pocket and called an ambulance.

Saturday

Call taker: Hello, crime stoppers.

07753390543: Hello.

Call taker: Thank you for calling crime stoppers. Your call is anonymous unless you want to claim a community action reward.

07753390543: I don't want a reward but I want to tell someone about what I heard yesterday after prayers.

Call taker: Ok, in your own time.

07753390543: I was at the central mosque when I heard two men talking about something very bad. I am a good Muslim and what these men was talking about was wrong. They were talking about taking a white girl to Sheffield for sex.

Call taker: Ok, what town are you in?

07753390543: Scunthorpe, they can't know who I am or they will make my family's life hell.

Call taker: Ok, that won't happen. Who are the men?

07753390543: One was Ranjit Quereshi and the other was Tariq Hasni.

Call taker: Ok, do you know who the girl is?

07753390543: No, but Mr Quereshi is the mayor of the town and is really big mates with the police. I am scared nothing will happen because he is so important. I have seen a white girl with some boys from the Acheron Street gang.

Call taker: I will pass it on. Sometimes the police do operations that you can't see. It doesn't mean that the police are not working on it.

07753390543: Yes, I know this. But the girl can't be taken away. It is wrong. These men are no true Muslims if they do this. I hope they are caught.

Call taker: Can I take your name?

07753390543: No.

Call terminated.

The call taker spun in his chair "Hey Mr Davies," he shouted up to the manager.

"What's up?" Replied Mr Davies.

"Can you listen to the call I have taken please?"

"Now? It's nearly my break time."

"Boss, it is urgent."

Mr Davies listened to the call. He then listened to it again to check he had not missed anything from the call. He picked up his telephone and called Special Branch. Special branch did not let Scunthorpe Divisional Police know about the call.

Tariq received the SMS late in the evening. It was from Abdul.

Abdul: Hello brother.

Tariq: Hello mate, how are you?

Abdul: Alright, thank you. How are you?

Tariq: I am fine. Did the package arrive for our associates as we planned?

Abdul: Yes they are very pleased with what you have given them.

Tariq: Good. Is the boy acting properly?

Abdul: Ranji says he is doing well.

Tariq: Thank you for letting me know.

Tariq was delighted. It seemed that the customers were pleased. Business would continue with these men into the future. They paid good money for their entertainment and that money would be going straight into his pocket. He just needed to complete the circle and have her brought back by Kharon and given crack. Then she would be able to continue to make them money to pay for the dependency that they fed.

He called Kharon.

"Hi Kazzy, how did it go?" Tariq asked on the phone.

"Thank you for calling, Uncle" Kharon remembered his manners nicely. "It went very well thank you"

"The girl?"

"She was ok, she performed pretty well. They liked it when she cried" Kharon reassured Tariq.

Pol Winchester sat in his office at the police station. He was checking through the incident logs that remained on his area. One of them caught his eye. It was a report of a girl missing from the children's home in Ashby. He knew the girl's name. This was the girl that he had loaded into the ambulance a week or so before. The incident was being handled by the duty inspector. It was not his boss, Mr Robinson, tonight. He read the text of the log.

Regular female misper. Missing from Cambridge house, Cambridge ave, Ashby. This is the third time she has been reported missing this week. No indication where she might be. Recently has had behavioural problems.

Pol picked up the phone and dialled the duty inspector.

"Hi Boss, it's Pol up at North, how are you?"

"Alright, thanks mate."

"Do you need any people to help with your search for that misper, I have got three cops and seven PCSOs on duty tonight. I can divert them to you if you need them?"

The inspector dismissed the idea straight away. "It's ok Pol. I don't want to waste your resources on this crap. She will be out with her boyfriend getting pissed or fucked in some alleyway"

"I saw her the other day with some of the boys from the Acheron Street Crew. I can get some of my guys to pop along there?"

"I don't know about that Pol, I don't know if the Acheron Crew even exist. But no, don't worry about it she will turn up. She is a regular misper."

"Guv, I suspect that she might be on my beat and with these boys"

"Yeah, maybe, anyway I have to go to the nick now. Catch you later mate". The inspector added.

"Yeah cheers, boss." Pol replied.

He put the phone down.

He was amazed by the apathy the inspector displayed, she was just a kid. She might be a regular missing person but should they just abandon her. If she was living with her parents in a nice middle class world she would not be treated like this. He had been foolish to make the call. He should have just deployed his people to do the checks. If he did now then the inspector would be able to claim that he has disobeyed his orders.

He picked up his radio and asked for all of the units on his beat to return to the station. Whilst he waited for them to return he made himself a cup of tea. By the time he walked back down stairs towards his office the constables and community support officers were all back in from the streets and sat around in their room.

"Ok troopers, give me a minute". He logged onto the computer nearest the smart board and found a picture of Jasmine. He projected it onto the smart board.

"Right, this is Jasmine Peters. She is a fourteen year old missing girl. She's in local authority care and I think she is pretty vulnerable".

He looked around the room as he wandered about keeping their attention as he spoke to them. The constables were all experienced and time served officers. He could see them as they examined the girl's face on the screen.

"Remember the girl I put into the ambulance with the injured fanny and arse? Well this is her. I can't direct you to go and look for her. The duty inspector has told me that we can't go out looking for her."

"Why not?" Asked Rachel, she was a good cop, over twenty years of good service now.

"He says we are too busy." Pol replied.

"Ok Sarge." She replied.

Pol closed down the smartboard and took a large gulp of his tea.

He closed the briefing by saying. "Thanks everyone, please return to your normal duties. I have no further taskings for you".

He knew they would go and look for her.

Pol put on his stab resistant vest and picked up his helmet.
He had a couple more hours left on duty and headed out
onto the beat to see if he could pick anything up on the
missing girl.

Walking out onto Ferry Road Pol's mind was buzzing with
where he could look for the missing school girl. He planned
his route to go down the alleyways behind Frodingham
road. He would stop off at Acheron Street and have a brew
with Sticks. Maybe check the Memorial Gardens and have a
chat with the street drinkers. He had heard that one of them
had received a really heavy beating from the Acheron gang.
The description matched that of Kharon Khan. But as normal
no witness would come forward. How could these people
expect to get rid of this gang of no one was prepared to
make a stand? They were happy enough to complain at
police authority meetings and at forums and in the street.
The gang were just a group of kids. They were nothing, this
wasn't LA or the tough East End of London; this was
Scunthorpe.

He patrolled down the alleyway. He didn't wear the
fluorescent yellow jacket that he was issued. He wore his
black issue T shirt and stab vest. He wanted to slide along
the alley way like some sort of predator. Unobserved and
quiet. This had been very effective for him in the past. The
streets and alleys were less busy than normal. The groups of
kids were not there tonight. He had hoped to bump into the
Acheron Street crew and do a few searches and try to shake
them up a little but they weren't on the street. Of course Pol
was not to know that Kharon and Nuelleh were in Sheffield
trading in the currency that was Jasmine Peters.

Pol arrived at Acheron Street without event. The evening was hot and he was ready to have a tea with his old friend. He knocked at the back door of Sticks' house.

"Hello Di, how are you?"

"Fine Pol, how are you?"

Di showed him into the house and through into the lounge. The huge dog grudgingly got off of the sofa and lay on the floor.

"He will be down in a few minutes, he is just in the shower. Can I make you a brew Pol?"

"Yes please, that would be really nice. Can I have tea?"

When Stu came down stairs he was looking well. He had lost a bit of weight in the last fortnight and there was a bit more definition to his shoulders and upper arms. It looked like he had been training hard.

"Evening mate." Stu greeted his old friend.

"How are you doing?"

"I had a bit of a run in with some of them little fuckers from the gang this afternoon". Stu understated what had happened earlier. He went on to explain what had happened in the back garden.

"Mate, they are little fuckers. They really need squaring up. They are making everyone's lives hell around here."

"Yeah well they won't come back round here in a hurry. They know what welcome I have for them".

"The thing is Sticks, they think that they are big fish but they are just low life thugs. The people are so scared of them they won't say anything." Pol aired his frustration.

"I don't think the tall skinny one will be throwing his weight about anymore. Well not with his left arm he won't be throwing anything around with it."

"That lad sounds like Ishan Hussein, he is their bully boy. It's a good thing it was him".

"Do you have to report it Pol?"

"I don't think so Sticks. It is a good thing. I certainly won't be reporting it."

"Ok mate, it's a shame we can't do them all over and get them out of the way". Said Hicks. It felt to Pol like he was exploring the possibility.

"Well, misfortune befalls all sorts of people" Pol sipped his tea and looked out of the window at the failing light. A blackbird perched on the back of one of the benches on the street. Pol watched as the bird lowered its folded wings slightly and started to sing. It raised its head high and opened its beak to sing. The song of the bird penetrated the double glazing and seeped into the room. The song in his ears provided a contradiction to the urban squalor in his vision.

Pol didn't know what he had just entered into.

Di woke in the night. She was not sure quite what woke her. Some feeling of insecurity made its way into the sleeping woman's mind and woke her. She lay for a moment or two in the feeling of indecision between sleep and awake. The bright colours and lights danced across the ceiling of the room. Yellow and orange flowed and swirled across the smooth white ceiling. It was the nose that woke her. She dragged herself from the bed and walked naked across the room to the window, she pulled the curtain to one side and allowed her eyes to focus on the scene below her. Their shed was alight. Flames licked out of the window and the doorway. The shed was sectional concrete and was full of their personal property. When they lost the house they stored a lot of things in the shed. The new house was much smaller than the old and the surplus, that the receiver hadn't taken, had to be stored somewhere. The shed was fully ablaze the flames grew every second she watched.

"Stu, Stu, wake up! The fucking shed is alight!" She shouted.

"Fuck, fuck!" He jumped up and was at the window with her.

"Bastards" he shouted at the shadows of figures that he could see in the alleyway.

"I am going to fucking get them". He ran from the room and as she watched out of the window he appeared in the yard. She noticed he had now put a pair of training trousers on over his boxer shorts. The other people in the alley way had slid away,

Di picked up her mobile phone and called for the fire brigade. She knew that by the time they got there the fire would have burned out and all of their belongings and furniture in the shed would be gone.

Stu stood in the alleyway as the fire spread. The anger left him and he felt drained and desolate. The flames would have burned through all of his old pictures and souvenirs that he had accumulated over his years of service. The memories were encapsulated in the pictures for Stu. The lump in his throat grew as emotion welled up inside him. He fought back the tears.

One of the girls from West St walked up the alley way and stopped beside him. He turned to her and said hello. She greeted him in a strong Eastern European accent.

"What has happened here?" She asked him.

"I don't know, I think some fuckers have burned my shed". He replied.

"Well it has burned, for sure." She replied.

"Who did it?" she continued.

He didn't look back at her he was entranced by the destruction of his memories in the flames. "I don't know, I think it was them little bastards in the gang that runs around here." He said quietly.

"I fucking hate them." She also was entranced by the fire.

"Yeah, I had some trouble with them earlier today." He said.

"The bastards raped me".

"Fuck, really? Did you go to the police?" He turned to face the young woman and saw the tears on her cheeks.

"It is a waste of time. I am Nadia" She said.

"I am Stu, I know the sergeant here. Do you want to see him?" Asked Stu.

"No, I can't. They own me now". She replied.

"I will talk to him, do you live here?"

"I work on the street".

As Blue lights started to appear she pulled her jacket collar up high her face and turned away.

Chapter 7

Scunthorpe, June 2011.

The morning after the night before. Stu sat at the table in the dining room with his old mate Pol. They looked passively down the garden without speaking. Di brought through a pot of coffee and sat it down on the table between the two men. She put three mugs down on the table with them and sat with the men. The coffee was strong, dark and with a rich aroma that filled the room with a glow.

They sipped the coffee from Help for Heroes mugs.

"I have these cups at home." Said Pol.

"Yeah, we were given them a few years ago, I did some stuff for them." Stu replied.

"Actually he ran the Marathon Des Sables for them, raised over ten grand in sponsorship for them, so yeah he did some stuff". Di was fiercely proud of her man's accomplishments. He was fiercely proud of her.

"All my souvenirs were in the shed, Pol." Stu looked down into his coffee as he spoke quietly. "There were photos and all sorts of things in there". Snap shots of my life.

"I know mate." Pol replied. He understood that those souvenirs were the only tangible link to some of the things that now started to fade into one another in Stu's memory.

"They are cunts" Stu said.

"Yeah" both Pol and Di agreed with him.

The trio discussed the run in with the boys from the Acheron Street Crew in the garden the day before.

"Did anyone see what happened?" Asked Pol.

"I don't know, maybe. I don't want them nicking for this". Replied Stu.

"It's not about that mate, we have got a young lad with a smashed elbow. He might say that you assaulted him and try to get you locked up". Said Pol.

"Yeah, I had thought about that. It is a worry for me". Said Di.

"For fuck sake, I don't think he will do that because he wants to be the hard man. He won't want to admit that an old boy like me kicked his arse, will he?" Stu doubted his own assertion.

"Mate, these little fuckers will do whatever they can to keep control of the streets and if that means using the cops to their advantage then they will do." Said Pol.

"The court will believe me, I will tell the truth and they won't be able to prove it. It didn't happen for fuck sake."

"Stu, they will report it as a racially aggravated assault and you will get nailed out for it. They will cook up their stories, no fucker will back you up and then you will be getting shafted in the showers at the scrubs before you know it".

Di put down her coffee. She looked directly at the cop. She

knew all about him. Stu had told her about the sort of ma that he was and she knew that they could trust him. "Tell us what we should do Pol".

Pol looked up at his friend's wife, he looked her straight in the eye and said to her. "Ok this is the deal. You both need to call the police anonymously and report that you have seen an incident in the street and tell them what has happened. Then there will be a bit of doubt in the case. If it goes to court then those two anonymous calls will give the court enough to doubt what the prosecution say in their bollocks witness statements."

Pol looked out of the window and saw a young blackbird perched on the wall between the houses. He wondered if the bird he had seen the previous night was the parent of this bird and was the young blackbird waiting for his breakfast. It wasn't singing.

"You know that you can't disclose this conversation. I will get fucked if you do." Pol added.

"Really? You don't say soft lad" Hicks laughed as he spoke to his old brother in arms.

Their eyes met over the table. There was an unspoken understanding and the shared memory of Tanjoc was a bond stronger than words ever could be.

Special branch did not operate out of normal police buildings. The Humberside and South Yorkshire teams had been merged and found residence in a nameless office building on an industrial estate in Doncaster.

Detective Inspector Steve Day was the senior officer of this team. He was a solid time served detective with only three years left to serve. He followed orders to the letter. He believed in what he did. He knew that the world was full of bad people and the good people of England needed his protection to keep on living the lives they did. He was a very intelligent man who followed his orders, but not blindly. He had an intuition and an understanding of people that quickly took him to Inspector rank but a resistance to follow corporate direction that meant he would never make Chief inspector. He said it was bullshit and he would rather spend his time catching villains and putting them in gaol.

He was early in the office, as always. On a Monday he liked to get a head start before his staff landed in the office. He wanted to get a look at any new developments and decide how best to allocate the jobs. He knew once the others came into the office he would not be able to concentrate properly. So he followed his routine. He sat at his desk, plugged his laptop into the secure server and whilst it warmed up he went for a piss and got himself a mug of strong Yorkshire tea.

The stack of emails in his inbox sapped his moral the second he looked at them. He followed a few simple rules. Anything from his boss he opened and scanned through to make sure that there was no immediate taskings. The emails from the admin assistants could wait until he had dealt with the serious business of fighting criminality. Most of their stuff would be leave requests and similar trivia.

Then he would get into the bones of the emails. The electronic intel reports. He liked to 'keep his finger on the pulse'. His team worshipped the ground he walked on. They thought of him as a copper's cop. They saw he was a bit of a Jack the lad and a bit of an old school detective. What they struggled to see was the razor sharp mind and steely determination.

At half past seven the team started to roll in. The teams briefing and official start time was nine but most of these guys also liked to be ahead of the game. Special Branch was staffed by officers who routinely went far and beyond the call of duty, the cream of the CID departments across the country. Dc Dom Watson was one of those detectives. He wasn't like the younger and flasher looking cops he worked with. He wore an old green coat, not a traditional detectives Macintosh. He was old and unfashionable. But he was in special branch because, like his boss, he had a nose for crime.

"Dom, come to my office please".

"Right Guv'nor, I will be right there."

Dom walked into the DI's office and was shown a chair. He sat and looked at the boss waiting for the briefing.

"Dom, there is something going on n Scunny. I am not sure quite what it is but it fucking smells. I know that much."

"Ok, Boss, What do we have?"

The DI placed a piece of yellow paper on the desk, an intrep.

"Crimestoppers call, says that Asian men are grooming white girls for sex."

The DI placed another report on the table.

"Report of a racially aggravated assault on a kid leaving him with a smashed elbow. The kid reporting it is, according to the force's intelligence, the local gang's enforcer."

The DI Placed two more reports on the table.

"Two calls to crime stoppers, reporting a local man has defended himself against a youth with a knife hurting the youth's arm, relates to the report of assault I have just mentioned, the dialogue is so similar it is believed they are related. It's almost like they are scripted".

The DI placed five or six reports on the table.

"A load of intreps from the local NPT Sergeant. Talking about the gang that the youth with the broken arm belongs too"

"Ok, what do you want me to do with it?" asked the detective.

"Go over there and weave all this bullshit into something that makes sense".

"Ok boss, what have we got on the two related Crimestoppers calls?"

"Not much really, checks have been done on the phone numbers that made the calls. Pay as you go, Tesco network".

"Alright then boss, I will have a look at it".

Dom Watson returned to his desk and logged onto his computer. There was little to go on. The call records from the two mobiles had been checked and on one phone there was a call to a local number and on the other mobile there was also a call to a mobile number. It was a start. Dom then searched on the two numbers he had come up with. The landline number was the number for a local pizza delivery service but the other one was more interesting. It was the number of the local neighbourhood sergeant.

A little over an hour later Dc Dom Watson was parking his car at the front of Scunthorpe North Police station. He was there to see Sgt Pol Winchester.

Pol and Dom sat in Pol's office drinking coffee.

"So what is it that I can do for you?" Asked Pol.

"A call was made to you the other day from a mobile number, 07852278934, to you. Who was it from?"

"I don't know off hand, let me check my call list". Pol replied. "Give me the number again"

"07852278934"

As Dom recited the numbers Pol searched through his phone history. He found the number. He realised what the special branch detective had come for. The number was Stu Hicks'. He put his mobile phone down on the table and looked up at the special branch man.

"Where is this going?" Pol sat still and spoke quietly maintaining eye contact with Dom. He knew he was compromised. His pulse raced in his head. He took a breath, refocused. This could be the end of his career. This potentially could mean time in jail for him.

Watson saw the split second of realisation in the eyes of Pol. He knew that he needed to act quickly or the sergeant would shut up shop and stop talking to him. "This intelligence is for use by special branch alone." Watson, dunked his hobnob. "You understand what that means?" he spoke quietly, he did not look at Pol, he changed his posture and opened to Pol, he looked him in the eye. He knew this would appear conspiratorial to Pol.

"Yeah, I think so", Pol replied tentatively.

"It means that the information will not be passed outside of the special branch. It means that it won't get back to division and won't get back to discipline and complaints". Watson ate his hobnob and watched Pol. He had collected himself and had started to think more clearly. The brief break in the man's poise was over. Dom didn't think there had been many and he certainly would not see another.

"Do I get that in writing?" Pol asked.

"Do you fuck as like." Watson replied. Both men laughed and a connection was made between them.

"Ok, I will give you it all," Pol said, his mind stepping ahead. "But not here, I don't trust that D and C haven't got this place bugged". Pol wanted control, he wanted a venue that he could set up. He wanted to record the conversation. Nothing would be in writing but he wanted some sort of insurance.

"Alright, Pol. Here is my card. Text me where you want to meet." Watson got up. The men shook hands and parted. Later they met. Pol gave Watson everything he wanted. He told him about Stu Hicks. He told him about his fears and about what he suspected was going on with the vulnerable young girls of the town. He didn't tell him about Tanjoc.

He knocked at the door and was greeted by a tall, handsome woman and a big fierce looking dog. "My name is DC Watson, are you Mrs Hicks?"

"Yes, I am. Please come in officer." Di invited Watson into the house.

"Is Mr Hicks home?"

"No he is out training at the moment but he will be home pretty soon. Can I make you a coffee officer?" Di showed Watson into the lounge and gestured for him to sit.

"Thank you, Mrs Hicks. That would be lovely. White with no sugar please." The detective sat down and stroked Winston who had also made his way into the lounge and sat beside Watson but on the floor. He was big enough that his head could rest on the arm of the chair.

Some minutes later Di carried through a mug of coffee for her guest. They talked about the weather and about the state of the town but Watson avoided anything about the local gang or the problems that Hicks had confronted just a couple of days before in his back garden.

Hicks came into the house through the back door. He was sweaty and heaving for breath. His training regime had really stepped up in the last week and he was starting to look and feel like his old self again.

"Stu, this gentleman is from special branch". As Hicks walked into the room Watson stood up. He extended his hand and Hicks shook it.

"How is it that I can help you?" Hicks asked.

"Well actually it might be better to say how can I help you". Watson said.

"Really?" Stu had been towelling himself down but now had stopped and watched the detective sip his coffee.

Watson was uncomfortable around Hicks, there was something about him that he could not quite quantify. Winchester had seemed tough but measured and controlled but Hicks just felt dangerous and explosive. Watson sipped his coffee and used it as a prop to hide his nervousness behind. Hicks recognised what he was doing and took a step towards him further pressurising him.

"How is it that you can help me then?" he said.

Watson put down his coffee. "Well we operate a scheme where in exchange for certain information we might be able to authorise cash payments. The payments can be quite big depending on what the information is".

"Like the grass system from Ireland?"

"Yeah, that's the scheme."

"I don't think I know very much though. Well not much that can be of assistance to you anyway" Hicks continued to towel himself down.

"You know Sergeant Winchester?"

"Yeah, I have known him for many years. We did a bit of soldiering together. Back in the day." Hicks sat down in the armchair opposite the detective. He studied the shabby, middle aged man. He watched him sip his coffee nervously. He saw the crumbs on his coat and the stains on his tie. He also sensed the sharp mind and the will to succeed that the man possessed. Watson told Hicks there were concerns about Winchester's performance and that they needed someone close to him to try to gather information about him. Hicks agreed to help Watson. Hicks talked to Watson about Pol's growing hatred of the Acheron street gang and that he felt that Pol would become so focussed on them he easily could cross into the realms of obsession. When asked Hicks told Watson that he didn't think that Pol would take the law into his own hands, he was far too disciplined to allow that to happen.

"So what does Pol tell you about this gang then?" Watson asked seemingly casually. Hicks knew this sort of man too well to believe that anything he ever said or did was casual.

"He doesn't give me specifics and he never names names but he opens up and shares his frustrations with the law and the processes that bind him."

"If he gives you names I need to know, we are worried about the security of the information he possesses". The detective knew that the ex-special forces soldier was lying to protect his friend. He might be trained in resistance to interrogation and torture but the cop knew for sure he was a liar.

Their conversation moved on to talk about Stu and Pol's time in the jungle before the detective handed a mobile phone to Stu.

"There is one number stored in the memory, it is under Mum. If you need me call me on that number. If it's urgent then you can call me whenever. It will only ever be me that answers. Do not text any information and don't leave a message on the voice mail." Stu took the phone from Dom and put it in his pocket.

When Dom left the house there were a couple of lads in the street near his car. He turned to Stu and said "If you want to discuss the claim for your shed any further please call the customer compliance department".

Stu immediately picked it up. "Thanks for coming round Mr Joyce, loss adjuster, my fucking arse!" he shouted and slammed the door.

He went straight in and picked up his phone, the same one he used to call Crimestoppers and text Pol. Pol replied almost straight away.

SMS CONVERSATION

Stu: We need a chat

Pol: Ok

Stu: Meet at Brigg swimming pool. 6pm. Bring your speedos

Pol: Ok.

By the time that Dom reached his office a copy of the text conversation was waiting for him on his desk. Exactly as he planned.

She looked like just another bag of rubbish laying in the alleyway. People walked around her on their way to work at the chicken processing factory or in the dwindling steelworks. She was just another piece of shit littering the shitty alleyway. With the burst black bags of rubbish and detritus. Her blue jeans bloomed into a darker shade where she had lost control. Her wild black hair was plastered to her face with mucus and vomit. The hoody she was wearing was covering much of her face. If the passers-by, had not been absorbed in the bubbles of their own lives, looked at her face they would have seen the pretty eyes of the fourteen year old. They would have seen the unblinking lifeless gaze of the girl as they started to cloud as the chill of death seeped into her. Finally at peace Jasmin Peters, fourteen years old. Abused by her stepfather and her own mother. Taken into care. Looked after by corporate institutions and professionals. Found comfort in the street gangs, finally she felt like she belonged. What did she know? She belonged to them. They possessed her, betrayed her, violated her and threw her away. Discarded and wasted, like any other commodity when its exploitation is complete.

The police received an anonymous call about her. They arrived a little after eight o'clock. After briefing and after a coffee. The marked Proton drove down the alleyway and stopped just short of the small figure laying in the gutter. The officers climbed out and walked over to the girl.

Pc Tommo Tomlinson and Pc Sarah Pyke approached the girl.

"Wake up!" Tommo shouted at her as he approached her.

Of course Jasmin did not respond.

"She's still pissed as a fucking bandit". Sarah muttered at a volume that only Tommo could hear.

Tommo bent down beside her and listened for her breathing. Of course Jasmin was not breathing.

"Sarah, she's not fucking breathing!" Tommo said to his colleague as he easily turned the small lifeless frame of the girl over. They both were trained to a good level in first aid but as they turned her onto her back they felt the stiffness in her limbs. Her lifeless eyes stared skywards. Of course she could not see the clear blue summer skies above her. She could not see the swifts and swallows as they wheeled and turned between the houses on scimitar wings.

Sarah looked down on her face and recognised her. "It's Jasmin Peters." She was difficult to recognise. Her face was distorted and misshapen, flat on the left where it had been in contact with the cold pavement as she had lay there in the alleyway. Her blood had pooled in that side of the face with post mortem lividity making the flat area from her nose, cheek and towards her ear blossom into a deep dark purple. Blood streaked mucous had dried in a slight trail from her nostril and its passage could be traced across to the distended, distorted and disfigured side. Her left eye was heavily bloodshot whist the white of her right eye remained clear and open.

"Control from Bravo Mike One Three," Tommo called up on the radio.

"Go ahead, BM13". The distant radio operator answered.

"Yeah, I can confirm we have a Sierra Delta, here". Can I have supervision please?"

"Roger, any ID on the SD?"

"Yes, I can identify her as the misper Jasmin Peters".

Whilst this radio conversation was taking place Sarah had taken a roll of police tape and closed off the ends of the alleyway. She had put her hat on and stood smartly about thirty yards from Tommo and the dead child. She looked down at the scene of her colleague crouching over the dead girl, he could see he was talking to her. She knew he had kids of about that. For fuck sake, she was only a kid. As she looked at them a woman walked up to the tape on the far side of Tommo and Jasmin. She lifted the tape and started to walk down the alley way. Sarah could not believe what she was seeing, she walked quickly back towards the woman and stopped her. By the time they met they were adjacent to Tommo and Jasmin.

"What on earth are you doing? Didn't you see the tape?" Sarah was incredulous.

"I need to get to work" The woman said.

"This is a police cordon, you can't just walk through"

"This is the way I walk to work every day, why should I change my route?" She was edging to walk past the constable.

"There is a dead girl there," Sarah pointed at Jasmin and

Tommo.

"Yeah, so? It's got fuck all to do with me now are you going to let me past or I will be late?" The woman asked Sarah.

Sarah was an experienced and professional officer. This was the first time in her eleven years of service that she felt like assaulting a member of the public.

"Walk back the way you came or I will lock you up and make sure you don't get dealt with until tomorrow, then you will be two days late for work". Sarah spoke in a quiet controlled manner.

The woman turned and walked back up the alleyway as she did she said "Power mad pig bitch!" despite herself Sarah responded. "Fuck you low life". How could she have known that six months and an investigation later those four words would cost her career?

She turned to Tommo. He sat on the ground beside Jasmine, he was crying.

"Come on Jasmin, wake up."

Of course Jasmin would never wake up.

At 1500hrs that afternoon Pol attended the afternoon Divisional management meeting. He sat round the table and represented neighbourhood policing. The Detective Inspector chairing the meeting moved his way through the agenda and came onto the commercial burglary section.

"Pol, we have had a further instruction from the Detective Super for you to focus your guys efforts in the area of Commercial burglary."

"Yeah, no problem sir, we have made some large scale reductions in that area previously by targeting the most prolific offenders with diversionary strategies". Pol knew how to talk the talk.

"Yes and that has been noticed and recognised. But the pressure is on to increase detection rates and lower offences. This is an area that, because of your previous success, has been earmarked as statistically crucial for the division. Can you pop to the office, after this briefing, and discuss the tactics that you intent to deploy on this please Pol."

"Yeah, no probs, Guv".

Pol knew that he was going to be tuned in by the DI about his persistence in targeting the Acheron street gang. It would be explained to him that the direction that they are given is determined by the division policing plan that is partly set at the home office.

The meeting progressed through the normal categories and each department made their normal contributions to them.

Pol thought to himself that he could almost write the script for this meeting day in day out.

He was waiting for the final section. The missing persons section. He was keen to hear any update on the vulnerable missing girl Jasmine. The DI gave the meeting the update on all outstanding mispers. There was no mention of Jasmine.

Pol interrupted the DI.

"Excuse me boss, any news on Peters?"

"No longer a misper it seems Pol." The DI replied curtly.

"Oh good, when did she get back?" Pol asked.

The Intelligence Bureau sergeant laughed and said, "Just another weed in God's garden, heroin works its magic again".

Pol looked directly at the still grinning sergeant and sad to him "Mark, you are a true wanker, she was just a kid."

The DI stepped in immediately. "Pol, that's enough, please keep your language civil"

"Civil? What's civil about laughing at a child's death?" Pol growled, never taking his glare away from Mark Sandford, the detective sergeant from the intelligence team.

The colour was rising in the cheeks of the DI he was angry. Pol was not sure what he was angry about. He knew that Sandford was his blue eyed boy. Pol guessed that the anger would be directed his way. Sandford could do no wrong.

"Leave the meeting Pol. We will talk afterwards and I will be making your inspector aware of your unprofessional outburst.

Pol stood up and picked up his note book and pen. He slowly placed them in the pocket of his Kevlar body armour and pushed in his chair. He looked the DI in the eye and said "Thank you sir". He said it in a way that made the 'sir' sound like an insult. The meeting was silent, the other staff sat and looked at their notebooks or their pens. No one gave any sign off support to Pol, even the Child Protection Unit officer kept her head down and looked away from Pol.

Pol stalked back to his patrol car, he didn't stop for a coffee with the drug team sergeant. He went back to his station and awaited the storm he had just stirred up.

On his arrival at the station George greeted him. "Hello young man, who have you been upsetting now?"

"Bloody hell George, how do you know already?" Pol replied.

"I know fuck all mate, but it's written all over your face".

Pol told George what had happened. George laughed and said to him, "When are you going to learn? For fuck sake Pol, you want to be an inspector? You have no chance they will make you leave"

"I know mate." Pol replied.

"I will make you a brew and then I will show that bloke from the college into see you."

"Yeah, good call mate. I didn't know Charlie was coming in

today?"

George looked after the admin and would often make appointments for Pol and put them in his diary.

"Neither did I, Sarge, he just rocked up." Pol walked off to his office and threw his body armour into the corner of his office. Pol thought that Sandford was a knob. It would be nice to see Charlie today. But the visit was not expected.

George came through and put the coffees on the table in front of the Pol. He showed Jackman in and directed him to a chair. George also put a small plate down with some home baked fruit cake on it. "My wife baked this for you, Pol. She said it would do you good. I say it could sink ducks".

"Thanks mate."

George left them to their coffee and slice of cake.

"What can I do for you today, Mr Jackman?"

"Well, you can start off by calling me Charlie." Replied the lecturer.

"Sorry mate, what's up?"

"You know I came in a little while ago and we spoke about Rhianna. Well she has had lots more problems at college of late. Her attendance has gone to rat shit and her attitude stinks. I am starting to think that she is kicking about with the Acheron street crew."

"Ok, that's, not good at all"

"No and Kharon is round at the college all of the time. He is in and out of the class rooms and workshops and he is causing a real problem. The other staff are too scared to say anything to him and he struts about like he owns he place".

"What do the college security do about him?" asked Pol.

"Them? Security, they call themselves. A crock of shit. They won't go anywhere near him."

"Oh, I see. So you don't have all that much faith in their performance?"

Both men laughed, both understood how serious the issues they discussed were but found each other's company could bring the humour out in both of them.

"You know, when she started she was obviously very bright but had come from quite a troubled background. I had hoped that we would be able to progress and really give her some direction in her life. To be fair she was a good engineer too." Jackman continued to enthuse about Rhianna. "Now, well I don't know how to reach her. She has changed. When she comes in she comes in late and without an apology, her attitude sucks now."

Pol and Charlie discussed options whilst they drunk their coffee. It was difficult for Pol to advise Charlie. Both men knew that without some sort of intervention the future of the girl was starting to look bleak. Pol knew just how bleak as he remembered young Jasmine as he had seen her when he loaded her into the ambulance; torn, broken.

When Jackman finally left the building Pol stayed in his office and looked out of the window. The summer evening was drawing in and the sodium light above his office window had just come on. It was on some kind of automatic device that detected the daylight.

Kids were playing football in the park and he could hear their laughter and shouts in the dusk. Moths and bugs had started to emerge and seemed to make their way toward the sodium light from all over the town. He watched them turn and circle attracted to the light's intense glow and butt against the lens. Time and again they would fly into the glass, they would turn around and then fly straight back into it, the glow of the light irresistible to them. Pol watched one of the bigger, clumsier moths carry out this circuit. He studied the insect in its flight, studied the angle and arcs it could turn whilst always striving to attain the collision with the glass covered sodium orange glow. The moth reached the apex of one of its arcs and turned to head back to the light. Out of the surrounding increasing dark a bat appeared. Within a fraction of a second it had swept, on its black blurred wings, through the light and back into the gloaming. It had gathered up and devoured the moth. Pol had seen this happen many times and he knew the bat would be back and would take the next moth, then the next and then the next. Moths would keep coming to the light and the bats would keep coming for the moths from the darkness. He had no choice. He picked up his mobile phone.

SMS Conversation.

Pol: Mate your Rhianna is in trouble?

Stu: What has she done?

Pol: The fuckers from the gang are after her.

Stu: Like what?

Pol: They want her like that poor kid I told you about.

Stu: Thanks buddy. I will sort it.

A transcript of the conversation was automatically emailed to DC Dom Watson. He had finished work and was at home enjoying a scotch when he received the email to his mobile phone. He quickly read the text, immediately understood the gravity of what he had seen. He emailed his boss.

Unit 21 Kings Cliffe Industrial Estate, Peterborough.

Meeting between Mr Green and Mr White.

Both men carried out the prescribed security checks before entering the office. When Mr White arrived Mr Green had already set up the projector and had opened his secure BlockMaster drive. But according to protocol he had closed it back down until the duress procedure was complete and he was satisfied. This was the biggest job that he had been involved in. He wanted to get this right, not let some minor procedural mistake detract from the work that he had done.

"Things are gathering momentum at Scunthorpe. Fortunately we have a source close to the Mosque where it seems that most of the transactions take place." Explained Mr Green. "There was a girl taken to Sheffield last week. Fourteen year old Jasmine Peters. She is dead. Heroin overdose"

"Ok, please continue." Said Mr White.

"They are looking at taking another girl. Our source is talking about it happening soon".

"Right, is that copper, Winchester, causing any more problems?" Asked Mr White.

"Well, not per se, but this came in through a technical channel" Mr Green, projected the conversation between Pol and Stu onto the wall.

"Mmm, this is interesting. Who is the other party?" Mr

White's façade slipped slightly with some excitement.

"It is a former SBS trooper, Stuart Hicks. Served with Winchester. We have recruited him, he is an asset."

Mr Green projected a large photograph of Pol and Stu walking into Brigg swimming pool together onto the screen.

"Let's run with this and see how it develops. These two could resolve our head ache. Update me on all developments immediately". Mr White directed.

Chapter 8

To Sarah and Brandon Byrne the North Lincolnshire village of Scawby seemed like a rural hell. They had been moved to The Grove from their home town of Rotherham. The reason they had been removed from their home was their secret. The care staff at The Grove were not allowed to have access to this information, it had been deemed too sensitive by senior social workers in Children's Services. They had promised each other not to tell any of the other kids at the home their secret. The Grove was a converted country house and was set in its own grounds and gardens. But it was a world away from the Yorkshire town of Rotherham. A world away from their comfort zone.

Brandon and his sister stepped out of the taxi that had transported them from their home town. They picked up the one shared bag from the boot. All of their possessions were contained in one small holdall. A figure appeared around the corner and walked towards them. The figure was a tall man, older. Brandon thought maybe fifty years old.

"Hello" the man called to them.

Brandon and Sarah stood together and looked at each other. They did not reply to the man. Another stranger in their lives.

"I am Matthew" He smiled and spoke with a friendly confidence.

Neither Brandon nor his sister replied.

"Come on then let's go inside it's nearly time for tea".

Matthew reached forward to try to take the bag for the fifteen year old Brandon. Brandon stood back and refused to hand it over to him. "Ok, it's Ok" Matthew's easy smile returned.

He turned and started to walk towards the door. Brandon and Sarah followed behind him. They walked together but with a larger gap between both of them and Matthew. He led them into the home and into the dining room.

A large table was set for them with five other children and two other care workers sat at it. This was intended, by Matthew to make the brother and sister feel welcome. It made them feel anything but welcome. They felt that they were under scrutiny and on show for the other kids and staff to examine. Both of them bristled defensively.

They took their place at the table beside each other. Under the table and unseen by their audience they held their feet and lower legs together. They sought their comfort where they could, where they had done so many times before, in each other. The only people they could ever rely on.

School was an easy transition for them both. They had been round a fair few schools in their educational history. The last, Brinsworth Comprehensive was pleased to see them leave. Brandon had exhibited very 'challenging' behaviour. This had included confrontations with fellow students and with teaching staff. The school valued its inclusiveness, almost as much as it valued the Byrne's pupil premium extra funding. Sarah had been of equal but more subtle concern to the educational authorities in Rotherham.

It seemed natural for Brandon to fit straight in with the lads at his new school that were most like him. The lads he sought out were the members of the Acheron Street Crew. He fitted in with them well. They felt they ran the school and he liked that. He felt an affinity to the two Latvian lads, Mikhail and Ludviks Skuja. They were dispossessed and far away from their home. He was away from his family, they weren't, and he felt that made him more desperate.

He walked into the town after school. Sarah would get the transport back to the grove as she was supposed to. Brandon didn't. He liked to go into town and run with the guys from the group. He liked the older lads and they liked him, he thought. He knew the language, the youth culture pseudo gangster speak.

Really Brandon was a lost boy, he wanted to fit in wherever he could. He had nothing in his life but his sister. The boys in the Acheron street gang made him feel like he belonged to something. He could be someone with them. Behind his façade of tough and cool he was alone and afraid. More vulnerable than he could imagine. Behind his blue eyes he was a child.

Kharon Khan returned to his house on Acheron Street. His uncle had asked him to come home. When he went in his uncle was sat in the lounge drinking tea from a small glass. The tea had been served in what had become a traditional way. Strong, with condensed milk and plenty of sugar. Kharon didn't like it much. But his Uncle Abdi liked to have his tea like this.

"Hello uncle." Kharon spoke quietly and diverted his eyes as a mark of respect away from the older man.

"Hello Kharon, sit down." Although this was Kharon's house and his home he deferred to his older uncle. He had stood and waited for the invite from his uncle. Kharon knew that his mother would be in the kitchen. She also knew how to behave properly and when a senior male member of the family came into the house she made her way into the kitchen.

"Lets' talk about business Kharon". Said Abdi.

"Yes uncle". Kharon looked towards Abdi, he had been working hard to keep things going, keep things expanding.

"What happened to the last girl that went to Sheffield?"

"She took too much heroin and died, uncle". Kharon did not know where this was going.

"Yes she did and you know what? That was a waste. We could have been supplying her heroin and crack for years and years whilst we creamed off her money on the streets, but you let her die?" Abdi looked hard and clearly at Kharon and then continued. "I hear good things from both Tariq and Abdul about your improving and increasing business acumen. But you need to learn from this and not let it happen again. Do you understand?"

"Yes, uncle." Again Kharon had diverted his eyes and looked down at the ground.

"What can you do to stop this happening again?" Abdi had given him the opportunity to show his intelligence, had trusted him to use his own initiative.

"I have been thinking about this a bit, uncle. In future when a girl comes back from one of the parties in Sheffield we could have one of the more experienced whores look after her. If we tell the older one that they can give the girl her heroin that will make sure the young one won't over dose, the older one will no doubt short change the young one. It will be in the interest of the old whore to keep the young one working. What do you think Uncle?"

He looked at the face of the older man and sought his approval. He got it. "Yes, Kharon, I like it. That will keep them close. It was an idea that I had been toying with, I am glad that you have had the same thoughts."

The young man grinned, he beamed with pride. This was the approval he sought. He sought to exploit his advantage. "Uncle, it is important that we control the supply of the drugs to the kaffir whores. I have been thinking about having one of the older ones and their boyfriend hammered by one of the boys. Then we can tell the others that we had heard she was getting her gear from someone else. If we go for one of the older ones it doesn't matter too much how damaged they are because they don't get many punters anyway."

That made Abdi smile in turn.

He knew that Kharon was starting to really grasp the business side of the business now. Abdi also aspired to step up from the operational level and become more of a manager to the people working for him. He had spoken at depth about how to best develop the lad with Tariq and it seemed that now their plans had started to take shape. It was also important for him to impress upon Kharon that he would be working for them and them alone, that he was also just a small part in the business empire that he and Tariq worked for.

"We can't have another white whore die like that, not only will it lose us money but if the police investigate it properly it has the potential to expose a number of senior people in the community." Abdi spoke to Kharon intensely again.

"What do you mean, Uncle?" Kharon looked at Abdi.

"Think about it, if the pigs took DNA from her …"

"Yes, Uncle, I see. They could trace where she had been and half of the men that she had been with. Those men might tell the pigs about who organised it".

 Kharon shuddered at the thought. He knew the repercussions of such a thing. He knew that if it had been caused by his own foolishness it would result in his sudden 'return to Pakistan' a euphemism for an unexplained disappearance and subsequent murder. He knew that there were some serious people involved in this business. He knew that they would make him disappear in the blink of an eye.

"This is how it works, you need to do something. We don't trust you, white boy, we don't know you, white boy." Kharon turned to face Brandon.

"So what should I do then Kazzy?" Brandon sought his acceptance from his new family.

"There is an old bitch that needs showing who the boss is." Kazzy saw this as a chance to get a new member initiated.

"She has been getting her gear from someone else. I don't want no other fucker muscling onto out patch". Khan continued, he was gesticulating with his hands, smacking one fist into his open palm and then changing over and punching the other palm. The slap of the punches punctuated his speech.

"Ok, what do I do?" Brandon was a puppy dog willing to please.

"Show the kaffir whore who's the boss, I want you to go and own that bitch"

"Yeah, no problem Kazzy".

Brandon felt his stomach lurch with anticipation and a little fear. He had been involved in fights and aggro before. But never had it been so calculated and never before used as a means to increase business. This wasn't like a fist fight with another lad. This was a planned beating.

"If you go down there with Ishan and Mikhail, they will point her out to you. She is a dried up whore. When you do it you need to shout out about getting her gear from the other fuckers. We own these fucking streets and we need to show them that they can't do what they want." Still the repetition of the slapping of fist into palm.

"Does he have a boyfriend?"

"Yeah, but he is a burned out junky that needs a smack if he starts anything".

Brandon, Ishan and Mikhail walked together down West Street. They were quiet, the conversation was not full of the bullshit and bravado that Kharon had shown them earlier. They knew they were going to do a job. They turned onto Gurnell Street.

This was where the old prostitute, Maureen Slight would be plying the oldest trade in the world. She liked to work here because the town's CCTV cameras gave good coverage. She wanted the punters that used her to be captured on film in case she was ever attacked.

As the boys rounded the corner onto the street. Ishan pointed to her and said "That's her the old one".

"Fuck me people pay to fuck her?" Brandon asked.

"Not as many as used to, she doesn't make much money for us anymore. You can smash her junky face in. We want her marked. Wait until I have got to the other end of the street Miki will stay here. Take her down the alley way. There are no cameras there" Ishan was calm and relaxed, for him this was normal business. He wanted a lieutenant and he thought that Brandon might be ideal. For sure, Brandon talked a good fight, they would see if he had what it took to hand out a kicking.

Brandon's breath was shortened as he felt the adrenalin had started to course through his veins. There were other whores on the street but Maureen was the oldest, the thinnest and most drug damaged. He needed the others to see the kicking and hear why it was given. He felt sick with anticipation. He knew he would have to exhibit a high level of violence to make sure that he found the approval he sought so badly. He saw that Ishan was now in position. Mikhail stood still. The whores on the street herded together, the boys were obviously moving into positions around them, with look outs posted at each end of the street. The women looked to each other with frightened eyes.

Brandon stepped into the mouth of the alley way behind the school. The five women watched him as he stepped into the alley way and he turned to look at them. They closed until they were almost touching each other against his circling menace.

"Maureen, I have something for you" He called out to them.

"What is it?" Maureen looked at him, the others looked away. Her blue watery eyes fixed on him and her sunken, hollow cheeks sagging. Her lank, greasy blonde hair rested on her shoulders.

"It's something from Kazzy."

She knew that the heroin she depended on came from New Mo. But she had guessed that it originated from Kazzy Khan. This was not what she was used to. But she knew that she had been working hard, giving what she had earned to the Acheron street gang. She had supplemented her tomming money with shop lifting. She had been getting here gear only from New Mo.

The palpable relief swept over the others. It was not their turn today. It was Maureen's turn.

Maureen walked slowly into the mouth of the alley way. Brandon stood with his left hand extended with his fingers closed as if to pass something to her. Maureen wondered if he actually had bought her some gear. Maybe in reward for her shop lifting. As she got close to him he could smell her. The cheap perfume failed to mask the body odour, despite the quantity that she had clearly used. She extended her cupped right hand to receive whatever this lad had for her. She watched with entranced attention awaiting a small foil or cellophane package full of her tonic, her nemesis, heroin to be dropped in. Her addiction had been her fate for the greater part of her life. Now it was an all-encompassing darkness.

No package dropped into her hand. Instead an arcing punch from the right hand of Brandon Byrne crashed into her cheek, the concussion of the blow was instant and she would have collapsed had Brandon not reached forward and grasped her by the front of her hoodie. He held her on her feet and pulled her close to his face. The daze of the concussion blurred his words. Maureen could not hear him. A wave of sounds overwhelmed her and rung in her head. She was barely conscious when he shouted within inches of his face the boy's saliva showered her face.

"You get your shit from us!"

He let her drop forward and as gravity took her down he swung a short and chopping uppercut into her face. The crunching of the bone was audible as her nose was smashed and split across the bridge. Maureen's head snapped back and she started to fall back backwards the last threads of her consciousness slipped away. The boy grabbed her hair and stopped her from falling.

"You buy your fucking gear from us, you fucking dirty bitch!" again he shouted at the unconscious woman.

The other prostitutes looked on and watched down the alleyway. They understood that a statement of intent and a declaration of ownership was being made.

Brandon let Maureen drop to the ground. He stood over her prone collapsed form and aimed a savage kick into her midriff. Her body absorbed the impact and was rocked back, almost lifted from the ground.

"All of you fuckers listen and fucking listen good. We run this place, you come to us you dirty fucking cunts". Brandon was shaking now.

He kicked the woman again. Her breathing had deteriorated into a low gurgling rattle. He turned to the women huddled looking down the alleyway, spat on Maureen, and shouted. "Get back to fucking work filth!"

Brandon stepped over the unconscious woman. He walked away leaving her lying in a pool of her own blood. Bubbles of frothy blood emerged on her lips as the jagged points of her ribs pierced her lung. Her life hung in the balance.

Later the same evening in the Acheron Youth Centre Kharon met up with Ishan, Abdi and Tariq.

"How did the new white boy do?" asked Kharon.

"He was good, he gave that bitch a real beating". Replied Ishan.

"Mmm good, will they know what it was about?" Abdi, as always was very business focussed.

"Yes, he made it very clear." Ishan reassured Abdi.

Tariq looked towards Kharon, "Kharon, we need to send another bitch."

"Yes, uncle, I know. The new boy has a sister, she is younger than he is. I will have her by the end of the week."

"Well done, Kharon, and the one you have promised to me? What are you doing about her?"

"Uncle, she will soon be ours, she is more difficult but soon, she will make a good video, she is spirited and disrespectful".

"Good, that will make us very good money". Tariq was pleased with this and Abdi nodded his approval.

Kharon picked up his mobile telephone from the coffee table.

SMS conversation.

Kazzy: You did good.

Brandon: Yeah, thank you.

Kazzy: Come into town tomorrow.

Brandon: Ok, Kazzy.

Kazzy: Bring your Sarah I will get pizza

Brandon: ☺ thanks.

He turned to Tariq, yeah we will have you a bitch for the weekend no problem.

Tariq in turn took out his mobile phone

SMS conversation

Tariq: We will have what you want for the weekend.

Uncle Ranjit: My associates will be very pleased, you are doing well.

Brandon sat on his bed at Scawby. His knees hugged to his chest. His face buried in his knees. He curled up. His shoulders shook as he sobbed. Sarah sat beside him. Her hand on his shoulder.

"Who was the text from Brandon?"

"It was from Kazzy, he was pleased with what I had done for him this afternoon."

"Good, you have some friends there." Sarah stroked the back of his neck with her fingertips.

Brandon lifted his face up and looked at his sister. His face was red and puffy from the tears he had cried. His eyes blood shot and red rimmed with sadness.

"She was like an old woman and I kicked the shit out of her." He looked pleadingly at Sarah, she did not know what he wanted from her. She could not offer him forgiveness for what he had done.

"Bran, you had to do it. If you want to be in with these boys you have to do what they want."

"I know, they want us both to go into town tomorrow night and they want to buy us a pizza because they are pleased with the work that I did."

"That sounds mint," Sarah said excitedly. She was also lost and without friends in Lincolnshire.

"Let's go straight after school, I will take my stuff in my PE bag" The girl planned.

"Yeah, that sounds good." The beating of the old whore faded away as the promise of pizza became more prominent in his.

Sarah's fingers continued to tease the hair on the back of his neck. She leaned towards him and placed a delicate and gentle kiss on his neck. Then another. He moved his head to one side to expose the length of the side of his neck and allowed her to kiss his shoulder, his neck and up to the ear. She nibbled the bottom of his ear and whispered "I can make you feel happier".

He turned to face his sister and lay back on his Buzz Lightyear quilt cover. She kissed him hard, urgently on the lips. She pushed him down onto the bed.

The next evening as planned Brandon and Sarah did not take the transport back home to the Grove. They walked into town together. Sarah was excited about meeting the boys from the Acheron street crew. Lots of the kids at school talked about them. It seemed that since Brandon had started to hang with them he had been afforded a really high level of respect by the other kids. Brandon no longer queued for his lunch. Because Brandon was treated like this it meant that Sarah was also elevated in status.

"What is this Kazzy like? He sounds nice". Sarah asked.

"He is ok, he runs the show really. I think he is the main man around here".

Sarah, hummed as she walked along with her brother, her

slight and boyish frame filled with exuberance and excitement about her brother's new friends. Between them they had earned some money working with the street gangs in Rotherham. She thought she knew how to handle people, especially men and boys.

They turned on to Frodingham road and walked down in the alleyways towards Acheron Street. She felt a little less confident along here. The voices she heard spoke in foreign languages that she did not understand. The alleyways, she knew, provided an alternative highway for the people that did not want to use the main roads, people that had something to hide or someone to hide from. She watched where she was walking, there was filth all over the place. Dog mess, spilt rubbish, fast food laying around amongst the detritus of the town's poorer areas and poorer people. Hidden, like those people.

Brandon seemed to grow an inch as he walked down the alleyway. His walk changed from a purposeful and direct stride to a languid swagger as they approached the small basketball court at the top of Acheron Street. This was also the court of Kharon Khan. The brother and sister emerged into the open area and joined the gang. Kazzy was standing in the centre surrounded by his entourage. New Mo was with him as was Ishan. They were the inner circle. Brandon saw the two Skuja boys chatting with another lad he did not know. They were talking in a language he didn't recognise but thought might be Latvian or Russian. As he came into the group Kazzy stopped talking to Mo and turned to Brandon.

"Yo, nigger. How are you doing blood?" He greeted Brandon with a clenched fist knuckle punch.

"It's proper mint man", replied Brandon. Sarah thought this way of speaking was ridiculous, but all of the boys liked to do it. They thought it made them sound tough and like gangsters. She thought it made them sound like idiots.

Kazzy looked at Sarah and turned to Brandon. "Who is this hot little bitch, blood?"

Brandon replied "My little sis bro."

Kazzy continually stared at Sarah as he continued to talk to Brandon. He looked her up and down, he paused at her hips and at her breasts. She felt the colour rise in her cheeks as she blushed with embarrassment. She was flattered and instantly felt attracted to Kazzy.

Kazzy recognised this. He was not attracted to this skinny, weak looking white bitch, but he had successfully made her thing that he was. That was his intention and the first step of the plan complete.

"Bran-dog, man, the Ishan man tells me you were the fucking business with the old whore."

"She had it coming Kazzy, no one fucks with your crew."

"Yeah Bran-dog, you fucking right on. Do you want to be in our crew? We have a place for you in our team." Kazzy rested his eyes on Sarah, as he spoke he reached up and touched her arm and turned her so she was facing away from him. He squeezed her arse, like checking a lamb before sending it to market.

"Blood, that would be so mint!" Brandon replied.

"Go with the Ishan man, you will work for him, he is our muscle. He will talk about our business and talk to you about your part in it he will get you a pizza. I am gonna take this little honey for a special treat." Kazzy had not taken his eyes off of Sarah.

Brandon was quite confident that his little sister would be ok. She knew her way about, she certainly knew her way around men. She had plenty of experience to fall back on.

Ishan motioned for Brandon to go with him and they walked down to West Street. The girls were working the street already. Punters drifted by, faceless, nameless men in cars looking to buy a piece of sanctuary from their worlds.

"Bran-dog, we run this bitches" Ishan boasted.

"All of them?" Brandon was surprised.

"Yeah, when a new one comes along we make sure that she gets the message that we run the street. Sometimes their blokes try to pimp them. That's where we come in. You and me, we give them the fucking they deserve. We make sure they know the score."

Brandon looked down at Ishan's arm which was still in a sling following his encounter with Hicks. "Yeah, we are gonna make the white cunt pay for this." Ishan said, he was conscious that his arm had put him on the back foot and was pleased to have Brandon with him to help regain the initiative.

They walked along the road and saw whore after whore. As they approached the tall blonde woman working near the memorial gardens Ishan said to Brandon, "This is Nadia, she can be a bitch, and we need to take her down a peg or two."

Brandon looked at her, she was a tall and good looking woman, she didn't have the husk like appearance that most of the girls did. "But we can't mark her up too much, Kazzy won't like that. She must earn us good money".

"You are a smart guy, you are right this is all about business and she is one of our assets". The real intellect of Ishan was obvious to Brandon. Brandon made s choice that Ishan would not be a good person to cross.

It was the first time that Sarah had ever been out for a meal and at the restaurant she was awe struck when Kazzy took her into the Bengal Raj on Frodingham road. When he entered and the waiters called him sir and bowed to him. She watched as the waiters rushed around him and treated him as if he was a local celebrity, a football player or a rap artist. The waiters bought out the meals that Kazzy had ordered in Urdu. They bought out wine for Sarah. As they ate their meals she looked into his eyes and thought she detected some kind of sadness that held them in common. She felt emotion inside her, she really liked this boy, he knew how to treat her and he clearly respected her for who she was. Why else would he have taken her for a meal? The other men that had her before never treated her like this.

"I want you, Sarah." He said quietly. Her heart fluttered. He watched her reactions. He had timed its delivery perfectly when she was looking deeply into his eyes.

"I want you too Kazzy, but we have to go to the kids home in Scawby. We can't be together."

"Go on the run, we can find places for you both to be. Then we can be together."

When they left the Bengal Raj much later that night, they left hand in hand. They didn't see Pol walking along Frodingham road on the way back from collecting his fish and chips. He saw them. The image blasted into his memory cells. The image reminded him of the images of jasmine peters and Kharon Khan just weeks before. He did not know this girl. But he guessed that soon he would know her.

The fact that they were leaving the same restaurant as he had seen Jasmine and Khan leave previously was not lost on him. This restaurant was owned by Ranjit Quereshi, the mayor of the town. A top player in local politics and a pillar of the community. Pol returned to the station, he ate his chips and drank a mug of tea. Out of the window he watched another moth circle the sodium lights.

SMS conversation.

Pol: hey mate, fancy a swim?

Hicks: yeah for sure.

Pol: Brigg at 8?

Hicks: no bus, make it Scunny.

Pol: ok mate

The electronic transcript of the conversation appeared in Dc Dominic Watson's inbox. He forwarded the message straight away to DI Steve Day.

Pol and Stu met up at the pool as arranged. They walked in together with their kit in old fashioned rolled up towels. The groups of teenagers ran past them as they were deep in conversation.

"Pol, what the fuck is up with you? You have a face like a smacked arse man." Enquired Hicks with his usual level of diplomacy.

"Buddy I am climbing the walls with frustration, what the fuck can we do to nail these little bastards". Pol looked emotional.

"What is happening?"

"Them little cunts that are running your street are really taking the piss. You know that young kid that died in the street the other day?"

"Yeah, you said about her. Jasmine?" hicks replied.

"Yeah, that's her. She was only fourteen years old. She had been running with that gang. I think that they had more to do with her death than we know". Pol explained.

"All sounds a bit like paranoia to me, Pol."

"Before she went she was seen hanging around with Kharon Khan. I saw her going in and out of Ranjit Qureshi's restaurant with him." Said Pol.

"Ok. And what?"

They were in the coffee shop at the pool and Pol ordered

them both a coffee and they sat down next to the window.

"Well," continued Pol, "I have seen Kharon with another young girl coming out of there today."

Hicks put his coffee on the table and looked directly at Pol. "you think that she is going to go the same way as Jasmin?"

"Yeah, for sure she will." Pol said.

"That sounds very likely". Stu agreed with Pol.

They sat quietly and considered their coffees for a few minutes together. Stu spoke first. "Do you think that the mayor, knows what's going on?"

"No I think he is up to his eyeballs in it."

Their conversation moved on and they talked about the old times in the jungle. They never actually mentioned Tanjoc when they talked like this.

"The worst thing is, you know Stu, that we know all sorts of things about the gang but we can't do fuck all about them because we don't have the resources and for some reason the bosses don't want us to get too close to them." Pol vented his frustration.

"It smells like some sort of shit to me." Added Stu. This was the first time that Pol had actually allowed himself to consider the possibility that there was a conspiracy and that he was purposefully being diverted away from investigating this case. He knew that given a bit of time he could unpick them.

"I know that Mohammed Nuelleh keeps his stash of drugs in the back garden of one of the derelict houses at the back of West Street. I can't even get the dog handler to run his drugs dog through the gardens as he has been told specifically not to do any on spec stuff in the town centre by the DCI."

The men finished their coffees and headed to the pool to start swimming. As they walked through to the changing rooms Stu said, "Well maybe a terrible accident will befall them".

Chapter 9

The screwfix shop was only a twenty minute walk for Hicks. Since he had made the decision he needed to be properly prepared. Previously when he had done this sort of thing he had not needed to be at all forensically aware. This time was different. He wasn't in uniform or in a foreign land fighting an enemy of the British people. He was in the town centre of his home town fighting, he believed, an equally insidious threat. This time he didn't have the law on his side. He knew that if he was caught he would go to court. No amount of previous heroism would save him from prosecution if he beat up an Asian kid. They would jump on the racism bandwagon and throw the key away. He had purchased what he needed to. A pair of navy blue overalls and a box of latex protective gloves.

The late summer sunshine was warm on his face as he walked along Normanby road. The road was busy as people had started to leave work and head out of town for the weekend. He hummed quietly to himself as he walked easily swinging the white carrier bag in his left hand. He felt a bit of purpose starting to develop. Hicks was a man who liked to know what his mission was. He had always known what he had to do when he was in the service. Not having that shape and that direction in his life had proved to be one of the most difficult transitions into his new civilian life. Previously he had been following the directions of those in air-conditioned, comfortable offices far away. The killing had been impersonal and professional. This mission was self-imposed. This was a personal battle that he had taken on. The weather forecast was overcast for the evening. That was ideal. The darkness was his friend, he seemed to fit comfortably in to the shadows, away from the casual observer and hidden away from his quarry coiled and ready to strike.

"Di, I have something to do tonight."

"Oh, right, Stu. Would you please pass the vinegar over?" They did not often have fish and chips for supper but Stu had bought these in. Di thought that Stu seemed really positive and have some purpose tonight. Maybe he had found himself a job. She hoped he had, he needed it.

"What is it?" She asked.

"I am going to sort out one of these little shits around here." They continued to eat.

"Which one?" she asked hoping he would say Kharon was his target.

"The drug dealer one. I know where he keeps his drugs and tonight I am going to persuade him to stop his drug dealing."

"Ok, is there anything I can do to help you?" She looked up at him over a fork full of chips.

"Yeah, I will be doing it just up the street, if you could sit in our upstairs window and watch out for the police coming?"

"Yeah sure, no problem. When are you going out?"

"Not for a bit, until it is nearly dark, about half past nine I would think. Can you make sure the washing machine is empty and when I come in I will strip straight down and go in the shower? If you put my kit straight through the washer with plenty of bleach."

They finished their food and Di took the plates into the kitchen. Stu took out the overalls and removed all of the labels. He placed them, and their small plastic ties into an ashtray on the coffee table. Opening the drawer in the table he took out a box of Swan matches struck one and watched the flame grow on the match stick before he ignited the small fire that consumed the labels he fed it one at a time.

SMS conversation

Pol: My people are working the other end of the town. I have changed the patrol matrix.

Stu: Ok it will be about ten

Pol: make sure you clean up.

Stu: Yeah, I will

The message stream was, as the others had been, sent directly to the email inbox of DC Dom Watson. Dc Watson sent the email directly to DI Day

The evening drew on and at eight o'clock Stu Hicks, slid into his new blue overalls. He stood in the kitchen near the open door as he dressed. He was determined to leave the smallest possible forensic footprint. He slowly and deliberately pulled on his rubber examination gloves. The gloves were tight and hot on his hands. He knew he would be in them for a couple of hours and he hated the way that they made his hands sweat but he knew he must wear them. He did not want to be exposed to any of the scum bag's blood. He didn't want to leave a fibre or a piece of hair from his hand on him.

He stepped out into the grey growing gloom of the evening and slid into the alleyway. He kept his gloved hands pushed hard into his pockets. He made his way through the alley way behind the remaining houses of West Street. Several were derelict now. Due for a large 'urban regeneration' project. Or at least that's what the town council spun it as. Streets of the Victorian terraces had been demolished and then gardens planted on the site. First it was half of Gurnell Street now it was to be a block of West Street. The empty houses had spawned galvanised steel shutters over the windows in a vain attempt to keep out thieves and vagrants. Hicks looked at the house he was headed for. The steel shutters had been pulled off. In the growing dusk the black, dark emptiness of the missing windows gave the empty house a deeper feeling of malevolence than their surroundings. An inky blackness that concealed all within.

The lead flashing had been stolen from the roof and, he suspected, the rain had got into the structure and rotted the timbers of the floors. But he didn't intend to go too far in, just in deep enough to tuck himself into the darkness. To merge with the darkness and gloom. To disappear from sight.

The garden of the house was a rubbish dump. Black sacks of household refuse covered the ground, many torn open by stray dogs and foxes, spewing their foul smelling contents across the ground. Empty beer cans and cider bottles strewn all around over the ground.

This was a very long way away from the pristine and smart vegetable garden that once this would have been. The steel workers of a century before took great pride in their gardens and the vegetables they produced supplemented their income. But that was in the days when the Lysaghts foundry was working and the town boasted near full employment.

Now the steel works was a fraction of what once it was. Immigrants that flooded in from all around the commonwealth to feed the furnaces hunger for man power had joined the ranks of the unemployed. Those communities closed ranks and formed enclaves within the town. Housing had changed and this was the result. Hypodermic syringes littered the doorway and ground floor of the house.

Hicks tucked himself into the kitchen and took a moment or two to let his eyes become accustomed to the dark. The ceiling hung down where the rain had come in. Floor boards had been torn up where the copper water pipes had been stolen and weighed in for scrap. Hicks took a couple of steps back into the shadows and stood still in the darkness, he waited. It was lighter outside and he knew he would be invisible to the people on the street or to anyone in the garden of the house.

From his vantage point he could see the back bedroom window of his house. The window was in darkness and the net curtains drawn. He knew that behind those curtains his wife would be watching. He sent her a text message telling her he was in position.

He did not have to wait long before he heard the clamour of a group of youths making their way down the alley way. He watched them pass. It was the Acheron Street Crew. His target for the night, New Mo, was with them. They walked passed and further down the street and away. He knew that Mo would not want the other members of the gang to know where the drugs were kept. Sure enough a few minutes later a solitary figure emerged from the alley way. Hicks controlled his breathing and mentally prepared himself. When he emerged from the door way he knew he would have to cover the ground to Mo quickly and soundlessly. The youth walked into the garden and looked around as he came in.

Hicks recognised him immediately. It was Mohammed Nuelleh, aka New Mo. This tall slim lad of Somali origin was the man in charge of the drug supply in this part of town. He was a distinctive kid with closely cropped hair and very East African appearance. He was wearing a quilted jacket and black jeans. He did not appear to have any weapons. But Hicks couldn't see what he had under his jacket. Pol had told him that there had been information that suggested that members of this gang had access to a gun. There was nothing to say that was not tucked into the waistband of Mo's jeans.

Nuelleh took a couple of steps into the garden and stood still. He looked around and looked directly at the doorway Hicks was concealed in. Mo did not see Hicks. Mo stepped towards the house and was now within five meters of the back door. Again he stopped, looked around himself and looked directly towards the shadow that was Hicks. Hicks could hear the boy breathing. Hicks had controlled his breathing and heart rate. He was calm and relaxed. He knew this feeling well. He had practised it many times in the past.

Mo then raised a hand to his mouth, he placed his thumb and forefinger in his mouth and let out a shrill and loud whistle. This was quickly replied by two other whistles from either direction in the alleyway.

So he was not alone. The other lads were not far away. Hicks quickly re-evaluated his plan. The whistles sounded quite a distance from the garden. What hicks had planned would only take a few seconds. Hicks had an alternative route out planned. He would hop over two garden walls, into the alley way and on to a side alley directly onto the street. He could still do it and be away without being seen.

Nuelleh bent down and pushed a brick aside with his hand, he carefully lifted a small glass jar out of a hollow in the ground under the brick. Hicks could not see what was in the jar from where he was concealed. He knew this would be the stash of drugs. Nuelleh emptied the jars contents into the palm of his left hand. Hicks saw that it was a plastic zip lock bag containing foil packages. Hicks knew each of these packages would contain a 'deal' worth of heroin or crack cocaine.

Nuelleh looked closely at the small packages in his hand. He lifted his hand to close to his nose. He examined the contents of the bag like jewels. He was entranced by the wraps. He knew that for him those wraps represented prestige and power and an opportunity to gain credibility in the community. Each of these bags contained either crack cocaine or street heroin.

Both of his hands were full, his attention rapt in the drugs. This was the time. Hicks exploded from the doorway. Nuelleh had enough time to look up and see the darkness leap towards him, his eyes wide with terror. He had no time to shout before the shadow fell upon him.

Hicks punched him on the right of his neck, hard. This blow caused instant concussion and dazed Nuelleh. As he fell to the ground, semi-conscious, Hicks struck again, against Nuelleh's momentum by striking with the knee hard under his ribs. This broke the lower ribs in Nuelleh's chest. It forced the breath to gush from his body. He lay motionless on the ground. He was conscious but dazed. Wracked with the pain of fractured ribs. Hicks took the packages still clenched in Nuelleh's left hand and thrust them into his pocket. He rolled the boy onto his back and crouched over him. He searched Nuelleh as he lay motionless. From the inside pocket of the boys coat he removed a roll of cash. The roll was ten centimetres thick. Twenty and ten pound notes rolled together, the proceeds of so much drug dealing, harvested from the misery of prostitutes and victims of muggings. He pushed the cash into his overalls pocket and bent over so his face was inches from Nuelleh's.

"Can you hear me?" Hicks said to him in a quiet and relaxed voice.

"Please don't kill me" the boy whimpered.

"If you tell anyone who I am or what happened here I want you to know I will kill you and I will kill your family. I will come to them from the darkness and take their souls to hell".

"I won't say, I won't." Nuelleh was crying now.

Hicks placed one hand on the throat of the boy. He felt the boys pulse from his carotid artery in his finger tip. He moved his thumb so it was equidistant from the lads wind pipe and then squeezed his finger and thumb towards each other. He was careful not to crush Mo's windpipe but he cut the blood supply to his brain just enough to render him unconscious. As Nuelleh's body relaxed his right leg rolled outwards away from his left. The leg rolled onto a discarded hypodermic needle. The needle penetrated the boy's jeans and his calf. The tiny pinprick in the leg carried the HIV virus from some unknown junky that would, in the fullness of time, prove fatal for the drug dealer.

The following morning the manager of the Red Cross shop on Cole Street was somewhat surprised to find a little over five thousand pounds in the donations box.

The latest intelligence from special branch about the situation in Scunthorpe caused some concern to Mr. White. It had become quite clear that the reports submitted by the sergeant had been correct. The local force had chosen not to pursue the mayor of the town and a key member of the local liaison committee. The information from the phone intel had shown a degree of collusion between the sergeant and a former military colleague of his. Hicks, the former SBS commando appeared to be on a vigilante mission in the town and it seemed that this was being supported by Winchester.

The danger was becoming clear to Mr. White that should the local police get involved with investigating the sergeant the situation would not be resolved and, more dangerously, the sergeant might go public. If the sergeant went public then the worst fears of the local force and of the agency could be realised. It would be exposed that senior members of the police force had been at best reticent and at worst colluding with a child abusing network headed by the local mayor.

It was time to remove the risk and start to pull these ends together a little. The situation in Scunthorpe could resolve itself quite nicely if all of the pieces fell together.

Mr White sat in his office and pondered the direction to take over a cup of coffee. His massive and heavily engraved oak desk crouched like a monument to the past. A monument to the victories his predecessors had enjoyed. The deep green leather top had been selected to match the aged two seat chesterfield sofa and his heavy oak framed leather chair.

The walls of his office were oak panelled. This timeless feel surrounded him and added gravity to the situation. The laptop on the desk was the only link back into the twenty first century.

It was time for him to earn his substantial salary and make the most difficult of decisions. He hoped if he allowed this situation to develop in the direction that he wanted the two key players Hicks and Sgt Winchester would, without their knowledge, become powerful assets for him to use.

Deliberately he placed the bone china coffee cup back on the saucer and he opened his laptop and started to compose an email;

To: Mr Green, Mr Black.

Cc: Ms X

Subject: Developing situation Scunthorpe.

Dear All,

As we have discussed in recent meetings we have a situation starting to develop in the town of Scunthorpe. The latest information that I am receiving from other sources and from Special Branch suggests that Winchester actively diverted police units away from the area in which Hicks subsequently carried out a vigilante beating of a seventeen year old Asian youth.

I have considered the way forward with this and pondered whether we need any active involvement in this. We are currently at a point in the development of this situation whereby the local police and Special Branch are showing some interest. It is crucially important that we prevent them from interfering with this rapidly moving scenario.

The following actions are to be applied

Mr Green. Please have the recipient of the telephone intelligence changed from DC Watson to Mr Black.

Mr Black. Please contact DC Watson and assume the role of handling both Hicks and liaising with Winchester. Please use the name of DC Black. This will prevent the subjects becoming suspicious of our activity.

Mr Black. Please report directly and immediately to Mr Green.

Mr Green. Please report to me as a matter of your discretion.

Mr Black. Inform both Winchester and Hicks that you are assuming this investigation because there is a suspicion of corruption and the intelligence that they are giving may not be secure. They are to submit all intelligence to yourself and not divulge any information in relation to the operation to any other person.

I will brief Ms. X and she will ensure local Special Branch and Humberside Police Force keep their difference and do not compromise the operation.

If there are any questions please do not hesitate to contact me. We will look to arrange a meeting within the next few weeks to fully update. Venue TBA.

Kind regards

White.

Kharon spoke easily to Sarah, he hid his revulsion.

"Sarah, I want you to meet someone".

"Who Kazzy?" Sarah was eager to please, as always.

"This woman works for me and she is going to help to look after you." He spoke softly and gently.

"I don't need to be looked after, Kazzy. Me and Bran, we have been through some shit times together and we have always been ok". She was not sure what Kharon was getting at.

"Listen to Kazzy, he is the man". Asserted her brother, Brandon.

Sarah looked back at Kharon, "I didn't mean to show you any disrespect, I am sorry".

Kharon nodded to Mikhail who turned away from the group in the basketball court and spoke into his phone. A moment later Sarah saw the tall and glamorously dressed Nadia walk round the corner. Nadia looked at Kharon, there was no disguising the pure hatred in her eyes. Sarah did not see it. Nadia's visage changed as Sarah looked at her. She threw a smile on like a coat. Her gloss red lips parted and she showed her near perfect smile. Sarah beamed in admiration at her.

"Hello, you must be Sarah?" Said Nadia.

"I am, who are you?" asked Sarah in awe of this tall and

beautiful Eastern European woman.

"I am Nadia, I work for Mr Khan, and I am going to help you when you start to work for him"

"What do you do for him?" Sarah gushed.

"All sorts of things, really whatever he wants." Nadia didn't lie and she gave no inclination of the disdain she felt for Kharon or for the things that she did for him. She would never have thought as a girl in a rural Romanian village that she would be here whoring for a youth. She dreamed the western dream of making a good living and having wealth. She dreamed of designer jeans and i-players. She had been a bright girl and had done well at school. She came to England in a container on a truck. In exchange for a doing some work the passage to England she thought she would have had access to her dream. She had no idea what that work would be. She stood in the wreckage of her broken dreams and looked at this little girl who had all of this in front of her. In her turn young Sarah's dreams would be smashed, stolen, destroyed, torn, raped and discarded in the alley ways by these bastards.

She had been told by Kharon what was to happen to this girl in just a few days. She was to look after her when she came back, make sure she didn't OD and die. They wanted to safeguard their investment and make sure she had a log and profitable future for them as a resource. Her brother knew what was going to happen but had done a deal and allowed her to go. He had sold his sister in exchange for acceptance into the gang. Another bastard trading in the misery of the girl as an asset.

"Sarah, why don't you go for a walk with Nadia, she will show you round our streets and then you can see what we do here". When Kharon made a suggestion it was not a request it was a directive.

"Come on, my darling let me take you back to my place and we will talk about what work you can do." Nadia smiled at Sarah.

They walked together and quietly until they got to the first floor flat in Berkeley Street. Another Victorian house lost to multi occupancy. Bedsits in the ground floor but a flat on the first floor. They woman lead the girl up the stairs and into the lounge. It was well furnished and well maintained. A large flat screen television was on the wall, a leather sofa and a rug on the wooden floor. All in the most tasteful of creams and magnolia. The open plan kitchen was just behind the lounge.

"Have a look around at my flat, I will make a coffee." Nadia had been scripted by Kharon and as Sarah looked around Nadia started the espresso machine. Sarah thought it was so sophisticated and she wanted this, she wanted to have this life. Kharon had developed this manipulation to an expert level.

Nadia hated her part in this plan, but she also knew it was a chance to help to keep the girl safe and maybe help her get away from the growing darkness that loomed on her horizon.

"Have a look in the bedroom, Sarah" Nadia called to the girl as she made the coffee. The strong aroma pervaded the flat,

"It's where I do my business" she added , there would be a point in this meeting where she would have to tell Sarah about what was in line for her and this was the time. Nadia carried the coffee through to the, again, tastefully decorated bedroom. A flat screen TV was also on the wall in this room.

"The flat is really lovely, Nadia. It must be really expensive." Sarah asked. Her coffee steamed from the designer espresso cup.

"No it is paid for by Kazzy and the gang". I get to live here and earn money here.

Nadia had expected Sarah to pick this up and pursue it with questions. Sarah didn't she just let it go.

"Sarah, do you know what I do?" she levelled with the girl.

"Yeah, of course I do. You are an escort or a hooker." Sarah's nonchalance shook Nadia. She had expected that Sarah would have been disgusted.

"Yes that's right, I am. What do you think about that?"

"Nothing really. I couldn't give a shit. Is this what they want me to do?" Nadia could not tell whether this nonchalance was real or some kind of youth powered bravado.

"Yes Sarah, it is. You will be working for them too."

"I don't care, it's nothing I haven't done before. I don't mind getting paid to fuck". Nadia would have suspected that Sarah was trying to big herself up in front of her but her attitude seemed too relaxed for that.

"Do all of their girls get a flat like this?" The girl asked.

"No some live in council bedsits or hovels, some live on the streets. They are the crack heads and they get treated much worse than I do. I am clean and I bring punters back here. Sometimes visiting business men that they want to impress." Nadia said.

She handed the girl a cup of Italian blend espresso. Sarah, took a sip and turned her nose up at it. "I don't like it much, have you got any orange?"

Two streets away on West Street Di Hicks was walking home from work. She had worked hard at the minimum wage cleaning job all afternoon. She took pride in her work, even if the work was cleaning toilets and scrubbing floors. Her hands were dry and cracked, she once enjoyed manicures and massages at the spa. But since Stu had not been working there had been no such luxuries. The idea of spending that amount of money on a manicure was repulsive when they struggled to feed the dog and themselves.

She was only fifty yards from home when it happened to her. Di passed a couple of lads on the wall of the corner shop when she turned into the alleyway. She had seen them before, they were foreign, maybe Poles or Russians. They hung around with the gang. She thought nothing of it. As she passed them they slid off the wall and followed her into the alleyway. There was another young lad in the alleyway, tall and slim with sad blue eyes. She had seen him with them before. He would not look at her, as she approached him she stepped to the side and to let him pass. He stepped the same way. He stopped straight in front of her. She couldn't pass.

"Give me your purse" The lad said.

"I haven't got any money", Di replied.

"Don't fucking lie" the lad flared up and seemed suddenly angry. His sad blue eyes lost their soft edge and became inflamed and angry.

"I haven't got anything, but I live round the corner and my

husband might come here at any time, so best get lost". Di was not scared of these boys.

"I don't fucking think so. Now give me your purse you fucking white trash bitch".

He stepped closer, there were only inches between them. She should see the fear in his eyes. At the same time she heard breathing behind her. She felt fear, this boy could not lose face. He had others with him. He would have to follow this through. She reached into her jacket pocket and pulled out her purse.

"Let me show you, I have got nothing."

She unzipped her purse, there was a few coppers in it. He looked down into the purse and with no further warning lunged his head forward. She had time to flinch and half turn away the butt landed heavily on the top of her right cheek bone. The thin skin, stretched over the bone split easily and opened a cut two centimetres long and down to the bone. She was stunned. A second later one of the boys behind her kicked her in the side of her left knee. The knee bent, the wrong way. The ligaments tore away. She collapsed to the ground. The flash of white hot pain from her knee took her breath away. She looked up at the boys from the ground and before the kick that knocked her out landed in her solar plexus she said, "He will come for you".

The three boys laughed as they ran from the alleyway. They were still laughing when they got to the youth centre where they met up with Kazzy and New Mo.

Kazzy said "What the fuck is up with you bitches?"

Mikhail laughed loudly "We just slapped some bitch in the alley near West Street"

Kazzy, focussed as normal on business "Did you get any money?"

"No, she had fuck all, the white bitch" said Ludviks trying to act tough with his brother.

"Any gear?" Asked Mo. He turned and faced the laughing trio. He was still stiff and aching the bruise on the side of his neck had made his whole body stiff.

"No, nothing at all. But it was on your streets Kazzy." Brandon replied.

"Was it one of the whores?" Kharon asked plainly.

"No, just some white bitch". Brandon spoke quietly now. He felt unsure of his ground now.

The atmosphere had changed, had become chilled and both Kazzy and Mo had become more questioning. He felt them start to develop a level of hostility towards him.

"So you just beat up a woman for fuck all?" Asked Mo.

"No, we wanted to get you some money" replied Brandon.

"Who was it?" Asked Kazzy.

"That bloke that has the big dog on West Street, the one who slapped Ishan the main man. It was his white whore bitch". Said Mikhail, "it will show him who runs these streets, bro."

Mo shuddered. His face became ashen and grey. He was

overwhelmed with fear. He knew that what the woman's husband was capable of. He stood up violently knocking the table to one side and spilling drinks across the floor. A mug smashed on the floor, the sound of the breaking chine made everyone look at him.

"I am not your fucking brother, cunt. You fucking idiots!" He shouted.

"Do you know what you have fucking done? Do you know what you have fucking done? You fucking dickheads". The club was silent. Mo was normally a quiet and calculating man. This type of outburst was unheard of.

Mo stormed out of the club. He had left his mobile phone on the floor amongst the cocktail of coffee and coke.

On the table at the end of the youth centre Shaizal Islam was playing pool. He waited a few moments until conversation started up again then he stepped out and went home. He hated what these boys were doing. They were not real Muslims. He called Crimestoppers again that evening.

Nadia swam every day. Fifty lengths in lanes. She knew that she needed to keep her figure good, she needed to keep working. Bide her time and wait for her chance. Towelling her strong thighs and flat stomach she planned her evening.

She pulled on her tracksuit and picked up her bag and left the cubicle. She made her way into the seating area to check her text messages. Normally Kharon will have sent her details of any special punters. She rummaged through her purse and found change for the coffee machine.

She recognised the man at the machine, it was Stu. She had been there when they had burned his shed down. He looked angry his firm jawline was set hard. He kept looking up at the door whilst sipping his coffee. The muscles in his cheek bunched and relaxed over and over.

"Hello, Stu" She said.

"Oh hello, it's Nadia, isn't it?" He said.

"Yes it is, are you ok? You look angry." She said quietly she touched his forearm.

"They beat my wife up, just beat her up." his voice strained with emotion.

"Are you waiting for someone?" She asked him.

"Yes, I swim with my friend, he is a police man but he you can trust him". He added impatiently.

"I will swim again, with you, I have something to tell you".

Pol walked into the room and saw them talking, he recognised Nadia. He had seen her working the street. She had clearly been in the pool, her hair was wet and her cheeks flushed.

"Pol, Nadia is going to swim with us this morning, she wants to chat". Stu said.

"Ok, I have something for you too." Replied Pol.

"Nadia has something for us both" Hicks said to Pol.

"I will swim again with you both", she said as she went back into the changing room.

Pol didn't give tell Hicks everything he wanted to. Whilst they swam together he listened but did not say much. He was not sure about Nadia. Later in the evening he sent a text message to his friend and gave him the names of the Acheron Street Gang members who had attacked Di.

Chapter 10

Tariq sat in the driver's seat of his new car. Business was good and the trade in the girls had been very good indeed. He had been able to buy this car comfortably and with cash. Walking into the show room with cash in his hand was a feeling he will never forget. He knew he had arrived. He was firmly established as a main player on the scene now. This car was a symbol of his ascension to management of the business. The daily running of most of the affairs would now be left to the lad. The seat was so comfortable, it managed to retain style and comfort. The full grain leather was a deep and lustrous plum red. He had collected the car and taken it straight to an associate's garage where some new alloys had been fitted. The lower profile tyres gave the jaguar a slightly more sporty edge. The thought of the big Audi or Mercedes four by four had receded when he had set eyes on the new XF. He wore a smart Western suit but with no tie and a pair of ray ban sun glasses. The reinvention of Tariq Hasni was nearly complete. In a few years' time his part in the Acheron street gang would have been forgotten and he will be a wealthy and successful businessman in the thriving Asian community of Scunthorpe.

"Do you like it then Kazzy?"

"Oh yes uncle, it is befitting of a man like you." Kharon had become quite used to giving the correct and overtly respectful answers. He knew that if Tariq heard what he wanted to he would be more likely to make sure that Kharon got what he wanted. Kharon thought it was an old white man's car.

"You don't think that it is a car for old men?" It was as if Tariq could read his mind.

"No uncle. But normally only older men, who have made lots of money in business can afford a car like this".

"Wait until we got on the motorway on the way to Rotherham tonight, she just purrs along nice and fast and quiet". Tariq admired himself in the mirror. Part of his new persona was a pencil line beard and moustache. He liked the look.

"Uncle, the girl will be expecting your old car. I will text her that we will be coming in this." Kharon sought approval.

"After that she will go in your car." Tariq said quietly as he started the jaguar.

"I don't have a car yet, Uncle. I want to save for a nice car"

Tariq opened a small compartment in his door pocket and withdrew the keys for his BMW. He handed them to Kharon.

"It is yours, you are doing good work and I want you to have it now. It will help you run the streets for me. You look after me and I will look after you." Tariq spoke quietly as the two men made their way out of Scunthorpe and towards Scawby where they would be picking up Sarah.

"Thank you uncle. You can count on me."

They drove quietly for a few minutes and as they powerful car sprung onto the open road of Mortal Ash Hill Kharon spoke, "Uncle, did you say we are going to be going to

Rotherham?"

"Yeah, Abdi has a unit there. Sarah is going there tonight. The night is going to be filmed and we have got a couple of guys coming in for it. The guys are Somali niggers with massive cocks. The film will make us a fortune and then the old mates of Randy Ranji can have their fun".

Kharon didn't know that Abdi had a unit in Rotherham, but he was not at all surprised. He had told the kaffir whore to just wear a tracksuit because they were going out and that he would arrange her wardrobe. He had her clothes in a bag. She could dress in the car on the way. She would be wearing makeup already, these white trash whores always wore the shit.

They drew up and parked in the car park of the village hall in Scawby. Sarah and Brandon ran from behind the building and over to the car.

They approached the car and as they did so Tariq opened the driver's window a few inches. He looked at Sarah and then at Brandon. He spoke whilst looking directly at Brandon, "Not you, only her".

"Ok", he replied, he looked crushed.

Sarah got into the back of the car and as soon as she did Kharon's visage changed. "Hello, baby girl." He flashed her a too white grin. She blushed.

"This is my uncle." He continued.

"Hello uncle" she said to Tariq, she was trying to engage

Tariq, but unsuccessfully. Within a couple of minutes they were on the M180 heading towards their destination, all three remained quiet.

"In that bag on the back seat is a dress, put it on." Kazzy said.

"Ok" she took out the dress and slipped it over her head. "It's pretty".

"Take of your panties and bra and put them in the bag." Kharon commanded quietly.

She did as she was told to do by Kharon.

"Did you shave your minge like I told you too?" He asked matter of factly.

"Yes, I did" she flushed again as she replied.

"That's a good idea, did you think of that Kazzy?" Tariq asked Kharon.

"Yeah, they will like it". Kazzy was proud of his thoroughness.

Tariq nodded appreciation.

"Am I going to work like Nadia does tonight?" Sarah asked.

"What do you mean sweetness?" Kharon turned to her, this was not expected.

"Well, you know, as an escort, turning tricks?" She continued.

"Yes, you are". He replied.

"Hmm, ok" she replied, and took a stick of gum from her purse and popped it into her mouth to chew.

"Do you watch Hollyoaks?" she asked Kazzy.

Kazzy told her he did not, she turned to face him as she slipped her sweatshirt over her head. "Well, Mercedes has stolen some money…"

She was cut short by Kharon. "Shut up and get changed, I don't want to hear about that bullshit"

SMS Conversation

Nadia: they have taken a girl to Rotherham. Her name is Sarah. She is just a kid.

Stu: Have you told the cops.

Nadia: I can't they will send me back to Romania.

Stu: Can I tell Pol?

Nadia: yeah, it's not from me.

Hicks put his phone back in his pocket. Since the attack on Di he had not been out much. He wasn't training much and Di needed all of the help she could. The ligaments would take a long time to heal properly. She might always walk with a limp after this.

"Who was the text from, Stu?" Di asked.

"It was from Nadia, she told me they have taken another kid to Rotherham for their fun and games, bastards."

"How old is she?" Di sat with her heavily bandaged leg elevated.

"I don't know, just a kid, Nadia says".

"Mmm, what are you going to do about it?" Di asked.

"I will give Pol a ring I am sure that he will be involved in the search for her. Maybe he can steer the cops in the right direction and get this kid found before it all happens to her."

"Yeah, I think you should, babe."

Hicks lifted his phone from his pocket and dialled Pol. Pol answered quickly.

"Hello mate," Pol greeted his old friend.

"Yeah, I am fine, you ok?"

"Yeah, Alright mate, you know, trying to get by the best I can. How is Di's leg, Sticks?" Pol asked. He had been really shaken up by the news that Di had been attacked. But he also knew that he would need to keep Hicks held in check. If Hicks had instantly acted on the information they had shared in their evening swim and taken out the attackers it could easily have compromised them both.

"Mate, she is struggling now, she has got it bandaged up an it is really playing her up"

"Fuck, what do the doctors say, Stu"

"The NHS are shit, Pol, they just seem to fob her off all of the time. I wish I was still in the mob, we could have her into a military hospital and get this leg sorted out" The emotion was strong in his voice.

"Look Pol, I need to tell you about some shit that them bastards are doing." Continued Hicks.

"What is it, sweat?"

"Mate they have taken a kid called Sarah to Rotherham, they are going to rape her over there." Said Hicks.

"Ok, who told you?"

"It was Nadia, but she can't have her name involved because she is an illegal."

"Yeah, know the kid she is from the kid's home, she has been reported missing by them. It was her brother that was involved in the beating of Di". Pol had suspected this had happened when he came on duty and seen the missing person incident report.

"Mate, will you be able to do anything about keeping the cops away from that bastard Brandon? He has an appointment with fate that I am going to take him to", asked Hicks.

"He is just a kid Stu."

"He was man enough to cripple my wife, he is man enough to take what is coming to him for it".

"Yeah, I will have everyone working in the alley ways around West Street and Acheron Street whilst they are looking to find Sarah. They are coming on duty at three, I will have them out there and doing searches after four. My guess is that Brandon will make his way into the memorial gardens out of the way of the police."

"Ok, Pol, I will see how it looks and try and catch him alone about then or maybe a bit later. Will you text me any change of plan?"
"Yeah sure I will, now you be safe Stu."

"Yeah, Pol, you too"

When the call was terminated a full recording was sent, as an attachment to Mr Black.

Pol was rostered to work a late shift. As he pulled into the staff car park of the station he noticed a silver ford Mondeo in the front car park of the station. He rode slowly round to the bicycle shed and placed his machine on its centre stand. He was glad to have the shelter to place the bike under the sky look black and pendulous. The weather was close and humid, the weight of the air signified the coming storm. He pulled his helmet and walked to the rear fire door of the station. As normal it was propped open with a fire extinguisher. He stepped into the station and the heat hit him. The new stations had not been built with air-conditioning.

George was sat at his desk, he was dunking a digestive biscuit into a large mug of tea with surgical precision. "Afternoon, Sergeant Winchester, how is that old moped of yours going?"

"Alright, George. How are you doing, old timer?" Pol replied with a wry smile.

"I'm alright, there is a bloke in the front office to see you, don't know who the fucker is but he looks like some sort of SB or Crime Squad wallah to me."

"Right O, mate. Just give me a few minutes to get my shit together."

"Yeah, ok Sarge, I will brew up for you"

"Cheers buddy," Pol stepped into his office and stripped off his leathers. He wondered who the visitor was. George was likely to be right about crime squad or branch, not much got past him.

When George came in with his tea Pol asked him to show the guest in.

"Come in, please." Pol stood up and extended his hand to offer a chair to the man. Pol thought he could be an insurance salesman or any number of other things. He wore his dark brown hair short and side parted. He wore a pair of black rimmed spectacles. A simple patterned dark blue tie and a dark charcoal suit. It was a nice suit but not tailor made.

"My name is Mr Black, i am from the home office".

"Pleased to meet you, Mr. Black. I don't often get visitors from the home office, are you from Her Majesties Inspectors?" Pol had heard that sometimes the HMIC would pay a visit to an officer that might be a little outspoken in person to avoid being fed the party line again.

"No, I am not. Is that your machine in the back garden? Let's pop out and have a look at it, I like motorbikes." Pol understood this. Mr Black wanted to step outside out of the office, he feared that there might be some sort of listening devices in the office. The two men stepped into the back yard of the station and walked languidly together to the bike shelter.

"Pol, do you mind if I call you Pol?"

"No, I don't really care." Replied Pol.

They stood beside Pol's machine. "Who are you and why are you here?" Pol looked directly at Mr Black.

"I am from a department that investigates corruption at the very highest level, Pol."

"Right, go on…"

"I have been reading the intelligence reports and the informant contact sheets from this area. I have been paying close attention to your suspicions and have caused some further work to be done on it by our people. The thing is Pol, you are onto something." Both men were quiet for a second and then Black continued.

"It seems that the rot goes very close to the top. Your people know what is going on, but they can't stomach dealing with it. They know the top players are in the circle but they won't deal with them because it will be too embarrassing for them." Black paused.

"Yeah, that's what I guessed." Said Pol. "But I didn't really think it was true"

"Well, Pol, they will be watching you pretty closely. You have to be very, very careful. Pol, don't put any more information through normal channels. You can't trust them. Everything you say will go to the top and they will not allow you to expose key members of the Divisional Equality Council."

"Ok, where do we go from here?" Pol asked.

"You talk to me, me alone. Not Dc Watson. Not the Intel

Bureau. Don't talk to your Inspector about this."

Did that mean that Pol's trusted friend and boss, Phil Robinson was also involved in the corruption? Pol found it very difficult to believe that could be the case. Phil was a young bloke, not hugely experienced but his morals and principles had always been above reproach. Moreover, Pol trusted Phil.

"Does Inspector Robinson know about this shit then?" Asked Pol.

"I don't know, but I know that he seems to be reporting on you to the DCI."

"Right, I see".

Mr Black left the station in his non-descript car and left Pol sat in his office. Pol's mind spun and raced as all of the possibilities seemed to come and go in front of his eyes. He knew that what he had been doing was right bit now he realised how close he was to the truth. Should he try and press on against these people and expose them for what they were? He thought about going to another police force and speaking to one of the senior detectives there. But it was all an old boys club, they probably played golf together and drank in the same lodge. His pathway had never seemed to obscure. The direction he should take was obvious to him. He should push this home and ensure these people got what they had coming to them. They had entered into the dark and sordid world of sexual exploitation of young girls. There could be no accepting of that insidious trade. The senior officers that were complacent in this abuse were as guilty as the criminals. It was beyond Pol how they could just turn a blind eye to the cruelty and suffering that this cruel trade precipitated. Soon the rest of the team would be coming into the station he would deploy them into the Acheron Street area. He knew he was wasting his time and their time, he knew that young Sarah was in Rotherham. If he disclosed what he knew then he would expose Nadia and he was not prepared to risk her.

Pol walked out of his office and through the main office on the station's ground floor. He passed George without saying a word to him and went up the stairs to the kitchen. The inspector was sat at his desk he was fully engrossed with his computer. Pol made himself a mug of tea and made another for the inspector. He took the steaming mugs through to his boss.

"Hello, Guv'nor."

"Hello Pol, how are things?"

"Alright, you know, not so bad." Pol replied cagily.

The inspector sensed the change in Pol's demeanour and looked up from his computer.

"Boss, I have fitted some new pieces to my bike, come and have a look." The inspector looked quizzically at Pol when he said this. Phil had never expressed an interest in motorbikes before and this was out of the blue. Pol winked his right eye.

Phil was puzzled and clearly quite intrigued by this. Without saying another word e got up and followed Pol into the yard of the station and together they walked over to the bike shed.

"What is up Pol?"

"I can't trust the security inside, boss. I don't know if the offices have listening devices in them". Pol replied. He knew, as he said it that he sounded paranoid. Like some kind of conspiracy theorist.

"You are having a fucking laugh, Pol". Replied the inspector.

"Boss, I respect you and I am loyal to you. We are friends as well as work colleagues. Please trust me on this".

"Phil, I had a visitor today, he confirmed my suspicions about the young girls is true. But he said other things as well."

"Ok, who was it?" Asked the inspector.

"I can't tell you, but I can tell you that the missing girl from Scawby kids home has gone to Rotherham as a part of the abuse ring. I can tell you that Abdul Mohamed from the youth centre is big in this, he runs with Tariq Hasni. I can tell you that our people know all about this. But they are all in bed with each other and don't have the stomach to front the fuckers up".

"You know that Abdul is part of the Divisional Equality Council?" asked Phil.

"Yeah, of course I do. That's why they are scared of outing him I guess".

"He swims with the big fish" The inspector observed cautiously in tone.

"Yeah he does, look Phil, I won't talk about this with you anymore. I don't want to put you in a position." Pol turned and walked away. The inspector, stood alone in the yard. He took a sip of his tea whilst he tried to digest the conversation he had just had and then slowly headed back inside and in to his office.

The next morning Sarah came home from Rotherham. She was taken straight to Nadia's flat by Kharon. The fourteen year old girl was carried between Kharon and Abdul. Her small frame was light and easy for the two men to carry between them. She was alive and partially conscious. When she had been finished with she had been put in the back of the car. Kharon had given her something for the pain immediately. She was taken to a flat in Rotherham where she passed the night in and out of opiate consciousness on a towel on the floor. She was not sure if she was in a nightmare or reality. The light came and went. In the early hours Kharon gave her more heroin for the pain. She subsided into a torpor and became comfortably numb. She would remember nothing of the journey back to Scunthorpe on a plastic sheet in the back of Tariq's car.

Nadia looked at the child the two men had brought to her flat.

"Put her on the sofa, it is leather, it will wipe clean." Her mind screamed outrage and hatred towards the men in front of her. She knew better to express is and give them an excuse to hurt her again and again. She also needed to try to protect this child.

Tariq and Kharon dropped her on the sofa and walked out of the flat, they said nothing more to Nadia. They would be busy today. They would have to get the distribution network in motion to get the maximum profit from the DVD. The money would come in to Tariq's account by an electronic transaction later in the morning. He had asked Ranjit to use cash to avoid any kind of trail being left by the money, crumbs to be followed. Ranjit didn't like to use cash, he said businessmen don't carry thousands of pounds around in cash.

She was so small, so fragile. Her face was streaked by tears. Her heavy makeup had run down her cheeks and into her dirty hair. Her bottom lip was swollen and there was a trace of blood at the corner of her mouth. She was in a short dress that was smeared with blood and other stains. The tops of her naked thighs were streaked with dried blood. There was no fresh running blood so she did not need emergency treatment. The hospitals were not safe for her. Nadia covered the frail and torn body with a blanket.

Pulling up the foot stool near her to girls head Nadia started her watch. She watched the child as she was wracked by shudders. Shudders of visions surfacing from the depth of the nightmarish world she travelled through. Sometimes Sarah wept as she slept, Nadia stroked her face and hair tenderly as if Sarah was her own child. "It will be ok, I am here I can protect you", She spoke softly and hoped some of her words would penetrate the fog and reach the child inside.

Sms conversation.

Nadia: The girl Sarah is with me. She is alive

Stu: I will tell Winchester

Nadia: They really hurt her. I don't know if she will be ok.

The morning sunshine gave way to the warmth of the afternoon and as the evening started to descend Nadia noticed the first signs of awakening from the girl. She groaned with pain and turned to her side. She pulled her knees to her chest and clasped them tight to her chest. She sobbed, the quiet and helpless sobs of one deeply hurt.

"Sarah, I am here." Nadia stroked her face again, she moved the girl's hair from her eyes and wiped the tears away.

"Oh Nadia, I hurt." Sarah gasped through the sobs.

"I know, little bird. I know"

"Can I have something for the pain, I need something."

Nadia felt the despair wash over her as the need for heroin was washing over Sarah.

"Try to be strong and I will help you feel better soon" Nadia tried to calm the girl. She knew the bastards would have given her heroin for the pain. To start the addiction and make her their property. She would depend on them for her heroin, it would be another way they would exploit her. She would have to work for them to earn enough to pay for her habit.

"My pussy and my bum hurt so much, Nadia. These two big men were there and I was filmed as the fucked me. They were too big for me and they have hurt me." She covered her face with her hands as she spoke.

"Sarah can I look to see if you need to go to hospital or

anything?" Said Nadia tenderly.

"Yes," In a tiny voice.

"Turn the other way on your side and pull your knees right up." Nadia placed a reassuring hand on her shoulder.

Sarah did as Nadia asked and pulled her knees up. Nadia gently rolled the blanket from the girl and then rolled her dress up. She tried to keep her emotion and outrage in check as he looked over the girls most intimate areas. Sarah's anus was torn in two places, but they were not so bad to need stitches. Nadia would be able to treat them with anti-bacterial wash. Sarah's vulva and pubic area was mottled with purple bruising and inflammation. There was a large amount of semen seeping from her vagina. Nadia felt the raw gnaw of her anger welling into tears.

"Sarah, you will need to go in the sower as soon as you can, wash their filth from you. I have some stuff for you to wash yourself in. I will get you some painkillers"

"Can I have what Kazzy gave me for the pain?" Asked Sarah.

"That was heroin, they gave it to you too make you work for them."

"I don't care what it was, I really need it badly".

"Let's get today out of the way and tomorrow we will start again, one day at a time now". Nadia tried hard to keep her calm.

"Ok."

That night Nadia found Sarah a tracksuit to wear and they phoned out for a pizza delivery. They sat together and watched MTV, ate pizza and drank coke. They laughed together as they both tried to forget what had bought them and bonded them together. At the end of the evening Nadia made up the sofa bed and settled Sarah in for the night. She knew that if Sarah could get through the night it would be a small victory, tomorrow would be another battle and tomorrow night would be another battle. It might be many years before the war against the desire, so recently set, for heroin passed. Each day was a challenge for her. Nadia hoped to be able to guide Sarah through and maybe; just maybe, if she won more than she lost then she would not end up as another faceless, nameless whore working the streets and descending into the darkness and oblivion that had closed over so many like water closing over a diver as they plunged to the depths.

At two in the morning Nadia woke to use the toilet, it was unlike her to wake like this, maybe something disturbed her. She felt uneasy and shaken, she struggled to identify what made her feel this way. She swung her muscular legs out of the bed and walked lightly through to the lounge. Sarah was not on the sofa bed, the tracksuit was gone.

"For fuck sake, you stupid girl! Why have you done this?" Nadia slapped the palms of her hands down on the work top. She felt the tears of anger well up inside her. She knew that Sarah was in the clutches of the gang and escape would be so tough.

Sms conversation

Nadia: Sarah has gone out on the street.

Hicks: Ok, when did she go?

Nadia: I don't know

Hicks: ok

Nadia sat down in the alleyway behind Frodingham Road. She had two punters in the hour since she had been back on the street. She was sore and in pain. The punters had used her and had given her the money for the pain of the tears deep inside her body. She sat with her face in her hands. Curled up with knees clasped to her chest. She looked small, lost and alone amongst the waste and debris scattered in the alleyway. The nightshift at the steel works provided the deep roaring mechanical sound track to the scene. The clouds reflected the orange light of the blast furnace smelting iron. The fine mist in the air also reflected the light of the furnace. The town was illuminated in the halo of the hellish heat of the furnace.

The mist slowly soaked through the pale grey tracksuit that drowned Sarah's childlike frame and gradually the colour darkened to charcoal. Her hair was now lank and wet against her scalp. Her eyes were wide and staring as she looked straight down at the ground. She hummed an indiscernible tune as she sat rocking in the mist. From the corner of her mouth a thin strand of saliva ran inexorably towards the pool of vomit in her lap. She made no attempt to wipe the vomit away, no attempt to clean the saliva from her face. She was unaware of all around her. She was wrapped in the soft warmth of the opiate womb. The cocoon held her close to its centre and closed out the pain that would have threatened to envelope her. One pain was substitute for another pain. The memories of the previous days and nights were merging into her dreams and nightmares, her consciousness was just a veneer over the nightmare welling from the depths of her despair and carrying her, and all that is her along with her.

The syringe lay on the ground beside the little girl. Kharon had been very happy to have her supplied with the heroin and have one of his white whores to help her cook it up and inject it.

Chapter 11

Tariq answered his mobile phone. "Hello". His caller was Ranjit Quereshi.

"The girl, last week was very good," Ranjit complimented Tariq.

"Thank you uncle, I hope that your associates were pleased with her?"

"Indeed they were, she was exactly what they wanted".

"Thank you uncle and thank you for the prompt recognition of that with the bank." Tariq continued.

As he spoke on the phone he sat in his lounge. He was watching a video on the large flat screen television on the wall. The video was the final edit for release of the previous weekend with Sarah. The addition of the two well hung Somali guys was a master stroke. The video would make him a fortune.

"I hear there is a video of the evening, Tariq", Tariq laughed to himself. Ranjit was a shrewd old fucker. Nothing got past him.

"Yes uncle, there is a video, I was hoping you might be good enough to accept a token of my esteem once we have sold some?"

"Thank you Tariq, what a lovely idea." Ranjit laughed to himself. His days of worrying about collecting money from businesses and running whores were long gone. Now people just gave him money for allowing them to do business in his town.

Ranjit continued in his oily smooth voice. "Tariq, we want another girl, not this weekend but in a couple of weeks for a meeting of important businessmen. Do you think you can help?"

"Yes, uncle I am sure we can, especially if these gentlemen are prepared to show us the same degree of respect as the others did".

"Well, Tariq that is the thing, these gents are very respectful, but they want something more special this time, you have been telling me you have a girl in mind for some months now, I think it is time to show her."

"Yes Uncle, I do have the ideal girl for you and I am sure that your associates will be pleased". Tariq assured the older man.

"Yes, I am sure you will do us proud Tariq. Good night"

"Good night Uncle, I shall see you at prayers tomorrow to sort the other matters out".

Ranjit terminated the call.

On the large screen on the wall the picture showed a close up of Sarah's face. The fear was painted, like a mask onto her young face. Tears streamed from her eyes as she cried out in pain. The shot cut to a full screen image of penetration, her cries were audible as she was forced.

"Good," thought Tariq, they will love this, this is money for old rope.

He sent a text message to Kharon.

Sms Conversation

Tariq: Come to mine.

Kharon: Yes uncle. 5 min.

Tariq: Bring Nadia

Kharon: Yes Uncle.

Five minutes passed before Tariq heard a subdued knock at the back door.

Tariq paused the DVD and slowly, smoothly and silently slid in to the kitchen and opened the back door.

"Hello uncle," Kharon said to Tariq.

Behind Kharon in the shadow and away from the light of the kitchen stood Nadia. Tariq smiled a little. He thought he saw fear in Nadia's eyes. Her blue eyes were wide and cold, but what he mistook for fear was a deep and pure hatred. A hatred bred from the pain that Tariq had subjected her to and distilled by the suffering she saw all around her. Further aggravated by the hell that he had put Sarah, and others just like her through.

"Come in, Kharon, can you go through to the lounge." He turned to Nadia, "You go up and undress"

Nadia turned and left the room without saying a word. She didn't need to say anything. She knew her role here, she knew what was in store for her. She prepared herself mentally for the ordeal she was about to endure. As she stood in the middle of the room that Tariq called his 'playroom' she undressed. She slid off her boots, slowly, deliberately. Placed them together in a pair by the door. She unzipped her fleece, and again, slowly with ritual like deliberation folded it and put it on the top of her boots. She undressed and stood in the centre of the room naked. There were no more rituals to undertake. There could be no more distractions to come. Her mind focussed on what was to come. This would be the last time.

In the lounge the men sat on the sofa. Tariq opened a beer and gave it Kharon.

"What do you think of the video?" He asked Kharon.

"It is well edited and put together". Kharon answered with a matter of fact business mind.

"I think it will sell very well." Tariq continued, he motioned to the screen with his hand.

"You see her crying? Well they will love that." The image on the large flat screen television was of the young girl crying in fear and in pain. Tariq enthused "This video will make a fortune for us."

"When will it hit the distribution network, Uncle?" Kharon could sense a good pay day coming from the video sales.

"This week, we have to ensure we get enough burned before the release because demand will be very high." Tariq sipped his cold lager.

"Kharon, we need another girl soon".

"Yes uncle, when?"

"Not for a fortnight, but this girl needs to be very special. She is for some important businessmen." Tariq, was looking directly at the younger man.

"I can get one for you, no problem." Kharon assured.

Kharon thought for a moment. Rhianna would be perfect for this one.

"I have one in mind that I have been working on for a while, she is a bit stronger than the others. I think she is just the one we want." Kharon continued.

"Okay, that sounds good. I need to keep me in the loop with this. It is a big deal." Tariq reminded him who the boss was.

Tariq stood and Kharon followed suit.

"Thanks, Kazzy". Kharon left the house from the back door.

"Morning all" Charlie Jackman walked into his workshop in the college. It was the confident and easy walk of a man confident in his ability and comfortable in his area. Not to be mistaken for the arrogant swagger of some of the students, students who knew too little to know how much they didn't know. Lecturing had been an unexpected career route for Charlie. He had spent the majority of his working life in 'Serious', as he would term it engineering. Years working with the research and development team at British Aerospace had come to an abrupt close when the, much vaunted, Eurofighter Typhoon failed to win its export orders and the R & D team was halved. Charlie's skills in the workshop were soon snapped up and he had found himself working on the circuit of professional motorsport. Motorbikes had been an enduring passion for him. His aerospace engineering skills and competence in the use of lightweight and strong alloys shone through as he worked in the superbike racing paddock. Leading projects on weight saving whilst strengthening crucial components he had been able to shave crucial kilograms from the Aprilia RSV that had romped to so many victories in the 2008 campaign. At the end of 2008 the regulations for the bikes changed and once again Charlie found himself in the market for work. Aprilia had made him a Euro generous offer to relocate and work with their factory in the crucible of world superbikes. It wasn't for him, long flights, no security, the relationship with, his then new girlfriend, Jemima had just started. She saw through him, she could see the dark shadow of his depression as it hid behind the success and confidence. No one else had ever seen that side to him. He could not let her go. In time she would become his beacon through the darkest of times and the wife he was absorbed in, the line between them blurred.

In his hand he carried a mug of Gunpowder Green, a strong green tea. He looked around at his group. When he entered teaching he thought he would be passing his hard earned expertise onto gifted students, cutting and turning them from the raw billets of high school kids and preparing them for polishing at the universities.

No, that had not happened. The engineering students in the college were academically challenged. They had been streamed into the 'vocational' bracket as the schools had tried to achieve their targets. Very occasionally a student would come through that genuinely showed promise – but how could they succeed whilst their peers where so poor?

The first period was to cover measuring. Charlie had completed this lesson twice with this group previously.

"Ok guys, if you could all collect a steel ruler, a Vernier gauge and a micro meter from the tool boxes". He spoke quietly and assuredly. Several of the group made their way to the boxes and collected what they needed, the other ten or so sat at the benches chatting or playing games on their mobile phones.

"Today we are going to look at the basics of measurements. Why?"

"I don't know, Charlie. You fucking tell us". A shabby spotty youth looked at him with a challenge.

"Ok, Ryan, please be civil. I always speak to you with respect and courtesy, I expect the same level of respect please."

"Yeah, whatever" Ryan replied. Ryan lived in the chaotic nightmare of heroin addicted parents. During his tutorial last month he cried. Charlie looked at him and saw the hopelessness and vanity of the boy.

"We are doing this because in engineering accuracy is everything. We are also doing this because in a recent test you guys really struggled with this area" Charlie stepped over Ryan's planned confrontation.

As Charlie walked around the room he passed out pieces of brass for the students to practise measuring upon. As preparation for the lesson he had written on the whiteboard

"10mm = 1 cm

100cm=1 m"

This was the level he was working with.

"Has anyone seen Rhianna this morning?" he asked the group loudly, she was one of the rare students. She was very bright indeed, academically she had achieved very little but her eye for precision was exceptional, as good as any that Charlie had seen, in all of his jobs.

"She was out with Kazzy last night, I saw her up town" Ryan shouted. The inference was that Ryan had started to hang around with the Acheron Street Crew. So Ryan would live to his preordained destiny, follow his script.

"Ok, thanks Ryan"

Rhianna did come in to the workshop, she was twenty minutes late. Charlie went over to speak to her.

"Evening, Rhianna," He spoke in a playful way. He understood the delicacy of the tight rope she balanced on.

"Hello Charlie." The respect was now gone from her voice,

she openly flirted with him. He felt this was to undermine him and to reinforce the change in her power dynamic. He stood beside her. As they spoke. He could smell cannabis on her clothing and her hair. The drug mixed with the smell of sweat and dirt. Her face, previously clear, pretty was dirty and had broken out in spots around her nose. She had a sore near her nostril

"Rhianna, we spoke previously about your ability in this subject. If you apply yourself my offer still stands, you have to choose." He had remained friends with several engineers in the race bike scene, he had offered her the chance of working on race weekends with one of these old friends.

Rhianna grinned and stepped away from the bench, "You only want to fuck me, is that what I have to do?" She didn't speak quietly, every member of the group heard her.

"Rhianna, don't bother please. Start to do the measuring exercise. Let's talk about chances later". She stood on the edge, on the precipice. College was the only shape to her existence. If Charlie reported this, together with her attendance she would be nudged and take the step. There is only freefall for into oblivion for her.

Lunch time could not come quick enough for Charlie. Jemima would drive in and meet him for lunch. The oasis in the centre of the barren day. He had to finish this session, a ten minute break and then the same group before lunch. Then dinner break, an hour with Jemima, he called her his Jem. The weather was bright and clear, he would get rid of the kids a few minutes early and wait at the picnic bench for her with a cup of coffee and a kiss. He looked at the clock in the workshop, 09:50, ages to go yet. He resolved not to look at it again until it was time to go.

In the run up to his little moment of sanity in the day, only ten minutes before he could see Jem the door to his workshop crashed open.

Framed and immobile in the door way was Kharon Khan. Kharon's eyes moved from Charlie and on to Rhianna, her bench was against the wall. She looked up and smiled.

Kharon walked into the room towards her, he swaggered across the room with an arrogance he had not earned.

Charlie walked quickly to the door. He stood in the door as Kharon got to Rhianna. Without saying a thing Kharon grabbed Rhianna and kissed her hard on the mouth.

"Come on, baby girl, let's get out of this shit hole" Kharon grabbed her arm above the elbow and walked towards the door.

Charlie and Kharon made eye contact. Charlie felt he recognised the spark of decency still within Kharon. A split second of apology crossed the boy's dark eyes.

"Hello Kharon, I wish you would come back to the class, you are really good at this. We are doing technical drawing." Charlie spoke quietly and reasonably.

The spark of humility resurfaced.

"I can't ever come back Mr", then anger flared hot "Jackcunt, you white honkey bastard".

"Ok, but don't take Rhianna, she is doing well too." Charlie's tone was cool and measured, he did not react to the provocation that Khan poured onto him.

Khan squared up to Jackman. He was taller but slimmer. Jackman was strong and fit, he looked after himself, and he climbed and cycled. His frame was solid.

"Do the cunt, Kazzy!" Ryan was stood behind Khan.

With no warning Khan pulled his head around to the right as if looking over his right shoulder.

In that instant Charlie knew what was coming.

Khan whipped his head back around and head-butted Charlie. The impact caught him under the left eye, later he would learn he had a compressed fracture of the cheekbone. Charlie did not react, he felt the hot blood running down his face.

"Yeah! Yeah!" Screamed Ryan.

"You can't take her past me." Charlie spoke in the same way as previously.

The alarm in the workshop sounded, it was the fire door alarm. Rhianna had run out of the fire door and left it open.

Kharon walked out of the workshop through the normal door and stepped outside into the sunshine. He walked as if he owned the place. He was proud of what he had done. He swaggered and strutted. Ryan trotted along behind him.

At that point Charlie made a huge decision. The girl was in

danger from this boy. Not some trivial issue that she would get over. A real insidious creeping danger that threatened to plunge her into a world of confusion, pain and death. Charlie was not going to let her go and step into that world. If that meant he needed to physically stop her then he would. If that meant he would have to restrain Khan then he would. The taste of his blood cemented that decision. This decision could cost him his job, but at least he would sleep at night.

He followed them into the bright sunlight.

Ryan was stood in the car park with Kharon and another two lads that Charlie didn't know. Rhianna was with the boys. They laughed as Kharon obviously re-enacted the assault on Charlie. The tall white boy laughed and the other lad, he looked like an East African to Charlie with his arm in a sling shouted "Show that old white pussy man!"

The car park was edged with a broad lawned area and a hornbeam hedge. On this lawned area were the picnic benches. Jemima had tucked herself around the corner from the engineering block so that she could surprise Charlie when he came out to look for her at lunch time. She had spread out a table cloth and a hamper on the table top. She was very proud of the hamper she had put together. As soon as Charlie had left for work she started to prepare it. His favourite cheese, a strong cheddar called Lincolnshire Poacher was cut into wedges. Jacobs's biscuits were spread with butter. In the centre of the table was a bowl filled with melon balls, raspberries and strawberries. She felt that this would refresh his pallet before he stepped back into the class room. The flask was filled with a rich Columbian coffee. Everything was made and prepared for Charlie. She had started to notice his decline the previous week. Charlie was a good man, a really good man. But the shadow of depression surfaced sometimes. When she first met him she thought he was paranoid or possessive sometimes. This was how the depression would manifest itself in this way. The plan was hatched in her head in the night. Try to break the cycle.

She watched the three young men and the girl in the car park talking about some fight that the Asian lad was involved in, she felt that it was like watching them through a window into their social world. A world she was so far removed from. They were not aware of her.

She saw Charlie appear from his workshop. He was wearing his fawn coloured storemen's jacket, she always laughed at this. For Jemima it was a throwback to the 1960's television shows she watched as a girl. He had something red spilled all down the front of the jacket. As she started to pour the coffee she saw Charlie walk purposefully towards the group.

"Kharon, you can't take her" Charlie spoke clearly and easily.

"I can do what I want" He replied. Kharon pointed his index finger on his right hand at Charlie's face.

"I will stop you if I have to." Charlie's tone had not changed.

As she watched quietly, not wanting to interfere in his work she saw the four young people start to split up. She initially thought they were going to leave and continued to pour the coffee.

As she looked back up at the group the lad confronting Charlie shouted in his face. "I am gonna fuck you up and smash your face in, cunt."

Reaching into her handbag she reached for her i-phone and started to video the group. Charlie spoke to the group but she could not hear what he said.

The lad raised his clenched fists.

"Don't do it Kharon, you don't need to do this" Charlie said loudly. Kharon Khan had no choice. He needed to keep his reputation building he needed this girl.

He pulled back his right fist and threw a long swinging punch towards Charlie. Charlie was nearly fifty years old but was fit and agile. With his open left hand he parried the punch away.

"Don't be so stupid Kharon" she heard Charlie say.

Charlie could handle this boy. She was confident of that. She carried on filming. The last thing Charlie would want is his wife getting in the way.

The boy stepped back and tried to kick Charlie. He aimed the kick like taking a penalty, it was a huge movement generating power from his legs and lower body. Had the kick landed it would have caused massive damage. But the gross motor skills he used made it easy to stop. Charlie stepped outside of the kick and it missed him harmlessly. The momentum took Kharon slightly off balance and stumbled forwards.

"This is your last warning, Kharon."

"Fuck, you!" The lad screamed, he was angry, this old guy with the piercings had made him look clumsy and slow. Jem realised what the spill on his jacket was. It was his blood.

He rushed forwards towards Charlie swinging both fists wildly. Charlie initially protected himself by deflecting the punches onto his forearms and away from his face. The blows rained down but Charlie was more than equal. It seemed that none of the punches would get through.

The young black man with his arm in the sling shouted, "Get in there Brandon!" The tall white boy, he looked much younger than the others stepped behind Charlie. The lad swung one punch that landed squarely on the back of Charlie's head.

The impact jarred him forward and for just a second his hands dropped. The flurry of punches increased and they found their mark on his face. Blood spread across Charlie's face. It was difficult to tell if it was from the existing cut or new injuries. She jumped up and started to run to help her man.

Charlie felt the sharp impact on the back of his head, it stunned him for a second and allowed Kharon to land telling punches on his face. He knew that he could not withstand too many more shots like this. With an open left palm he struck Kharon in the stomach. The Strike was from his front left hand but with the power he produced in the eight inches of travel he knocked Kharon clean off his feet and left him curled on the ground.

Charlie turned to face the other boy, he held his hands high, like a boxer. The boy threw straight and powerful punches, no huge haymakers although he was younger he was more dangerous. Charlie watched his eyes as he acquired the targets for the next punch. The boy looked down towards Charlie's genitals and aimed his kick. This was not a large swing like Kharon's but a short sharp flick out with his foot.

Charlie stepped outside of the kick and immediately drove his right knee hard into the boy's leg. The powerful knee strike landed in the middle of the boy's quad muscle.

Brandon dropped onto one knee. The dead leg had incapacitated him instantly. The fight had left him and he wanted to go home. He felt physically ill. The old man could really hurt him if he wanted to.

Jemima had closed the gap to the group and as she came within a few feet she saw the flash of a knife held low in the hand of the slim boy with his arm in the sling. She saw it for just a fraction of a second before it was plunged into the thigh of her husband. One single stab in the top of the thigh, the boy pulled the knife out and turned to her.

Jemima knew she was going to be next. When she ran across the car park she had carried the steel flask with her. She was going to hit her husband's attackers with it. But as she looked at her husband's thigh and saw the red rose of his blood blooming fast across his thigh and running down his leg. She threw the contents of the flask over the boy with the knife.

As she did she heard the Asian boy say "Fuck, Shan, you are

the man!"

With the attack stopped she crouched over Charlie. As soon as he realised what had happened and that the attack had stopped he lay on the ground and pressed his hand onto the puncture wound. He knew this was serious, he felt the shock coming on. He knew he was losing blood, his life was running from the wound in his leg and into the car park in a scarlet pool. He lay on the ground and undid his belt. Jem appeared in his dimming vision, he knew he was near death and he felt his angel had appeared. She pulled his belt out and put it above the wound. Jem pulled it as tight as she could to stem the flow. He felt it tighten and knew the tourniquet was on. His conscious started to fade. He tried to tell her he loved her but as he faded away the only voice he heard was Jem's. "Don't you fucking die on me. I need you with me". As he slipped into the warm arms of unconsciousness he resolved today would not be his day to die.

Kharon had regained his feet and the pain in his abdomen was subsiding. He watched the woman put the belt around Jackman's leg. He saw her kneeling over him asking him not to die. Jackman was laying on his back with his head towards Kharon. How fucking dare they embarrass him. He needed to make a point, he needed to show the others he took no shit. He took five running steps towards the Jackmans and kicked Jemima square in the face with the top of his foot, her head snapped back and she rolled into the puddle of her husband's blood, her nose was smashed and fragments of her glasses were embedded in her eye.

The whole incident had passed in less than a minute, in the next minute Kharon Khan, Ishan Hussein, Brandon Byrne and Rhianna Taylor piled into Kharon's car and they screeched away from the scene. Hussein had blood on his hands and Khan on his feet.

The police were on the scene of this confrontation in only five minutes after the call. The general patrol officer first on scene was an experienced veteran with twenty five years of hard earned experience. The police had received a call informing them of a stabbing. The call was anonymous. PC Dowson's experience showed as he stopped the patrol car short and ran to the couple laying on the floor, the woman was lying across the man and the blood suggested that this was a serious job. He immediately called on the radio for back up, a sergeant and scenes of crime to attend.

"What have we got, Dave?"

Pol had known Dave for ten years, he was a trusted and competent constable. Pol was the nearest sergeant in the town so volunteered to attend. By the time that Pol had arrived on the scene the paramedics had arrived and were working on the Jackmans. Pol left them to it and started to look into the police investigation.

"It's difficult to say, Sarge. We have an adult male and female, male has a puncture wound to the thigh, looks nasty and has bled extensively but there is a tourniquet above it. The female is unconscious with nasty facial injuries, her nose is smashed and maybe her jaw."

"Ok, any witnesses?" Pol replied.

"No one on the scene and this is as far as I have got at the minute."

"Dave, please look after the scene." They both looked at the pool of blood and the set of foot prints leading to the car park. "Make a big cordon mate, can you start a major crime log in your pocket book please." Pol left Dave with these directions, he could think of no better person for the job. He knew he didn't need to give the instructions to Dave. Dave knew he didn't need to call Pol Sarge. But both of them respected each other enough to use formal speech in an operational situation.

As the back-up officers arrived at the college car park Pol detailed two to go to the hospital to seize the clothing from Charlie and Jemima for forensic examination.

Two further officers were detailed to talk to the students from Charlie's group, they had all stood outside and watched.

Pol was an experienced sergeant and managing the scene of a serious crime was second nature to him. He would gather all of the evidence here in a formulaic fashion. The mental tick list exhausted.

He strode over to the officers taking details from the group of witnesses. They recorded names and addresses from all of the students that Charlie had taught for a year.

As Pol joined the group he spoke to Pc Penny Mulrane. "Got all the details Penny?"

She turned to the Sergeant "Yeah, but none of them saw

anything" She was angry. One of the boys from the group looked at Pol and said "We seen not a thing five –oh".

Pol turned his back on the lad, he could hit him.

"Thanks Penny".

He left the scene and made his way to the accident and emergency department of Scunthorpe General Hospital. The department was, as always, mayhem. Just before lunch and the drunks were already in residence. The paramedics and nurses fought vainly against the flooding tide of humanity at its ugliest.

Pol strode through to the cubicles and saw his two officers stood outside of the resuss room.

"Hey Chris, alright?" Pol said.

"Yeah, I haven't got any clothing evidence bags." Chris was embarrassed. He didn't work for Pol directly but he knew that Pol was a professional and would challenge him over this.

"Chris, you know the score, you get the kit you need before you go on Patrol"

"Yeah, for sure Sarge" Both men were happy that they had performed their parts in the equation.

Pol stood outside of the resuss room and briefly chatted with the two officers. They reassured the sergeant that both casualties were stable and not life threatening. Pol was happy that the officers knew their brief and just took a quick peak through the window before leaving. He instantly recognised Charlie on the table.

"Fuck, he is my mate." He said to himself. Chris overheard.

"I will keep you posted on him Sarge, I think the woman is his wife. She has some nasty facial injuries."

"I bet this is the Acheron Street Gang". Sarah, the female officer said.

"Yeah". Said Pol. "Let's get this job done well and nail the fuckers, they have got it coming".

Chapter 12

Pol ensured that the initial investigation into the assault on Charlie and Jemima was flawless. All the opportunities to capture evidence had been taken to the best of his ability. The attack seemed to have been over very quickly. The college had been checked for witnesses, none would come forward, the college had not maintained the Closed Circuit TV due to cost so it no longer was functional. Both Charlie's and Jemima's clothes had been recovered for forensic examination and to check for transfer of fibres or of DNA. Pol knew that was a waste of time. He knew the DI would never authorise for the cost of that examination without a witness that would stand up in court. But he was satisfied that he had carried out his duties to the best of his ability, little consolation that would be to the Jackmans. And so, when it was time for Pol to finish work that evening he sat at his desk and wearily pulled on his bike boots. Looking from his window early evening sun set the nights had started to draw in. The swallows lined up on the telegraph wires ready to make their miraculous journey back to Africa for the winter months. Another summer was coming to an end and the colder days of the winter marched inexorably closer. Pol envied the swallows. He wanted to fly away, be somewhere else, somewhere far from here. Maybe he could book some leave and he and Fleur could jet to the sun. Since joining the police he had never felt like this. He wanted out. He wanted to shut the door on the politics and the policies. The police were tied up and paralysed by fear of being called racist or sexist or homophobic. Emasculated by lack of resources and 'budgetary restraint'. He could see what was going on in the town all around him and feel the growth of the misery and pain that bred in the shadows of poverty and crime. He felt he was impotent to deal with it. His hands had been tied. With the recent visit from Mr Black he didn't know who he could trust. No one was who they seemed. The respected pillars of the community abused kids, the senior police officers knew but had not go the stomach to take them on. Mr Black had confirmed not only that Pol's fears were true but the degree of complacency within the job had horrified him. He walked out of his office locking the door behind him.

Pol rode straight up to the hospital to check on Charlie and his wife Jemima. Pol walked into the A and E department and was met by one of the staff nurses. In a small town like Scunthorpe the nurses and the police felt a close allegiance to each other. The considered the worked together to deal with the lost and the feckless of society.

"Hello Pol, I didn't recognise you with your clothes on"

"Hi Sue, how are you doing?" Sue had been an Accident and Emergency nurse at the hospital since before Pol had joined the police.

"I am ok, have you come to see the Jackmans?"

"Yeah, how are they getting on?" He asked the older staff nurse.

"She is awake, you can see her."

"And Charlie?"

"He lost a lot of blood Pol. He is lucky to be here. The stab cut his popliteal artery. Up in intensive"

"In English?"

"One of the major arteries in his leg, it is a good job his missus knows about a good old fashioned tourniquet or he would have bled out and died on the street". Sue picked up a wad of patient notes and walked from the nurses' station. Pol took a quick glance at the cubicle list and then went down to see how Jemima Jackman was doing.

He pulled the curtain to one side and stepped into the cubicle. He had not met Jemima before.

"Excuse me," he greeted her as he stepped into the curtained cubicle.

She was laying securely strapped to a back board and neck brace. Her short blonde hair was thick and matted with gore and blood, it was plastered flat to her scalp. She had a deep and ragged tear in her skin over her nose and a large piece of medical gauze was taped over her right eye.

"I am Pol, I am a friend of Charlie's, how are you doing?"

"I am ok, no pain really" she replied, Pol quickly gained respect for her.

"What have the doctors said?" asked Pol.

"I have a shard of glass in my eye, I have a smashed nose and cheek, I will have to be transferred to Sheffield for my operation, I think my modelling days are over". She laughed at her own joke. Pol liked her.

"Is there anything I can do for you guys? Do you need anything bringing in?" Pol offered.

"Yeah, do you know where we live? I could do with a few bits bringing and I don't know if our daughter knows about it."

"I don't think she does, what do you need?"

Jemima gave Pol a list of what she wanted from the house. He took the address and left Jemima to collect her clean underwear, pyjamas and tooth brush. He rode home and collected the car. Then returned to the hospital with Chloe Jackman, Charlie and Jem's nineteen year old daughter.

"Will you give a statement about this?" Pol asked Jemima.

She fixed him with a cold and hard stare. "I maybe blind in one eye now, of course I will give a statement. I would prefer it if you just shot him in the street like the sick dog he is".

"If only" Pol left the two women together and made his way to the top floor of the building to the intensive care unit. The lights were always subdued up here as doctors and nurses quietly and diligently went about the business of keeping the handful of the sickest patients alive.

"What do you want?" A male nurse dressed in green coloured surgical clothes challenged him.

"Two minutes with Charlie Jackman is that ok?"

"Yeah, but no more, he is very tired, lost a lot of blood." The nurse turned sharply and walked into the next room. Pol was quite happy to have been challenged in this way, the nurse had more important things to do than exchange platitudes with visitors.

Pol walked in to see Charlie.

"Hey, Jacko, you are a lucky boy"

Charlie was on the bed, on a drip, with an oxygen mask on. His eyes moved slowly and with great effort until they rested upon Pol.

"Don't - call – me – fucking – Jacko. I – don't – fucking – like – it" these words were a struggle for him. Like his wife down stairs Pol felt his respect grow for Charlie.

"Is she ok?" he whispered.

"She will be fine, she has to have some surgery" Pol spoke quietly and calmly.

"Me too, tomorrow. My face is fucked up"

"Don't worry mate, it always was, no one can tell". Pol couldn't help himself, sometimes that humour that kept him going in the dark days of the jungle would raise its head.

Jackman smiled. "You are a cunt" he whispered.

Pol crouched down and put his hand on Charlie's shoulder in a very unusual, for Pol, show of support.

"Mate, you get better. When this is over we will have a few beers"

"Yeah, I reckon so mate" Jackman was tiring he rolled his

head away and breathed heavily through the mask.

Pol left and went home. Later as he lay in bed holding his softly snoring wife in his arms he felt a sense of desolation and hopelessness growing within him. Nothing he did mattered, he could not stem the tide and the malignancy that was all around him. His belief in doing the right thing and in good shining through was shaken.

Stu came back into the house from training. He had really pushed his fitness up in the last few weeks and this evening he had ran five fast miles. The dog had been training with him and even he was heaving for breath.

"Fuck, that was good" He said as he drank in the air. Sweat beaded on his forehead, each bead grew, joined its neighbour and ran down his face in small rivulets, dripping off his nose and on to the lino flooring. Winston licked up the droplets of sweat. Stu's grey t-shirt was wet in large charcoal areas from sweat.

"What's up?" Di was sat at the table, head in her hands. She turned to face him and he saw her eyes red rimmed from crying long and hard. He saw pain and loss in her expressive eyes.

"Rhianna is missing" Between sobs.

"Oh no, what's happened?" he sat down beside her. He put his hands on hers on the table and held them protectively tight.

"Our Shelley phoned. There was a big fight at college today and one of the staff got stabbed. Then Rhianna left in a car."

"Whose car was it?" He asked.

"You know that creep Tariq? It's his old BMW. They say Kharon was driving it."

"Has Shelley told the cops yet, Di?"

"I don't know, you know what she is like, I doubt it. I will tell her to" Di reached for her phone and text her sister, Michelle. As she text Michelle Stu text Nadia and also Pol.

Sms conversation

Stu: they have got Rhianna

Pol: who have?

Stu: Acheron gang.

Pol: have you called the cops?

Stu: no her mum has.

Pol: Keep me posted.

Stu: She was seen getting in a car at college after a teacher got filled in.

Pol: Who with?

Stu: Kharon from the gang.

Pol: she is in danger.

Further Sms conversation.

Stu: Nadia, my niece is missing

Nadia: Have they got her?

Stu: I think so. Keep your ears open.

Nadia: I will

Di stood up and turned to Stu. "Will she be ok?"

Stu pulled Di close to his chest and held her tight. She buried her face against him and took comfort from his broad chest and the strong arms around her shoulders. She sobbed into his chest. He stroked her hair and let her cry.

"Will she be ok?" Di repeated her question, she was looking for some reassurance. Stu knew he had none that he could give.

"I don't know if she will be ok. I will get changed and go out and look for her".

"No, stay with me. I need you here with me. The police are looking for her now." Di held him tight. "Just stay with me, hold me".

Stu knew that she would be out there, that she had been taken by the Acheron Crew. He knew what would happen to her.

"Di, we have to do something. The police will be too slow, I have to get out there and look for her".

"I am worried that you will get hurt or get in trouble if you get all wrapped up in this and I can't get by without you." She remained locked in his arms.

"I know you worry, but you don't have to be worried about this lot. They won't harm me or you again".

"My leg is knackered, my niece, poor little Rhianna, is

missing and these scumbags have her. I don't want them to take you from me or get you locked up."

"I will be careful, but we need to find Rhianna or at least find out where she is so I can tell Pol and his people." Stu spoke quietly but urgently.

Di knew he was talking sense. She knew that if it was left to the police Rhianna would just become another statistic and disappear from society.

"Ok, but I want you to promise to come back to me when you have finished. I will not be able to sleep if I know that you are out there somewhere looking for her with them out there too".

"I promise I will come back, I won't get hurt, I won't hurt any of them and I will come back safe and sound and in one piece tonight. I just want to go out there and see what I can find out"

Di peeled herself from his arms and stood back from him. "I love you Stuart Hicks" she said to him.

"I love you too, Dianna Hicks. How about you make me a coffee whilst I get a shower and get changed then I will go out there and look for Rhianna".

"That is no problem for my man".

Both of them sought refuge from their fears in their respective rituals. Di made the coffee, just the way that Stu liked it and he got himself in the shower.

Stu showered quickly he massaged his thighs and calf

muscles with shower gel under the hot stream. He could feel
the build-up of lactic acid in the muscles after his training he
wanted to be free from aches or stiffness before he went back
out. He had told Di that he would not get involved in any
confrontation this evening but he needed to be ready in case
the confrontation came to him.

He dressed in a pair of old olive green fatigue trousers and a
grey fleece top. Before stepping out into the night he held his
wife tight to him again and promised her he would be
careful. He put on his woolly hat and stepped out of the
back door leaving the warmth of the kitchen and stepping
out into the cold darkness of the town at night.

The night air was cold and damp, the fine but constant
drizzle wet the streets and alleyways and immediately
started to wet his fleece. The sulphurous fumes of the
steelworks gave the air an unpleasant taste. He headed up
the alleyway behind his house on Acheron Street and
towards Frodingham Road. He knew that the gang would be
hanging around the lights of the street. The lamp post in the
centre of the alleyway no longer worked. Someone had
crashed a stolen car into it a week or two previously and
since then the alley way had no lighting. Animals scurried,
unseen but heard, across the alleyway in the darkness as he
silently prowled along. Rats moved over the bags of waste
and the discarded fast food scraps. Stu moved into the long
alleyway that ran the length of Frodingham road when he
got to it. He did not want to step into the brightly lit main
road. He wanted to stay in the shadows, the shadows where
the Acheron Street gang did their business. He joined the
others that did not want to be observed in the shadows of

that long alleyway. He wanted to have a close look at the gang and see if he could find his young niece.

Staying in the shadows and out of sight he found he could quite easily watch the basketball court that the Acheron Street Gang seemed to frequent, like their territory, like a gate post the dog pisses on. The boys were there. The two lads from Lithuania, they were only boys; the new young lad in the area, taller, thin and angry. He knew these were the boys that had hurt Di so badly. He hated them. But they were just children, they were too young to sort out in the way he would like to. A couple of other lads and a few young girls moved in the glow of the street light. He had not seen the girls before but there seemed to be a constant stream of girls willing to be with these boys. They had no idea what they were exposing themselves too. He watched the girls as they flirted with the boys, they sung pop songs and danced in the way that children do. They moved into the full glow of the light and then away into the shadows, like moths, drawn to the artificial light, whatever the cost maybe.

Kharon, from his street was not there. There was no sign of him at all. He was normally in the centre of them; holding court. Stu watched for a few more minutes from the shadows, Kharon did not appear. Stu slipped, like smoke, into the depth of the shadows and was gone. The youngsters had never been aware that he was there, unseen, unheard.

Shortly after 10pm and he was on West street. The same cars ran their circuit round the street and slowed beside the desperate prostitutes working their patches. The drizzle continued to hang in the air around the street lights illuminating the drama being played out in the sodium halos. He was on the street here, there was no alleyway to seek cover in. He approached one of the girls. She turned to him with the gappy grin of a methadone user, "Do you want business, lover?" she asked him she was almost pleading with him. Her sad eyes riven with the need for heroin.

"No thanks, not tonight" he replied and strode past her skeletal frame.

At the end of the street he saw the familiar figure of Nadia. Stu had never seen her out on the street corner like this before. She looked tired, as if she had lost some weight. Declining. The evenings spent with Tariq exacted a heavy price on her.

"Hello Nadia", He said.

"Hello Sticks," since hearing Pol call him Sticks he had also adopted this nickname for him. She smiled, he thought she was a good looking woman, she was clearly intelligent but they had her trapped somehow. They had her where they wanted her. He hated them for it. She didn't fit in this grey world of squalor.

"Nadia, do you know if they have taken another girl?" Stu asked her directly.

"Yes, they took her today, I don't know where too. Normally it is Sheffield."

"Who will know?"

"Tariq is the main man now. He will have sent his puppy dog Kharon with her".

Stu thanked Nadia and walked on.

His mind raced now. He knew she was in danger. Pol had told her what happened to Sarah, he had seen Sarah working since then. Seen the weight fall from her already slight frame as the addiction bit into her frail teenage body. She would no doubt follow the same path that the other kid, Jasmin, had. He could not be sure where she had been taken, but he knew Tariq would tell him, given a little persuasion.

For the first time in his adult life he was stuck, he didn't know what to do and how to resolve the situation. With what he had been told the last time he spoke to Mr Black he could not trust the police. If he took the law into his own hands he would be risking a long jail term. He resolved to ring Mr Black and tell him what he had discovered. Hopefully Mr Black would put something in place and get this sorted out. He turned back towards home and on the short walk home he called the mobile number Mr Black had given him.

He stepped in the back door and Di was in exactly the same position that he had left her in.

"I was worried about you, Stu". Di's voice was small and lost.

"I know you were, but I am back now". He placed his hand on her shoulder.

"Did you find her?" Di looked up at Stu hopefully.

"No, I didn't but I know they have taken her for sure. I am going to ask Pol to pop round for a chat about it". Stu replied.

It was early when Pol arrived at Stu's house. He had not slept well and was up very early. Pol was working hard on trying to piece together something solid to find Rhianna. He was heading to the office an hour earlier than rostered.

"I don't have any specifics for you Pol" Stu said.

"No I haven't got much either, just that she has been taken by Kharon to maybe Sheffield" Pol had confirmed what Nadia had told Stu.

"How do you know that?" Asked Stu.

"We have a grass at the mosque that they go to." Pol sipped his coffee.

"I fucking hate them, Pol."

"I know you do, Stu"

"They are bastards, they just prey on sorrow." Stu was angry, Pol could see it in his eyes. The gang had taken his niece and he wanted her back but this was more, this was an outrage at them and their operation in general. "I am going to do them. I am going to get Rhianna back and I am going to step it up and I am going to do them. One at a time."

Pol had seen Hicks kill on a number of occasions, he had seen him do it with a cold blooded calculated efficiency that Pol had found frightening. Stu delivered death easily and with no feeling. But he had never seen any real grain of emotion in his old friend when it those moments.

"Stu, you need to be careful, you have an emotional attachment here and it will compromise the way that you work if you don't keep it in check". Pol watched the animated Hicks as he spoke.

"Yeah, you are right, I need to think about this just like we always thought about things in the past. Calm and professional".

"For sure, the last thing I want to happen is you end getting locked up." Pol again spoke with quiet assurance.

"Yeah," Hicks nodded.

"Make a plan, Stu, and execute it. Find out where Rhianna is and go and get her".

"If you find out where she is will you let me know first, Pol?" Pol, placed his mug back on the coffee table. He studied Hicks for a moment. They both knew the gravity of what had just been asked. If Pol agreed to this he would have stepped a long way over the line and there would be no going back. They made solid eye contact and reinforced the bond that had been forged in the jungle so long ago.

"Stu, I will tell you everything I know. I will meet you for a swim tomorrow at twelve noon"

Pol got up and said his goodbyes to Di and Stu. He left their house and drove to work.

Mr Black received the call from Sergeant Winchester shortly after arriving in his office. He was a little unsure of why Winchester had called him. Initially he gave information about the missing girl but he went on say that he thought that things would soon be resolved. Black sensed that Winchester was deeply troubled by the events unfolding before him. But, he felt that very soon Mr White's plan would reach fruition.

Chapter 13

Stu was becoming desperate for information. The police, apart from Pol, of course, seemed to be totally disinterested in the missing girl. It was Friday and she had been gone for a day now. Stu silently dressed in his running gear in the half light of the autumn dawn. He had tried not to disturb Di as he got up early to train. He didn't know but she wasn't asleep, she had lay in the bed watching the first signs of the morning open out her vision. The monochrome first light had given way to the still quietness of early morning.

"You don't have to sneak about, Stu. I am wide awake" Her voice emerged slowly, wearily and far away from the pile of duvet on the bed.

"I am going for a run and then I have some things to do today".

"I expect I will still be here when you get back, I didn't sleep well."

"No nor did I really" he said as he pulled on a pair of running tights. "I need to get out there and blow the cob webs away."

He bent over the bed and kissed her.

Winston reluctantly slid from the sofa and stretched on the floor. "Don't you fancy a run this morning?" Stu asked his canine mate.

Early morning Scunthorpe was a very different place. The streets were quiet, occasional local Muslims walked on their way to morning prayers. The newsagent vans were making their deliveries when the man and his dog started to run along Frodingham Road. Hicks pushed the pace fast, he was working on improving his fitness. He treated every run as a challenge and a chance to race himself. He was incapable of taking a morning jog. For Stu Hicks everything was a competition that he could not lose.

Rubbish blew along the street in the fresh autumn breeze. Gulls and jackdaws patrolled along the road before the people filled the pavements picking up pizza crusts and discarded chips and food. The town would soon wake up and the shift workers would start making their way to their daily tasks. Many oblivious to the undercurrents that flowed so powerfully just below the surface and the sharks that swam in those treacherous currents.

Stu, now in his forties, found the first few hundred yards of is run tough. The aches and pains took longer to heal now. The impact of the road on his joints jarred up his bones. He pushed through the pain and extended the pace. As soon as he found his rhythm the aches and pains eased and he settled in to it. His mind cleared as the endorphins started to circulate round his body. Winston had settled into an easy canter and loped along beside Stu with his tongue lolling from the side of his mouth. Stu started to formulate his plan. He ran past the station where Pol worked. Pol's bike was the only vehicle in the car park. Stu was not surprised, he knew Pol and he knew he would be in the station working hard to try to find Rhianna. The man was wasted in the police. Stu extended his pace and pushed on down Ferry Road. The kernel of an idea in his mind had started to take shape and grow into the seedling of a plan.

Pol did not see Stu run past. He was at his desk. Trying desperately to legitimise the intelligence that he had been given by Stu without revealing its source. Trying to raise the profile of yet another missing teenager.

Stu and Winston returned home. Their training complete for the day. Winston resumed his position on the sofa and promptly fell to sleep.

Stu went up to the bedroom, sure enough Di was still fast asleep. He left her comfortable sleep had eluded her of late and she needed all she could get. He took his clothes from the drawers silently, he padded down to the shower. The plan was set in his mind and he needed to get a move on to make sure he was in the right place at the right time. He needed to get something solid to take to Black or Pol a location where to find Rhianna. He would go and get her back but he needed something to go on.

It had been some years since he had worn the urban camo combat kit. The materiel was a stiff and coarse weave, resistant to the abrasion of working your body along walls and over roof tops. The knees and elbows were double thickness. The pattern was not like the swirls and curves of traditional camouflage but straight edges and squares the fawn and red colours with darker lines blended surprisingly well into the colour of masonry or brick work. Because of the variety of different building materials used there was no one pattern for this type of work, this was as near as he had. He

pulled a pair of loose tracksuit bottoms on over the trousers
and the combat boots he wore. Over the top he pulled on a
large blue hoodie. He returned to the bath room and from
the cupboard he took a bottle of baby oil. The last time he
had taken that out of the cupboard it had been to spread on
Di, not this time. He squeezed a small pool into his right
hand and then rubbed it into his short hair. Immediately he
looked dirty and unkempt his hair appeared to be greasy.
He let the bottle drip onto his hoody and then rubbed his
greasy hands over the top to give it a dirty and stained
appearance.

He took his combat gloves from the kitchen drawer and
placed them in his trousers pocket. From the same drawer he
pulled a used Sainsbury carrier bag. He squirted a small
amount of washing up liquid into the bag. He held the bag
around the neck and pullet the top of it back over his open
hand.

"Hey sexy, nice look" He had not noticed Di stood in the
doorstep.

"Thank you, this what everyone in London and Paris is
wearing"

"Yeah right, do they call it the evo stick look?" she joked
with him.

"Watch and learn, the transformation will take place
imminently." He said.

As he spoke he allowed the proudness to seep from his
square shoulders, he hung his head forward towards his
chest and let his mouth flop open. He took a couple of steps

towards Di. He lifted his feet high but relaxed his calves and lower legs so the steps were clumsy as those that have nerve damage caused by solvent or alcohol use walk. He shambled towards her. He had shed all that she recognised in him. She knew that if he walked out into the alleys and streets like this he would disappear from view and consciousness, he would be another glue sniffer sitting in a corner. He would become invisible.

"I will be out all day, keep Max in with you and keep the door locked" he spoke gently with his gentle eyes locked on hers.

"Are you scared that something might happen?" She mistook what he intended to be concern as fear.

"No, not at all. But I want to be sure that you are ok, can you make sure the washing machine is empty,"

"Yeah I know, loaded with bleach and set for a hot wash".

"You know the drills."

He turned and walked out of the door. As he got in the alleyway she watched him flick the switch and become the vagrant again. He even lifted the bag to his face and inhaled from it a few times to complete the 'new look'.

He did not have far to walk to his destination. He walked in the stooped and ragged style he had earlier showed to Di. He knew how he would slide from view and no one would notice him. This time he did not use the alleyways as his first choice. He used the main road, he wanted to escape the view of the Acheron Street Crew. They frequented the rat runs and the alleyways. He walked straight down the street. As he turned towards West Street and along Teale Street he saw Ishan, the gang's enforcer in the mouth of the alley way behind. He placed a hand against a car lamp post adjacent to him. He was close to Ishan. Only a few meters. If Ishan recognised him there would be no way he could continue his plan. He raised the bag to his lips and again, feigned inhaling solvent from the bag.

He watched Ishan in the reflection of a parked car window. He saw Ishan watch him with the bag and watched the expression on his face turn to one of disgust.

"Piece of fucking white trash" Ishan shouted at him in the street. This was the crucial moment. If Ishan, injured arm or not, decided to attack him there might be nothing he could do to avoid compromise.

Ishan turned and walked away in disgust. Stu shambled on slowly.

The Mosque was a converted terraced house. It fronted onto West Street but was on the south side of the street in a small block with Gilliat Street, Frances Street and running parallel to West Street was Scunthorpe High Street. Behind the high street and running between Frances and Gilliat Street was a small alleyway. He needed to get into the alleyway near the High Street. Easily he moved down West Street until he came to the junction with Frances Street, He turned into Frances street and could see the entrance to the alleyway, his target only eighty meters in front of him.

Between him and his target he saw a police officer and a

police community support officer out on patrol. They were walking up the street on the same side as him and directly in front of him. He averted his eyes from them. If the stopped him that would be the end of the days job and he would be no closer to Rhianna. If they searched him they would find the knife and other tools he had concealed. As they got closer to him he recognised the police officer immediately as Pol. The sergeant was out in his patrol vest and helmet. As they got close the PCSO spoke to him.

"Hello, what's your name?" He asked

Stu looked at Pol, Pol recognised Stu instantly.

"Danny, what's it got to do with you?" Stu slurred a very effective Scottish accent.

"Come on Mike, we don't really have time to deal with this, we need to keep our eyes open for that misper" Pol spoke to the PCSO.

"Alright Sarge".

Stu continued his unsteady progress and finally made his way into the alleyway. Typical of most of the town alleyways it was dirty. The smell of urine was strong and the ground littered with the human and animal waste that seemed to accumulate in the corners away from the main stream view.

These alleyways had been constructed to give access to the rear of the houses on three sides and the shops on the high street side of the block. Stu shambled along the first section of alleyway until he was at the junction with the piece that ran behind the houses and between Gilliat and Frances Street. He moved int the alley with the intention of slipping off his outer clothing and climbing up on to the roof tops. In the centre of the alley way stood a group of people. This was the last thing that Stu needed. He wanted to be up and on the buildings to give himself maximum time to gather the information that he needed. The group consisted of three men and two women, they were all shouting and arguing in an eastern European language, maybe Polish. In their hands they held various drinks containers, vodka seemed to be the tipple of choice for them. Stu guessed they had been on the night shift at one of the large factories and where now relaxing in the style they seemed to enjoy the most.

The rear of the mosque was within his reach but now this group of drunks looked like they might prevent him from reaching his objective. Stu considered his options and decided he would have to go into one of the gardens and climb up onto the buildings sooner than he had initially hoped.

Some of the back yards into the alleyway were fenced and others open, some of the yards had steps running own from first floor flats. He chose one of these yards. It was open and concreted but with rusty steel stairs leading up to the first floor. The stairs landed against the building and in the angle created by the back of the house and the kitchen that projected into the yard. The ground floor rear windows were shuttered with the metal sheets of dereliction and the door partially boarded with ply wood. One section of the timber had been pulled away from the frame and it looked like the ground floor was a squat. Ideal for what he wanted.

Hicks moved along the garden and to the door way, the piece of ply wood that was pulled away would be big enough for him to squeeze through. Slowly and quietly he looked inside the house, he allowed his eyes to adjust to the gloom. The room was empty. It had been the kitchen of the ground floor flat. The cheap units lay with their doors hanging off. Filth and rubbish littered the floor, paper plastic bags and the ubiquitous needles and syringes. This was perfect for his purpose, this was the place he could slide into and disappear. He climbed in to through the door, crossed the threshold and into the darkness and filth. His foot crunched on something as he stepped in. He looked down and underneath his foot he saw a shapeless thing that he initially did not recognise for what it was. The thing, shapeless and melted moved on and pulsed. He crouched to see what this thing was. As his eyes had become fully accustomed to the gloom he saw this thing was the remains of a dead kitten. The movement provided by a writhing, pulsing horde of maggots, the agents of decay had consumed the frail body leaving nothing but the husk and outline of what once it was. Stu stepped off the corpse and placed his carrier bag on the work top amongst the other detritus he removed the tracksuit and hoody that he had worn as he approached the house and the alley. He pulled on the leather combat gloves and from the inside of the urban combat jacket he removed his hood. He pulled it over his head. The hood was of a tight fitting cut and enclosed his full head and face. He could see through the fine weave of the eye panel. The Silk hood had been designed to reflect light from the outside but to allow him to see almost as clearly as if he did not have it on. It flattened his features, merged them into the pattern of the urban camouflage he wore, his face disappeared, he became a part of the shadow, without identity and without substance, moved into the shadow with ethereal silence.

The highest risk part of the job was getting on to the roof tops in the first place, he would climb the stairs to the flat above and then using the kitchen window ledge climb up. He was not as agile as once he was but he was fit and he was strong, this would be no problem.

The drunk Poles had left the alleyway and were nowhere to be seen. The alley was empty, mid-morning was a quiet time. The Junkies that used the alley for moving about the town to shop lift had been out at nine and scored their first bags of gear, they were now in their bedsits and flats with the blanket of heroin pulled warm and tight over their squalid and desolate worlds. People that worked or shopped in the town didn't venture into the dangerous edgeland of their worlds' that the alleyway represented.

Hicks padded up the stairs to the flat, allowing each foot fall to settle before placing the next. Combat boots were not the best for this, but he no longer had the sticky climbing shoes. But with careful placement he could prevent the stairs from resonating and continue his progress in silence. With every step he paused for a second to check the windows. The back window directly to his front had a sheet pinned over it, the sheet was still and made no movement. The more imminent danger came from the kitchen window to his side. The room was dark inside and he would struggle to see anyone in there until they had moved, the light was off and he hoped that anyone using the kitchen would turn it on as soon as they stepped into the room.

The platform beside the door was only two more steps above him when the sheet in the back window moved. Hicks instantly crouched down to the wall. He was not able to see what had caused the movement, the bottom right corner of the sheet had lifted just an inch or two. He guessed for someone to look out of. He was confident that even if they had caught sight of him that they would not have recognised the shape on the stairs to be a person. The Clothing disrupted his outline very effectively and the hood made his face invisible. Without the outline and the head the human mind would not be able to place the shape on the stairs in the identification box that said "human".

He waited frozen on the stairs for a second and then, when there was no more movement he made his way on to the top platform beside the kitchen window and crouched amongst the discarded cigarette ends on rusted steel platform. As he watched the kitchen intently the door into the kitchen from the back room opened. A human shape stepped into the kitchen in front of him, if they saw him here she would be compromised. It was a young woman, she stepped into the kitchen and walked straight through in front of him without looking out of the window. She was naked, her long mane wild and unbrushed. Her thin body was adorned with poor homemade or amateur tattoos. She disappeared from view into a door at the end of the kitchen, Hicks assumed it to be the toilet. This was his chance to get up and on to the roof, but he needed to be quick and silent, the woman was only ten feet from him and might only be in the toilet long enough to go for a piss. Silently and with cat like agility he sprung from the plat form and one foot landed on the window ledge. On hand under the barge board around the roof and the other on the gutter bracket he swung the other leg flat onto the pitched kitchen roof. With a quiet secondary moved he flicked the foot from the window ledge and placed it gently beside the other on the roof and rolled his body up the roof once. H exhaled slowly and calmly as he lay on the small pitched slate roof of the flat. He hear the toilet flush and the soft pad of the woman's bare feed as she made her way back from the toiled and through the house. That was as close as he wanted to get to being compromised during this outing.

Remaining low on the roof and spreading his weight through his hands, forearms knees calves and feet he moved along the roof to the main line of the terrace roofs. Now the route to the mosque was simple and straight ahead. Even in the low and crouched position he covered the ground distance quickly and efficiently, he kept below the line of the roofs and away from the edge. His movement was close to invisible to anyone on the ground. He was aware that the town boasted a superb CCTV centre that had been fitted ten years previously but he also knew that the monitoring centre was understaffed and that many of the cameras were now unserviceable as the council had not been able to afford to maintain them properly. With the streets becoming busy he was quite sure that the few CCTV operators would be monitoring the shops and streets for the thieves and drunks, they would not be watching the roof tops.

When Stu got onto the roof of the converted house that now

formed the mosque he lay still for a few moments. The front door opened on the other side of the building so he felt safe to rest for a moment. It was still only 11:30, prayers did not start for another hour, but he wanted to be in situ before the building started to get busy in the hope that should anyone come into the building early he would be there to hear them.

At this point it occurred to him that there was a chance that his targets might speak Urdu. Or another Asian language. He crouched on the roof and could not believe how stupid he had been by omitting this possibility from his planning. It was too late now he was there he needed to take the chance.

He positioned himself half way along the roof and half way up. From a large pocket inside the back of his jacket he removed a stethoscope and a long thin handled pair of cutters. The cutters would have been as equally at home in a surgeons tools as the stethoscope would be. He placed the stethoscope on and placed the end flat against the roof. He could hear deeply muffled conversation from inside the mosque. Experience told him that the sound was from a distance and that the attic had not been converted. With the long handled snips he reached under one of the slates in front of him. He felt the two copper nails that held the slate in place. He cut through them both and released the slate which slid down to his hand silently. The first slate rested against his knee he cut through the nails of two more slates, one either side of the first, and lifted them to his knee and lifted them to his knee. The removal of these slates enabled him to remove three below opening a gap. He gathered the slates together and took them to the edge of the roof where he delicately placed them so the edges were held in the gutter. The hole in the roof was not yet complete with the lats still in place. He returned his tools to the pocket in his jacket and pulled out from the pocket a multi tool and opened the saw blade. Easily and quietly he sawed one of the lats out leaving a hole he could comfortably get through. Again he took these lats and placed them in the guttering then made his way back to his hole. Reaching in he gripped one of the trusses and swung his legs in, he landed lightly and softly on the beams. No one in the room below would have been able to hear the soft transfer of his weight onto the timbers. He stretched out and lay along two of the beams, the fibreglass insulation would deaden any noise he made. Again he removed the stethoscope and held it to the plasterboard or the ceiling below him. There was some sounds of movement from the room below. He lay still and quiet, waiting for an opportunity, the room became quiet and he heard the click of a door latch. Another sixty seconds of quiet and he removed a ten millimetre drill bit from his pocket and started to drill through the plaster board, every half turn he paused for five seconds and listened. Before starting again he brushed the dust away. He continued until the plaster was gone and the thin piece of paper on the back was all that remained. He replaced the drill bit and using the small, razor sharp blade of the multi-tool he cut a cross in the paper. Through the small hole he placed a small fibre optic lens and attached it to a small hand held endoscope. He lay and he waited.

Years of close surveillance had taught Hicks almost unbounded patience. He could maintain a high level of alertness whilst his mind wandered. It would take the very slightest stimulation to bring his mind back into sharp, monochrome focus. And so it was, he listened through the stethoscope and heard the prayers being given on the ground floor and the lessons being given to the children in the school room. He heard the sound of running water and the noise of a kettle being filled and turned on.

The door to the meeting room opened and Hicks heard the people come into the room. Immediately his mind left the Caribbean Beach and zoomed in on the room below. He moved the eyepiece of the endoscope and looked into the room. The meeting room slowly filled with men. They were of all ages and some dressed in traditional Muslim dress whilst others dressed in smart western suits, some casual and some scruffy. He listened to the speech, some of the men spoke English but most spoke in other Asian languages. He waited and listened. He saw Tariq move close to the Mayor, Quereshi.

"Hello uncle" Tariq spoke to Quereshi.

"Hello Tariq, how did you enjoy prayers?"

"Very much thank you, uncle. We have everything in place for your associates in Rotherham."

Hicks focussed hard on the conversation, picking the most important parts out.

"Very good," said Quereshi.

"This time we are going to use a unit that belongs to Abdul"

"Which Abdul? And I don't want my associates going to

some dirty garage with a mucky old mattress on the floor."

"Oh no, Uncle it is not like that, it is a two story unit with nice accommodation upstairs which we have nicely sorted out with furniture and downstairs is a bit more open, we will put her in there then your associates can go upstairs when they have finished or they can have a break in comfort. It is Abdul Mohamed from the youth centre. We can trust him, he knows the business."

"That is good, I might pop over and partake myself."

"Well, will be there hosting it for you anyway, the guests are invited for ten and we will have her there for eleven."

"Thank you, Tariq. I am sure that the normal respect will be paid to you early next week"

"Thank you, Uncle. It is always a pleasure to help you and you associates".

"Tomorrow, the pleasure will be all mine"

Both men laughed. Hicks felt the anger boil inside him. They were talking about his niece, about Rhianna. She was just a kid. Half an hour later he was walking back home, once again dressed as a vagrant.

As he got in the back door Di, who had been sat at the table rose to greet him. "I know where she is."

"That's fantastic," Di said. "Tell Pol"

"Ok, I will just let me get changed and I will get straight onto him."

Pol stepped into the back yard of the police station and pulled his mobile phone out. He walked slowly towards the cycle shed where his motorbike was stood. He dialled the number from the phones memory.

"Hello," The voice was detached, non-descript and without accent.

"Is that Mr Black?" Pol asked.

"Who is this?"

"It's Pol Winchester."

"Yes this is Black"

"I have some information on the location of a missing girl, tomorrow she is going to be gang raped by a group of animals in Rotherham" Pol said.

"Right, is it Rhianna Taylor?"

"Yeah, how do you know?"

"I have various sources, technical and human, and I knew that she was missing"

Pol knew that Stu spoke to him, they had discussed this on a number of occasions, but they both had agreed not to let Black know they both spoke to him and not to mention him in any electronic communication.

"She is in Rotherham at a place owned by Abdul Mohammed." Pol appraised Black of all of the facts he knew.

"Ok, where did this information come from?"

"I also have sources," Pol replied jokingly.

"Yes, Quite." Black replied, dry with no humour.

Pol said "Her Uncle, Stuart Hicks found it out",

Black replied "Ok, I don't know how much we can act on without compromising him".

The reality of what Black had said to Pol started to sink in. He was declining to help. He was backing out of rescuing a fourteen year old girl.

"I am sorry, Mr Black, are you declining to help?"

"I am not declining to help, I am just thinking of the bigger picture, Sergeant"

"So what should I do? The local police can't help because they are all bent and now you are saying that your agency, who the fuck they might really be, won't do anything?"

"Look Pol, I know where you are coming from and I understand the way that you feel, but we have to keep a grip on the bigger picture or all is lost."

"I am sorry I swore. I served in the forces with her Uncle, I guess I sort of know her by proxy".

"I think if he went to recover her then it might be the best thing" he didn't say anymore. He just left the suggestion in the air.

"Ok, Mr Black, I will leave it with you"

"Thanks Pol, keep me posted"

Sms Conversation

Pol: Swimming pool 10 min

Hicks: Ok

When Pol got to the pool Hicks was already waiting for him. He was pacing up and down in front of the main entrance. Pol told Stu what Black said to him. Both men stood and looked at each other without speaking a word.

"Do you know where we are going?" Pol asked Hicks, by way of accomplice.

"I will by tomorrow." Hicks said simply.

Chapter 14

Tariq was out late that Friday night. By the time he returned to his house the rays of the morning light were starting to infiltrate the sky over Scunthorpe. The natural light took away the reflective orange glow of the steel works and replaced it with a slowly increasing gentle lightening of the sky. The town was quiet now, there was little movement on the roads and the partiers and late night drunks had by and large made their way home or to were ever they would be spending the last few hours of the night sleeping. On the back of one of the benches a cock blackbird perched. He ruffled his feathers and slightly drooped his wings before starting to sing his greeting to the day and the proclamation of his ownership of this part of the street. His bright yellow bill chattering with his song. When he finished his song he flew away from the bench and between the houses towards the few patches of green gardens that remained behind the houses. He knew that the sparrowhawk would also be looking for his breakfast and working his way along the gardens and alleyways. The black birds ownership was proportionate and dependant on the tenure that the predators allowed him.

Tariq parked the Jaguar in the street outside of his house and stepped out into the growing morning light. As he looked down the street his car was the best in the street. It breathed the style and presence that was part of the new Tariq Hasni. No longer a street gang member but now a respectable businessman. He soon would invest in a couple of houses and maybe a restaurant. Then, when he could, he would move out of this house and into one of the bigger houses on

Doncaster Road or maybe Normanby Road. Yes, his time was coming, he was arriving.

He walked to the front door of his house and as he did so he turned and locked the car. He just loved the solid click of the central locking on the jaguar. Felt and sounded like quality. He opened the front door of his house and stepped in. Whilst the light was gathering outside his flat remained gloomy and dark. Closing the door behind him he turned and reached for the light switch. The room was washed with the sterile white light of the bulb. Tariq dropped his keys on the small table beside the door and thought that a quiet beer on his own would be a pleasant end to the evening. Turning to walk through the room he became aware of Hicks. Hicks was stood in the middle of the lounge. Tariq knew Hicks, he lived on the same street. Hicks was wearing a simple cotton tracksuit in pale grey. There was no mask, no disguise. Tariq noticed that Hicks wore a pair of blue latex gloves.

Hicks did not speak, he watched Tariq, stood easily and calmly. Fear started to grow in Tariq. Why was he here? Why didn't he hide his face? Why wear the gloves?

"Get the fuck out of here" Tariq said, he wanted his voice to be strong and commanding but instead his voice betrayed his fear and wavered.

"No Tariq, that won't be happening."

"Why are you here?" Tariq asked.

"Well, me and you are going to have a short drive out and then we will have a chat" Hicks was calm and contained.

"Are you going to hurt me?" Tariq asked, scared.

"Yes." Replied Hicks, he knew he was going to hurt Tariq so badly.

"Are you going to kill me?" Fear was painted on Tariq's features, his strong Asian features had drained of colour and he was an ashen grey colour.

"That depends on our chat, but maybe".

Tariq moved slowly his right hand outstretched and leaning against the table he had just put his car keys in. Hicks watched his movement and allowed it to continue.

"What will we talk about" Hicks knew that Tariq was stalling for time, he also knew why he was.

"You know, business and stuff". Hicks replied.

In his mind Tariq was trying to work out if he could open the table drawer before Hicks could get to him. Hicks glanced to the window, the curtains were open and the light was on inside the house, this would make him more visible to anyone looking into the house. He turned obliquely to the window so his face could not be clearly seen.

As Hicks moved this was the chance that Tariq had been waiting for, Hicks was distracted for just a second, that was enough, he thought. Quickly and smoothly Tariq opened the drawer and pulled out the pistol. He raised the pistol and pointed it directly at Hicks. The muzzle of the browning hipower looked huge the nine millimetre barrel looked to gape wide open to Hicks. Tariq loved the browning, it had been part of a deal he had done for a white girl he had supplied to a group of Kurdish men. It had been a sweet deal, she was young, they were very grateful. In the holdall with the money they had also left some coke and this pistol. It was in excellent condition with the serial numbers milled off and refinished with a silver inlay. He cleaned it regularly and when he could get ammo for it he practised his shooting.

"I am going nowhere with you, white cunt". Tariq laughed, the power had changed and now he was the one calling the shots, quite literally. Once he squeezed the trigger and the hammer fell the hollow point bullet would smash into Hicks. The bullet would travel the full width of his body causing massive damage and exit his back.

Hicks slowly lifted his arm to the side parallel to the floor at shoulder height. He opened his clenched fist. The ten rounds from the chamber and the magazine dropped to the floor and bounced lightly on the laminate flooring.

Tariq had watched the hand open, the fingers extend slowly and the small brass cylinders of the rounds tumble end over end onto the floor. As they fell, in the fractions of a second before they got to the floor, he understood what this meant. The pistol in his extended arm felt unbearably heavy as his arm dropped back to his side and the gun dropped onto the floor. He exhaled and his shoulders slumped.

"Nice browning, I have used them a lot, good weapons." Hicks commented as Tariq watched his every move and the formation of every syllable from Hicks' lips.

Hicks stepped, over the pistol rounds on the floor and towards Tariq. "Time for me and you to go for our little drive out in the countryside, Tariq"

"Where are we going?" asked Tariq, he thought the more information he could illicit from Hicks the better, it would help him to find him later.

"I have an industrial unit out at Santon, the problem is we can't drive straight there through the steel works because of the CCTV cameras".

Maybe if he spoke to his captor enough he might make some kind of human bond that might make a difference and save his skin.

"Please can you put your hands together and in front of you?" Hicks politely asked Tariq. Who duly obliged. Hicks removed a long and thick black cable tie from the sleeve of his tracksuit and looped it around Tariq's wrists and pulled it tight. The plasticuff, pulled tight cut into the skin of his wrists and he let out an involuntary gasp. In his mind he had determined to resist whatever Hicks did, he would not make this easy for him. And so when he heard his own gasp he was disappointed.

"Yes, it's pretty tight. When we get to my lock up you will be ready for that to come off, it will cut the circulation off to your hands. Maybe that will be enough to get our chat going."

Hicks picked up the keys to the Jaguar. Tossed them in the air and put them in his pocket. "I have always fancied one of these, I bet it's nice and quick". He crouched down and picked up the browning. Then turned on his heal and took the few steps to pick up the rounds on the floor. He quickly loaded the magazine with the rounds. "Nice rounds these hollow points, highly effective man stoppers." Loading the magazine into the pistol he pushed the pistol into his hoodie pocket. The weight of the pistol pulled the slack grey cotton down at the front. Hicks pulled a scarf from round his neck and covered his lower face and pulled his hood up. Only his eyes and nose were visible.

Tariq saw him covering his face. He had allowed Tariq to see his face but now he covered it to prevent others from seeing it. It dawned on Tariq that Hicks didn't conceal anything from him. Tariq understood that Hicks was not concerned about what he might or might not see because he would never be able to tell.

"Let's go." Hicks opened the door and they stepped into the street. He opened the jaguar using the remote control and walked with Tariq across to the car.

In a house opposite Mrs Hussein was up early. On a Saturday morning she like to get up and go to the grocers to get her veg fresh. Mrs Hussein came to Scunthorpe in 1963 as a young woman with her husband. He had worked in the steel works for the next forty years before he retired. They came from a village in Bangladesh and had kept themselves to themselves, her husband was one of the Mosque committee and she viewed him as an important part of the community. She watched out of the window as Tariq was lead to his car by a man she didn't know. The man with the hood was not a teenager, she couldn't see his features but he was a solid and deep chested shape that moved with an assurance and confidence of a mature man. She saw the fear in Tariq's face and she saw that although there was a jacket over his wrists in front of him they were tied together.

She had seen Tariq grow up, when he was a little boy he was a lovely boy, respectful and polite. Then Mr Hasni had returned to Pakistan. Mrs Hasni struggled with young Tariq and he became a surly youth, he lost his respect. Mrs Hussein watched his behaviour get worse and worse, watched him start to hang about with the gangs on the street corners. The whole community knew that Tariq was involved in the drugs and prostitution that had blighted the area. So when she saw the hooded stranger leading Tariq to his flash new car she didn't open the door and challenge him, she didn't call her husband to phone the police, she turned and went back to the kitchen and switched on the kettle. She would have a cup of tea before walking to the shop. Tariq had it coming to him.

This was the first time that Tariq had sat in the comfortable cream leather passenger seat of the Jaguar. His wrists were starting to hurt now. He had seen the plasticuff before, he had used them during his sex games in the past. When this man had pulled them tight he felt the skin underneath them burn with the friction. The circulation had been cut off. Initially he had pins and needles in his fingertips, the discomfort had grown and spread into a slow but deep burn in his fingers then into his palms. The burn was deep and throbbed. He felt real fear for the first time in his life.

"My hands hurt". Tariq looked at the hooded stranger

beside him. He knew this man from Acheron Street. He had seen him out running.

"Yes, I am sure they do". Hicks replied.

"What is this all about?" Tariq asked.

"My name is Stu Hicks, my friends call me Sticks. My wife is called Di. She has a niece called Rhianna." Hicks pulled his hood down and pushed his scarf down from his face. He turned and faced Tariq. "You see, Tariq, I know that your people have Rhianna. I know, you know where she is. I also know that you will tell me where she is so I can go and get her."

"I can't tell you anything" Tariq spoke quietly and softly, "If I tell you then they will kill me".

"It is quite likely that I will kill you anyway, so if you want to survive start talking to me and we can try to get keep you alive." Hicks informed him matter of factly.

Tariq looked out of the window of the car and saw the fields passing by. It was light now, the clouds were breaking up as the orange disc of the sun started to claw itself into the autumn sky. A few whisps of early morning mist shrouded the stubble fields on the flat of Trent valley. Geese were flying in to feed on the discarded corn laying on the surface of the stubble, they seemed impossibly big and heavy to fly. It was the first time Tariq had taken any notice of them. He had seen them flying over the town, high and arrowing through the deep blue of the autumn skies. He had not seen the beauty of their flight before. A group of them flew low over the stubble and flared their mighty wings open to land.

The transition between the powerful flight and landing was a clumsy flapping of huge wings and massive webbed feet. Tariq promised himself to take notice of the beauty around him, if he came out of this alive.

"Where are we going?" Asked Tariq.

"I have a lock up down in Gunness."

Hicks pulled the car up to a compound and unlocked the gate. The compound was surrounded by a large palisade fence of eight foot high steel spikes. Inside was a grey concrete building with a line of roll down steel doors. The doors were in a selection of rusty and painted finishes. In the compound outside of the garages were piles of tyres and rusting vehicles in various states of decay. Several of the units had large waste disposal skips outside full of rubbish that seemed to well from within, fill them to the brim and overflow onto the concrete on the ground around them.

Hicks drew the car up to a one of the roller doors and stopped. "I am going to open the door now, if you try to run or get away I am going to hurt you and hurt you real bad. Do you understand?"

"Yes, I understand, I won't run" Tariq said.

"Ok, good lad." Hicks smiled at Tariq as he got out of the car.

The roller door was locked at the side with a combination key pad. Tariq watched Hicks walk to the lock and punched in his combination. He held a button down on the pad and the electric motor grudgingly burst into life. The door edged up slowly inching away from the concrete floor. Bright artificial light ran out from below the door. Tariq watched the slow exposure of the inside of the lock up. The lock up was deeper than he guessed it would be. It took a few minutes for Tariq to understand what was different about the back of the lock up. The first section, was simple concrete floor and grey concrete block walls. But the back section of the lock up appeared to be a pale blue gloss, it had a shine to both the floor and the walls. He finally recognised what the blue colour was. The rear of the lock up had been lined with plastic sheet. On the floor in the centre of the plastic sheet stood a solitary wooden kitchen chair.

Hicks returned to the Jaguar and drove it onto the concrete. He turned off the ignition and turned to Tariq. "Ok, laughing boy, time to get out and start our little chat."

Tariq could not move, he was paralysed with fear. The colour had drained from his face. His pencil line beard contrasted harshly against his grey skin pallor.

"Oh, are you a little bit scared?" Hicks laughed as he spoke.

Hicks got out of the car and moved to the passenger door and opened it. "Step out Tariq"

Tariq tried to move but he could not coordinate his movements. "Let me help you decide if you want to do what I say." Hicks grabbed Tariq's hair in his left fist and held his head firmly. With his right hand palm upwards using the tip of his longest finger and index finger he traced the strong line of Tariq's jaw line. His touch was light and fluid, a smooth lover's caress. When Hicks found the sharp angle of

Tariq's strong jaw line he used the gentle fingers and pushed hard against the inside of the mandible. The skilled touch of the former Special Forces soldier found the tangle of nerve fibres and the lymph node that made up the pressure point. He jabbed his finger against them and pressed hard. The flash of pain illuminated Tariq. Tariq's body went rigid with the pain and he exhaled sharply. The level of pain was something that Tariq had never experienced before. He instantly felt mentally confused as the shock had run straight through the nerves and into his head. "That hurt?" Hicks asked the obvious question. "Ok, well if you don't want more then you best get out of the car". Hicks did not allow Tariq time to answer after the question.

Tariq swung his legs out and stood unsteadily on the concrete. As he stood on the concrete his bladder voided with fear, the hot stream of urine coloured his mid blue trousers dark and pooled at his feet. He felt ashamed and afraid.

"Let's have a seat shall we?" Hicks lead him on to the plastic sheet to the chair. "Sit down, sweetheart" Tariq sat quietly as directed. He watched Hicks with wide open, dark fascinated eyes.

Hicks walked across the plastic sheeted floor and to a large plastic storage box at the back. The box had been placed underneath the plastic sheeting. The sheeting seemed to flow from the box, the inside was lined with the plastic. From the box he lifted out some old newspaper and a five litre chemical container. As he walked back past Tariq he spoke again. "Dear me, don't want you leaving any of that tell-tale

DNA here amongst your cocaine riddled piss do we now?"

He placed the newspapers on the puddle of urine to and on top of the newspaper he poured some of the contents of the chemical can. Tariq could smell the strong bleach as he watched the fluid drain from the container. He continued to watch Hicks as he returned the container to the storage chest. Hicks placed the container back in the box and lifted something else out. He was not sure what was in the hand of the man in the grey track suit. Tariq watched Hicks as he walked back towards him. It became clear that the item in the Hicks' hand was a mobile phone. Hicks lifted the phone to his ear. He could only hear one side of the conversation.

"Hello Black …. Yeah I have him … no not yet….I need a clean-up …. Yeah a Jaguar car… give me two hours."

He turned and spoke to Tariq, "Ok sweetie, let's talk."

Tariq spoke "Ok, what do you want to know"

"Where is Rhianna?" Hicks spoke quickly and quietly.

"I can't tell you" Tariq felt he had scored a point.

"Ok, this is how this works, I ask you a question and you tell me the answer. Do you understand?"

"I really can't tell you."

"I haven't got time to fuck about, I am not playing games."

Hicks took a step towards Tariq and crouched directly in front of his face. "Tariq, you leave me no option."

Hicks stood back and with his open left hand he slapped

Tariq on the side of the neck. The explosively powerful slap
was aimed at a pressure point on the side of the neck. The
aim was critical, if the impact hits too far forward the slap
could damage Tariq's windpipe and kill him. Too far back
and Hicks could damage his hand on the hard cords of
muscle or neck bones. The slap compressed the flesh in his
neck causing a shock wave of pressure to penetrate the nerve
clusters. If Hicks weighted this too hard then one slap would
render Tariq unconscious.

Tariq let out a shout of pain.

"Where is she?" Hicks was calm when he spoke.

"Fuck you, cunt" Tariq spat back.

"Good, I like that, shows some character." Hicks said.

Hicks hit Tariq again, this time he used the heal of his left
hand and struck the man in the cheek bone. The thin skin
over the high cheek bone split open. The cut bled heavily
and immediately.

"Fuck you, fuck you, fuck you" shouted Tariq.

"Ok, we will have to be a bit more subtle wont we. Looks
like you have had a spanking or two."

"I am not going to tell you a fucking thing, you will have to
kill me" Tariq was anger, his dark eyes flashed with fury.

Tariq was not secured to the chair, up to now only his fear
had kept him seated. But now his anger overcame his fear
and he stood up. He was on his feet for only a second before
Hicks struck him hard in the sternum using the point of his

left elbow. The wind was smashed out of Tariq's lungs as the overwhelming pain of a cracked rib pushed him back into the chair.

"Very naughty, Tariq." Hicks spoke in a calm and easy manner. Hicks walked back to the plastic storage box in the corner and returned to Tariq carrying a carpenter's chisel and four more plasticuffs. He crouched in front of Tariq. Hicks secured him to the chair with the plasticuffs. Tariq could not move, tied down by the ankles to each chair leg and at each elbow to the vertical back of the chair. "Tariq, I have here a chisel, I have sharpened the edges as well. Do you see it?"

"I see it". Said Tariq. Hicks held the chisel in front of Tariq, The bright edges were razor sharp.

"I am going to use the sharp edge to open the skin on the front of your leg and the point will get dragged along your shin bone. The pain will be excruciating. It's a method that was used by the Russians in Afghanistan."

Tariq looked at the chisel and looked at Hicks again. "You don't understand, if I tell you then they will kill me and maybe my family." He was pleading with Hicks, "I can't tell you."

"The thing is Tariq they won't get a chance to kill you because I will kill you this morning. You have a choice whether you want to die quickly and with little pain or whether you want to visit hell and die in a world of pain crying for your mother."

Tariq closed his eyes, he started to sob. His life was coming to a very finite conclusion. His hopes and visions for himself, his ambitions and aspirations were ebbing away.

"Do you want money?" he asked.

"Money made from having little girls fucked by gangs of old men? By drugs being pushed into the town? I don't want your money, you filthy fucker."

"I want to know where Rhianna is, you tell me that and the pain can go away, you will fade into my darkness and slide away". Hicks bent close in front of Tariq's face as he spoke in quiet and defined words.

"I can't tell you where she is." Tariq sobbed, his large dark eyes pleaded for his life, begged to be spared.

Hicks looked straight into his eye, into his soul. "Ok, let's do this then, I don't have all day."

Taking the chisel in his right hand and using the sharpened bevelled edge on the long side of the blade he slit open Tariq's trouser leg from the knee down to the hem.

"I am going to ask you one more time, where is Rhianna?"

"Fuck you, white trash cunt". Shouted Tariq in defiance.

"Ok, any time you want me to stop you just need to start talking to me and I will stop and listen". Hicks used the edge of the chisel and pressed it into the dark tight skin on the front of Tariq's leg. As he pressed onto the leg the skin parted easily and the blade entered the fine sheath of muscle covering Tariq's tibia.

Tariq looked down and he saw his blood flowing dark and easily from the wound, it ran down his shin and into the top of his shoe where slowly it pooled behind the little dam that each of his laces made before flowing over the top and trickling down the instep of the shoe. He watched in fascination as his very blood formed a pool that slowly, slowly rolled out it's boundary across the plastic sheet. The pool expanded under the bright neon light of the unit. Tariq was surprised how little pain he felt. The chisel was razor sharp and cut through him easily, almost surgically. He looked down at hicks who squatted in front of him. Their eyes met. Tariq could not fathom the darkness behind the easy eyes of Stuart Hicks.

"Not too bad?" Hicks smiled.

What sort of man could smile whilst he did this? What sort of man knew how to do this? Tariq smiled back at Hicks. "No, not bad. Not bad enough for me to tell you what you want to know, anyway."

"Ok Tariq, you have it your way" Hicks looked down at the large vertical wound down Tariq's leg.

With the forefinger and thumb of his left hand he held the wound open. He looked into the wound and carefully using the very sharp tip of the chisel he again made a vertical incision down the same line as the first. This incision opened the sheath behind the muscle. And again Hicks pulled the layers of Tariq's leg apart. The skin, peeled back over easily, the muscle was tough, Hicks thought that Tariq must work out or do some sort of training to make his muscle this tough. The smooth white length of Tariq's tibia was exposed.

"Tariq, I want you to watch what I am doing, I will be upset if you look away" Hicks knew that if Tariq was watching the chisel parting his flesh he would be so much more susceptible to the pain that would be overwhelming him in just a few seconds. Tariq looked down, his attention fascinated by what was happening to him.

"If you want me to stop then you tell me ok?" Hicks said again.

"I can take this you fucking white bastard". Tariq growled.

"Gosh, I could be offended by your racist language" Laughed Hicks.

Taking the chisel back to the top of the cut he again held the skin apart with the fingers of his left hand. He placed the corner at the very tip of the chisel against Tariq's shin bone. He struck the back of the chisel with the palm of his left hand firmly. Tariq screamed in agony as the shock of extreme pain overtook his body and mind in wave of pure desperation.

"No, no, no please don't, no more," he cried.

"Shall we talk?" Hicks continued in the professional detached tone of one who does not give a damn about the pain of his fellow man.

"Fuck you!" The steel point of the chisel was embedded just a couple of millimetres in the bone. Slowly and precisely Hicks twisted the blue plastic handle of the chisel. The tip of the chisel pressed hard against the bone under the torque of Hicks' grip. The level of pain that Tariq felt was ratcheted up. He had never felt anything like this. When the chisel caused a small chip of bone to shear away from the tibia in a long splinter he let out another scream of pure agony and fear.

"Shall we talk?"

"Ok, will you let me go?" Tariq's voice was a small echo lost in a gale.

"No, but you won't have any more pain"

"She has gone to a unit in Rotherham, 19 Stadium Court."

"Thank you" Said Hicks "what time are they all due over there?"

"They won't be there until ten, maybe later". Tariq looked straight up at Hicks "If you let me go I will cut you into the deal, you can have what you want and I will never tell about this"

"What you will never tell?" Asked Hicks.

"No, I will never tell a soul, let God help me" Pleaded Tariq.

"What about security?"

"None, will you let me go?"

Hicks pulled the chisel out of the deep wound in the front of Tariq's leg. He stood up straight and walked behind Tariq. "My legs were aching with all that squatting down. Although probably not as bad as your legs ache."

Tariq didn't speak he sat looking straight forward in the

chair, the relief of the cessation of his torture softened the pain throbbing from his fractured shin bone. The tip of the chisel felt cold as it touched the back of his neck just above the hairline.

Hicks held the chisel over the atlas joint precisely with his left hand. He formed his right hand into a fist and with the bottom of his hand like a hammer he thumped the chisel handle on the end. The razor sharp Sheffield steel of the blade smashed through the skin, ligaments and muscle, the tip divided the atlas joint where the skull meets the spine and the cold steel severed the nerve. Tariq's legs twitched against the bonds as the few confused signals from his severed spinal cord ended.

The pain left him, the sharp pinch in the neck was over in an instant signalled a sudden detachment from the pain in his leg. In the seconds before the darkness enveloped him he heard Hicks' voice say "you will go to Hawiyah". There was no pain, there was only darkness, Tariq did not see heaven or hell, he saw nothing, nothing overwhelmed him and he became part of it.

Hicks looked around, this part of the mission had been accompanied easily.

Tariq was dead on the wooden chair in the middle of the garage, his blood had been nicely contained on the plastic sheet. He was quite pleased, there wasn't much blood. The less spilt the less time in clearing up.

He reached into his pocket and using the remote control of the Jaguar he opened the boot. Walking over to the Jaguar he looked in. Hicks was surprised at the room inside. Much more than he had anticipated, really good accommodation for such a car. He returned to Tariq and taking hold of the back of the chair he dragged him across the plastic sheet and lifted him into the boot, still taped to the chair. The boot would not shut. The chair was just too big. Hicks didn't mind that too much, the cleaner would deal with everything like that.

Hicks rolled the plastic sheeting from the garage floor back and into the large plastic storage box. He placed the box in the Jaguar and as he did so he opened the driver's side window and closed the door. Standing beside the door he stripped off his tracksuit. Underneath the tracksuit he was wearing a set of paper, disposable overalls, he stripped those off as well. He was in his running kit underneath.

Just inside the unit door he had placed his trainers in a bag on a previous visit. He slipped the shoes on his feet and waited for the cleaner.

The seven and a half ton curtain sided lorry arrived at the compound exactly on time. Hicks spoke to the driver. "Hello, can I help you?"

The driver replied "I am from Mr Black's cleaning company"

"Ok, can you back up to unit five please?"

The driver did as he was asked and within a few minutes, the Jaguar had been dragged onto the back of the lorry.

"I will deal with it" The driver said to Hicks.

"Thanks mate" Hicks shut the door of the garage and jogged steadily out of the compound and back towards the town. It was a nice morning. The sun was shining now. The town starting to wake up and people were starting to move about now.

Chapter 15

The two men sat at the table drinking coffee. It had been many years since they last had planned an operation together. Technology had moved on significantly since the days in the jungles of Central America. On the screen of the laptop the google maps image of the target was clear and in colour. This technology enabled the men to plan in a way that they could only have dreamed of previously.

"There can be no killing in this" Pol said quietly.

"No of course not. Just a straight in and out extraction". Hicks replied.

"The thing is I am a cop now, not a soldier. We aren't soldiering now. We could go to prison for an awfully long time if we do any killing".

"Mate, these people are villains, we need to go tooled up in case it goes out of shape, I hope it doesn't but we need to be ready". Pol suspected that Stu was talking them into turning this into a Special Forces operation.

"I am really worried that we are going to end up with this all going to rat shit." Pol voiced his concerns.

Stu lifted a black canvas holdall on to the table and unzipped it. He slid his hand into the bag and pulled out the contents one item at a time.

The first item out was the Browning Hipower that Hicks had taken from Tariq.

"For fuck sake, Stu. Where is that from?"

"You don't need to know where it came from. But I also have a few spare rounds for it." He placed two boxes of fifty rounds on the table. The rounds were the superbly efficient man stoppers. The Hornady hollow point bullet was designed to expand explosively on impact. It is unlikely that the rounds would shoot all the way through a human torso making them ideal for close work where shoot through casualties were a real risk.

Hicks pulled the next item out and for Pol things went from bad to worse. The Beretta 9mm pistol was the standard issue for the American forces for years. Superbly reliable, relatively accurate. "Lovely piece, brought it home from a job in the Middle East." Hicks spoke lovingly as he placed the pistol on the table.

Pol leaned back in his chair and sipped his coffee. He looked at his old friend closely and thought about the ops they had in the jungle. He remembered what had happened to the little boy and the old man at Tanjoc. His memories had been flavoured and sanitised by the passing of the years. The years had passed and he had forgotten the horror of the killings. The horror of the relaxed attitude that Hicks had to the taking of the life back then came flooding back to him. The loving voice in which Stu spoke about the weapons and ammunition gave Pol a deep and strong feeling of uneasiness.

"Ok so what time shall I pick you up tonight?" Pol asked.

"Well let's get in the bushes behind the unit at about seven. That way all the office people will be home and we will be in situ for when they turn up with Rhianna so we need to be across there for about half past six. Set off from here about five?" Hicks ran the clock backwards in his head as he worked out the timings.

"Yeah ok, Pick up point at Asda?"

"No, let's meet up outside the scrap yard over the road. There is no CCTV there and we will be invisible". Suggested Hicks.

"Ok, no problem"

Pol rode home on his 1200. His mind was a confused turmoil of thoughts and emotions. He was excited by the prospect of going to collect Rhianna. In the dark side of his history was the memory of the adrenaline thrills of military operations. Try as he might he could not put the anticipation of this thrill back in its box.

As he parked his machine in the yard, Fleur opened the back door of the house when she heard the rumble of the big Suzuki pulling in. "Hey, Winchester, the kettle is on".

"Thanks, Fleur."

"What have you been up to, Pol?"

"I have got myself into something that I have to see through." Pol spoke slowly.

"What is it?" Fleur asked.

"Well, I am going with Sticks tonight to get Rhianna back". Pol had spoken to fleur about Rhianna. He told her everything. He knew that there were some things that she shouldn't know. But he trusted her implicitly.

"The thing is Fleur this has got the potential to really go fucking wrong. If it goes that way it could get seriously ugly".

"Pol, you know this is the right thing to do. The cops won't touch it so someone has to and that person has to be you, I am right behind you, this kid is more important than the policies of the cops".

"Thank you sweetie. Right I have to go and try and get an hour or so in bed."

"Ok, I will bring you up a coffee in a couple of hours."

Sleep came to Pol far easier than he thought it would. It was deep and dreamless sleep. So when, a couple of hours later Fleur slipped into bed with him he was refreshed and ready to head to Rotherham. Fleur had other ideas for him, he was quite happy to oblige her.

Pol stood under the hot stream of the shower, he allowed the water to wash away the gloom that had washed over him after Fleur had gone back downstairs singing to herself. He cleared his mind and once that gloom had departed he started to focus on the task ahead of him. Started to mentally rehearse various scenarios. It was a technique he had been taught whilst playing rugby. The mental preparation and mental rehearsals were crucial when trying to perform to the highest level. In his mind he was remembering and running through the drills for clearing the Browning of jammed cartridges. He hoped that he would not have to reach for the pistol at any time.

Fleur had cooked Pol a large bowl of pasta, he sat quietly at the table and ate it in silence. He was not hungry. He felt nervous and a little shaky with tension but he knew he would need the energy later on in the evening and he needed to replenish his tanks before he left.

Pol put his holdall in the boot of the car and set off to collect Hicks.

Their journey to Rotherham was quiet. They did not speak

much to each other. Both of them submerged in the unknown depths of their own individual worlds and doing their own preparation.

As they got closer to the South Yorkshire industrial town Hicks broke the quite oppressive silence in the car.

"Ok, Apollo, nearly there now, are you ready?"

"Yes Stuart, getting towards it. Sunday names for this job?" Pol glanced across to Stu and they laughed together as old brothers in arms. They had easily assumed the roles they had left twenty years behind them and fell comfortably n to where they left off in the filth and heat of the Central American jungles.

"I have a car on the other side of the target address so we have a different egress and extraction. We will leave your car in a mate's garage just round the block." Hicks continued.

"Ok, you are on top of this little job, aren't you mate?" Pol continued to laugh.

"Yeah, for sure, you know me. Proper Prior Planning and Preparation Prevents Piss Poor Performance. The eight P's. I still roll with that". Hicks was able to reel off the old mantra easily.

Hicks directed Pol to an industrial estate and onto Cornish Way. This was a shabby light industrial complex of small lock up units. Pol slowed his car down to a crawl and awaited further instructions from his passenger.

"Ok mate, it is the third unit on the left" Pol drove up to the unit and Hicks stepped up to the roller door.

"We can come back and pick it up tomorrow or the next day, I can use the other car to bring you back and I will drop it back in the garage."

"Ok Mate, got the gear?" Pol asked.

"Yeah, come on, you know me." They walked from the garage closing the door behind them, both men wore baseball caps pulled well down and navy overalls. They could have been from any unit on the estate, both men dropped into an easy slouch that was foreign to them.

The walked down Cornish way and to the car park of the unit that stretched the whole length of the road on the right. At the end of the car park Pol saw there was a line of trees. The trees would mark the edges of a water course as shown on Google maps, they extended both north and south of his view point.

"Keep your head down, there are cameras on this unit." Said Hicks.

Pol thought that the extraction of this girl had taken more planning than one man could have achieved in one day, especially as Hicks had spent the morning with him drinking coffee and chatting.

"I hope the water is not too deep, I don't fancy sitting in wet boots for the next three hours".

"Yeah for sure, we will see. I don't want to sit listening to you moaning for the next three hours either".

Again the easy laugh of the old comrades. To Pol this felt more like a good day out with an old mate at the moment. A stark contrast to what would happen.

The wire at the end of the unit's car park had been cut and the two men in their overalls slipped through, they could be any two men looking for a shortcut home or seeking some privacy to smoke a joint. Stepping under the trees Pol saw there was a large plank across the small stream, he would not, after all, have to sit in the bushes in wet clothes.

"Right mate, the unit we are looking at is on the left as we look at it, the third one up. It used to be a washing machine repair place, not any more. One of them uses it for storing smuggled in drugs and whatever else he is pedalling at the time." Hicks spoke in hushed tones, they had left the slovenly posture and gait as soon as they had stepped out of view. Both men had returned to the fluid stealth that they were most comfortable with.

Pol crouched and moved forward towards the edge of the bushes. The front of the unit was quite easily visible to him. It was a two story building of concrete and steel construction. The ground floor had a steel roller door, a pedestrian door and a set of steel stairs ran up to the first floor offices. At this time the unit was in darkness, no cars were parked nearby and all of the doors looked locked.

"On the map there is no exit to the rear, is that right Sticks?"

"Yeah, seems to be there is a staircase in side to the right of the roller door which will go up to the offices. I suspect they will set up the ground floor for their fucking show." Pol detected a sniff of emotion and anger in Hick's voice. He was crossing the line. He was dangerous, this wasn't the calm and clinical Stu Hicks he had known all those years ago, in Pol's darkest hour. Maybe he would be able to control himself when it really mattered and it was time to go in there and get the girl.

"Are you going to be ok to do this tonight, Sticks?" Pol asked.

"Yeah," Hicks turned to face Pol, he knew his feelings had been compromised and he knew that Pol recognised the potential weakness that this could expose them too.

"Its fuck all, of course I can do it. It's just that the kid is Rhianna and I really want to get her home safely" Hicks reassured Pol.

"I don't want to be involved in a punishment beating, we are not the fucking IRA." Pol pressed his point.

"Well what the fuck do you think we are?" Hicks had been angered by Pol's answer. "Look at yourself, you are wearing a set of overalls, in this bag I have pistols and daggers. We are not Mary fucking Poppins are we?"

"I guess not."

"We need to get her out and keep her safe, if some of them get hurt, then fuck them, it is collateral damage. If they had not abducted her to fuck her and hurt her then we wouldn't be here would we?"

Both men sat quietly, watched the place quietly through

binoculars. Pol reflected on what Hicks had said to him, 'who the fuck do you think we are' burned into his brain cells. He certainly wasn't a cop when he was sat watching this unit knowing that in just a couple of hours he would be going through the front door with a loaded automatic pistol on his thigh. He wasn't a soldier, the enemy on this were British people. There was no mission to follow. No orders that they could hang a killing on.

After a quiet hour Pol put his hand into the hold all and pulled out a stainless steel flask.

"Mate, we are soon going to have to get ourselves in the zone, let's have a quick brewski before we really start fucking things up for them." Pol passed the steaming cup of coffee to Hicks. They would have not have had a coffee in the jungle, the smell could be detected for hundreds of meters. Here, in Rotherham the chemical smells of industry would mask the subtle scent of the Gold Blend.

"The power cable runs in at the back, it has been prepped so that I can knock the mains off as we go in, we will go in in the dark. They won't know what has hit them. In and out, grab Rhianna and gone, by the time they realise that they have been done she will be in a car and gone." It was the first time that Hicks had spoken for some time. The anger he was showing earlier had seemed to subside.

"Yeah of course" Pol felt a little reassured by the seeming change in Hicks' attitude.

Hicks put his hand in his pocket and pulled out two small camouflage face paint compacts. He tossed one over to Pol.

"Here bro, time to put on our make-up, we are on stage soon"

"Cheer mate". Pol had not worn this stuff for many years, some of his hunting buddies used it when they went deer hunting. Pol always thought that was bull shit.

He opened the compact and looked into the mirror, he looked at himself, at his eyes, into himself. Pol covered his face in a light layer of grey, this would stop the reflection from his skin and take away the bright white disco of his face. He built up layers of darker cream over the higher points of his face. And in vertical lines, this had the effect of flattening his face out and breaking it up into shadow and light.

Hicks had done his. Pol thought it dehumanised him.

The evening was starting to draw in now. The industrial estate was empty a few beacons of light shone out where a unit might have been working shifts or just staying late. The street lights were illuminated around the estate except for Stadium Court, the street lights in the court stubbornly remained off in spite of the increasing gloom. The pleasant afternoon had turned cloudy and the autumn evening air was starting to chill a little. A light breeze had started to pick up and there was a feeling in the air of dampness. It wasn't raining but mist blew in on the breeze as the dampness grew over the town.

By eight o'clock it was dark, the two men in their black clothing, merged and joined the shadows around them. The edges of the darker shadows blurred the outlines of the men.

They were experienced and skilled in fighting in the dark and they each carried a small head torch and hand torch. Their lights had red lenses to make them as inconspicuous as possible. The light mist had now drenched both of them to the bone and they were starting to feel the cold.

Pol became aware of headlights moving slowly down the road towards the unit. The driver moved slowly as if lost, or looking for something. The car was the small BMW that both Hicks and Pol had seen Tariq driving but recently had been driven by Kharon. It swung onto the concrete hard standing in front of the unit. Pol and Hicks were in the bushes only twenty meters away and when the car stopped they clearly recognised Kharon as he got out of the car. The passenger also got out and walked towards the unit. He was another Asian man, "Do you know him?" Whispered Hicks.

"No mate, never seen him before". Pol replied.

Pol heard Kharon speak quite clearly. "Go and get the place ready"

"Ok Kazzy, aren't you coming in?" the other lad said.

"Are you scared of the shadows, Ibby?" Kharon laughed at his friend.

"Fuck off man, I was going to get a beer before we started man"

"No drinking, you need to be sober and clean, no booze and no weed. If it goes wrong you have to be with me to do whatever we need to do." Kharon stopped laughing in an instant.

"Ok, Kazzy, you are the man"

"Go in and get sorted, get the cameras ready and check we have enough beers in for them. I have to pop and get our investment"

Pol heard hicks murmur when Khan said 'investment' "Fucking investment, she is a little girl". Pol knew he wanted out of this. But he had come too far along the line now. He could not go back and leave Hicks here on his own. The BMW backed out and left its passenger stood outside the unit. The young man was short and stocky, he was dressed in a pair of black slacks, a white shirt, and a waist coat. He could have stepped out of any restaurant's waiting staff. The lad took a bunch of keys from his pocket and as Kharon reversed the BMW of the front of the unit he unlocked the door and stepped inside. A moment later the lights on the first floor flickered into life.

From their vantage point in the bushes the two watchers were able to see quite a large proportion of the first floor. The venetian blinds were still up and they could see the top of the lad in the waiters' clothes moving around the place, making it and himself ready.

As the time crept on and the darkness fell Pol started to feel that old and familiar comfort of his adrenaline starting to circulate. Earlier in the evening he had regretted coming with Sticks to do this, now he could not wait to go in there and get on with their job. As he stood, in the shadows, he went round the mental checklist, he reached down with his right hand and patted the pistol in the thigh holster. He ran his hand up to the small of his back and felt the dagger clipped onto his belt centrally in the small of his back. The dagger was far shorter than the Sykes-Fairbairn dagger that he had been trained to use long ago. This dagger's blade was shorter and broader. Double edged like the Sykes but only five inches in blade length and thick through the centre section and the blade was wider. Made of a tough and super sharp carbon steel the blade had been blacked in the same way that a gun is blacked. This meant that there could be no flash of light from the blade when it was drawn. The thick tang was simply wrapped in a single covering of paracord. The nylon cord gave texture and a solid grip so that even if the knife was covered in blood the user would be able to grip it strongly.

Several other cars had drawn up to the unit now, a Mercedes and large BMW saloon, long low and dark. Their occupants had gone straight into the building.

"I am counting them in, I think there are five in there now."

"Yeah," agreed Pol, "the waiter and two from each of those two cars,"

As they looked up at the first floor windows they hoped to establish where in the building the people were the blinds on the first floor windows were closed.

Pol glanced at his watch. Time was getting close. It was 21:33hrs, soon they would all be here. Soon they would bring Rhianna in and soon the two ex-soldiers would burst in there and fall upon them from the shadows.

More cars drew up and more Asian men went into the unit. The large wide shape of the black Audi seemingly silently drew up on the frontage. The windows were darkly tinted but both men had seen the car before in Scunthorpe. The door open and they both recognised the mayor of Scunthorpe, Ranjit Quereshi. Quereshi was well dressed in an expensive suit and moved with a self-assured confidence that could easily be described as arrogance. Quereshi opened the unit door and light from the unit flooded out into the increasing evening gloom.

"I don't think it will be long now, mate". Pol whispered to Hicks.

"No, how many have you counted in there?"

"I am up to nineteen now." Replied Pol.

"Yeah me too, once she gets here we will give it ten minutes or so for things to settle down then I will cut the power and we will go in." Hicks spoke quietly.

"Yeah, ok mate. The same as we discussed at your place?"

"Yeah. Exactly what I said."

At a few minutes after ten Kharon's old BMW pulled back into the frontage of the unit.

"She's on plot" Pol whispered to Hicks. He could see a girl in the front of the BMW. As soon as Kharon opened the driver's door of the car the interior light came on and illuminated the girl. He recognised her straight away.

"Get out of the car, if you try to run I will catch you and things will be even worse for you."

Hicks and Pol heard the threat clearly. Pol was scared that this would cause Hicks to lose his temper and go straight in to the unit.

Rhianna got out of the car. She was stood in the light of the open car door and both of the watchers could see what she was wearing. It turned Pol's stomach. He felt enraged. It was disgusting and only underlined that the men in the unit knew exactly what they were doing. They knew how old Rhianna was. She was wearing a school uniform. Flat black shoes and white ankle socks. Her long coltish legs bare and a short pleated grey school skirt a white blouse and a tie. Her hair was tied high on her head in pig tails.

"This is fucking sick" Rhianna spat at Kharon.

"Come on Baby, you know it's what I want and if you do this I will know how much I respect you" Kharon replied.

"Fucking bull shit," Rhianna replied.

"Listen to me, bitch. You go in there and perform, if you don't go in there by choice I will drag you in there kicking and screaming and then afterwards I will make sure you go in the foundations of some motorway bridge. Do you understand me?" Kharon was cold and calm. There was no room for doubt in what he said. He was earnest and serious. Rhianna clearly sensed this and the fight went out of her, she deflated by inches.

Kharon reached into the car and from behind the driver's seat he pulled out a small ragdoll. "Ready?" He threw the doll to her and she held it tightly in her hands as she went in.

Hicks looked at his watch. He did not say a word, he didn't need to. Both men didn't need to speak. In military terms they understood they would operating "with extreme prejudice".

Pol did his checks once again. Checked his pistol, checked a round was chambered. Checked his knife. He even bent down and tightened his boot laces. He did not want to trip over his laces in the middle of this rescue.

"Ok, let's do it." Hicks said.

"Yeah, fucking right" Pol agreed.

Both men drew their pistols. Pol gripped the top slide of the browning and checked, again that it had a round in the chamber. It felt reassuringly heavy in his hand, solid, dependable without character or foible. Both men advanced along the tree line to the edge of the building and at a low crouch crossed the open ground to the corner of the unit. The lack of lighting in the court put them in shadow throughout their advance. Light spilled out from the bottom of the unit door and around the blinds in the first floor. Pol felt the familiar surge of adrenaline as it coursed round his system, he knew he must temper it. If he went into the building so adrenalized then he would not be as in control as he needed. He regulated his breathing and consciously slowed down his heart rate.

Hicks swiftly and silently hunched down and moving like a shadow within a shadow. He passed the ground floor door to the unit and pressed his back against the wall. Pol followed him along and pressed his back to the other side of the door. Hicks reached to the edge of the door frame. He pulled a thin piece of wire from the side of the door frame.

Pol had placed his head torch on and he looked over to Hicks. Hicks had put his on and with a nod they both switched them on. In the same second Hicks pulled on the wire. The rhythmic music from within the unit stopped and the lights went off. The unit was plunged into darkness and as the voices of protest rose from within. Both Hicks and Pol stepped into the unit and shut the door behind them.

The red beams of their head torched played across the furniture inside the unit on the ground floor.

Pol surveyed the scene. It had been set up as an arena. In the centre was a double bed but with only a dark coloured rubber sheet, in the red light of the head torch it was difficult to differentiate colour. There were a several sofas set out around. They were matching leather Chesterfields. It seemed that no expense had been spared to convert this industrial unit into a theatre to display the commodity that was Rhianna's innocence.

The stairs at the rear of the unit were their target, they had expected to find Rhianna on the ground floor but she was not there. They would have to make their way up stairs and onto the first floor. As they approached the base of the stairs they switched off their head torches. They moved through the shadows and darkness with silent intent. Softly rolling each foot fall down to the floor silent, crouched and ready to deal with whatever they came across.

A voice; a man's voice cut through the darkness and the

silence. It was a voice they did not recognise. The man said
"I will go and find the fuse box and get the power on."

Abdul Razak was part of the network that Tariq worked for.
He was a key player and had achieved progress through the
organisation very quickly. He was a bright and intelligent
young man. He also had a huge propensity towards extreme
violence. This skill set had made him a very attractive
prospect to the senior members of his network. He knew
that the fuse box would be down stairs, probably near the
single door. He blundered forward in the darkness. He felt
for the hand rail down the stairs and as he found them he
slowly started to descend into the stairwell. His footsteps
audible from the steel risers of the stair well.

At the base of the stairwell he felt his foot land on the solid
concrete of the ground floor. He had his lighter in his pocket
and reached for it. He had become slightly disorientated and
could not quite get the location of the door straight.

The small flame of the lighter gutted into life. The meagre
light spread a weak slash around the unit. Razak didn't
immediately recognise the two shapes either side of him. It
took his mind a second or so to process the images carved
from the darkness. The blackened dehumanised faces did
not easily fit into the patterns his brain would easily
recognise. The eyes did. The whites of Hicks eyes were
bright. But it was too late for him, he did not get the chance
to make any sort of noise, call for help or say his final words.
The leather gloved fist of Hicks struck hm. Hicks threw the
punch in a hugely powerful but short uppercut action. It
was unlike hicks to use a punch. But this had to be quick and

quiet. Voices had started to rise in the room upstairs, they would not have heard the thump of the punch that connected to the point of Razak's chin. Razak's head snapped back he lost consciousness immediately. With an economy of movement Hicks was able to throw left arm around the throat of the unconscious and falling man. His left arm came around Razak's lower face. Hick's fingertips found the angle behind Razak's jaw. With a sharp exhalation of breath he pulled Razak's head sharply towards him and against the momentum of his fall. The skilled hand of Hicks snuffed out the life efficiently and professionally. Hicks lowered Razak to the floor of the unit. He ensured he lowered him to one side of the staircase to allow an easy escape without tripping over his prostrate form.

Neither Hicks nor Pol noticed when the impact of the punch caught Razak the zippo lighter flew from his hand. The lighter skidded across the concrete floor and slid under one of the chesterfield sofa. The sofa was old. Too old to be made of any sort of flame retardant filling. Old enough to be stuffed with horse hair and fibre. The small and weak flame of the zippo was focussed on a piece of the hessian lining underneath the sofa. Slowly the flame blackened the natural brown fibres and they started to smoulder. As Hicks and Pol started to ascend to the first floor so the fire started to lick through the sofa, at first very small and very slowly but soon gathering momentum and size. As the two men stepped foot on the first floor for the first time the fire had become established in the sofa and started to accelerate through the old piece of furniture.

"Now!" Pol whispered to Hicks. They both turned on their

head lights at the same time. They were in an open space, a room, not quite as wide as the full unit and with a door at the opposite side of the room. There was a small raised platform in the middle of the floor, maybe a coffee table, Hicks could not be sure as he looked across through the red light of the torch. Chairs and sofas around the walls of the unit were lined with men. Rhianna was displayed on the small platform, she stood high yet alone amongst this group of customers. The men sat transfixed by the events unfolding in front of them. Both men stood in the traditional Weaver stance with one foot slightly forward and the pistol held in the extended right arm and pulled across the chest with the left arm. The weaver stance was side on and exposed the left shoulder to the enemy, a narrower target to engage. The left hand gripped the bottom of the right hand round the pistol grip. The left elbow bent but low making a solid platform and providing an additional barrier to an attack to the ribs and side. Hicks and Pol held their pistols high with their lights running down the sight line, where the men looked the pistols pointed. The men in the room could easily see the weapons in that eerie red light.

"We have come for the girl, if no one moves, no one gets hurt!" Pol shouted.

"Rhianna, come with us" Hicks spoke in his normal menacing calm.

She stepped down from the display platform and walked the few paces across the floor towards the men.

As Rhianna walked towards them Pol became aware of the door at the other end of the unit opening. He swung round and levelled his pistol at it. As the door opened he saw a figure step through the door and into the red light of his head torch. The figure was Kharon Khan. Kharon's right hand went behind his back. Pol knew what he was doing "Don't do it" he shouted at Kharon. The room watched Kharon as he pulled the old Tokarev pistol from his waist band. Pol recognised the pistol immediately, he recognised the threat that the Soviet bloc pistol represented. The door was twenty feet away from Pol. The Browning was not an accurate pistol.

Pol selected a chest shot instantly and pulled the pistol onto Kharon's sternum. The browning barked twice. The concussion in the small room was deafeningly loud. The first bullet struck Kharon in the base of his rib cage. It tore through the soft cartilage of the sternum and expanded quickly into the familiar mushroom shape as the impact forced the hollow point to open and peel back. The pressure wave in the wake of the bullet opened a temporary wound cavity where all of surrounding flesh was smashed and torn. This included the bottom of Kharon's heart, both ventricles were smashed. The bullet exited through the young man's back and continued into the door. The second shot was ten centimetres higher than the first. Again the bullet smashed through the breast bone and ripped through the chest cavity above the heart. The wound cavity from this shot ripped open the young man's aorta and the top of his heart was as smashed as the bottom. The second bullet struck the inside of one of his vertebrae. This caused a marked deflection of the bullet which exited from the side of Kharon's rib cage.

The bullet, now deformed and expanded had lost its superb

ballistic qualities and tumbled through the few meters until it smashed into the bloated beer gut of one of the men sat in the room. There was no deep penetration just enough to rip open his abdomen and tear his stomach open.

As Kharon Khan dropped to the ground in the darkness, red blooms of blood on his shirt front, Jarminder Begum started to scream. The pain from his stomach was excruciating.

With Rhianna pushed behind them and facing the men in the room Hicks and Pol slowly backed towards the stair case.

"It's on fire" Rhianna shouted. Both men turned to look what Rhianna was shouting about and saw the orange glow of flames in the stair well. The smoke had started to build and they knew it would be a matter of time until they would not be able to leave by the stairs.

The young man Ibby, which Khan had dropped off earlier in the evening saw his opportunity to become a hero in front of the senior people in his network. He grasped a beer bottle by the neck and taking the second of distraction when Hicks and Winchester had looked at the stairs as an opportunity he leapt from his seat and tried to close the gap to the two armed men. As he got up he drove powerfully with his legs. He saw how smoothly Hicks turned to him. He saw the pistol come into the bottom of the red torch beam. He had taken only two strides when the Beretta's report rung through the room. Ibrahim didn't feel the sledgehammer blow of the pistol bullet as it smashed through his nose and through his medulla oblongata. The bullet continued through him and smashed into another watching man's face

Steve Wash

striking him in the cheek bone. Ibrahim cashed to the ground, his chest fell hard on to the platform in the centre of the room.

The two injured men screamed out in agony. Smoke started to fill the room from the increasing inferno below them.

Pol turned, he took hold of Rhianna by the shoulder. "Let's fucking go".

He pulled her forcibly onto the stairs. Taking a deep breath he bounded down the stairs. Behind him he heard four further pistol shots.

When he got to the concrete he was greeted by the inferno. The sofa was well ablaze and the one adjacent to it had also ignited, both spewed clouds of black smoke. One breathe of this and he would be down, he knew it. He bounded across the floor and out of the doorway.

As they had planned before he sprinted across the car park and back to the cover of the bushes all of the time he dragged Rhianna with him.

"Thank you, thank you" she repeated over and over. Hicks crossed the ground a second later.

"Fuck man, that went pear shaped" Pol said to Hicks.

"We got her out alive. That was a success. I don't think killing them fuckers could even be counted as collateral damage." Hicks replied, both men stripped off and put their clothes and equipment back into Hicks' holdall.

"Let's get the fuck out of here" Pol said.

330

Looking back over to the blazing unit several men had got out and were running to their cars. The fire was quick and strong, the soft furnishings burned with a savage ferocity that send clouds of black noxious smoke through the unit.

Rhianna, Hicks and Pol made their way along the stream and to the bridge where Mangham road crossed the small water way. They climbed out of the undergrowth and got onto up onto the pavement. Behind them they heard the roar of the fire as it had grown and enveloped the whole unit and had started to ignite the cars parked outside.

The Ford was parked on Mangham road. "This is ours." Hicks pointed at the Ford.

"Ok, what about CCTV?" Pol asked him.

"Yeah, none of that here."

"Are you sure?" Pol asked.

"Oh yeah, quite sure" Hicks added.

Hicks crouched down and reached behind the front wheel and on the suspension arm, as arranged, he found the keys.

"Right, lets fuck off" Stu unlocked the car and they all climbed in. As they moved away a fire engine passed them in the other direction.

They drove in silence, each in the labyrinth of their own thoughts.

Chapter 16

Nearly a week had passed since the excursion to Rotherham.
In the first hours after his return home Pol had expected the
knock at the door of the local police. He had burned his
clothing, showered and scrubbed his fingernails and hair.
There were no forensics, no gunshot residue to be found by
the scenes of crimes officers, no matter how well they
looked. The following morning he sat and watched to local
news. The story was shown. He had been amazed to see the
local Detective Chief Inspector had stood in front of the
cameras and informed the media that there had been a tragic
accident at the unit where a business meeting had been
taking place. Twelve people had died in a fire. Leading
lights of the South Yorkshire business communities and a
great loss to the inclusive community of Rotherham. Pol
knew it would only be a couple of days until the pathologist
found evidence of the gun shots. Then it would be ramped
up and the media circus would start, the murder of twelve
people would be a huge story and some fucker would have
to pay for this. Someone would have to carry the can and go
to gaol, there would need to be a scapegoat. Every morning
of the week Pol got up to watch the Sky news before work.

As the week progressed Fleur began to notice this more and
more. On the Thursday morning she came down stairs to
speak to him. He sat on the leather sofa with just his boxer
shorts and a tee shirt on. Curled up beside him on the sofa
was his Labrador gun dog. Fleur walked into the room and
shooed the dog off the sofa.

No mention on the local news of the fire. By now it would be out. By now the pathologist would have recovered the bullets and they would be at the ballistics lab in Wetherby.

"What is it, Pol?" Fleur snuggled in closely to her man, she rested her head on his shoulder.

"You know I went for Rhianna?" he spoke softly, he did not avert his eyes from the screen as he spoke. As if removal of eye contact equated to removal of culpability.

"Yeah, sure, I know you got her back."

"Yeah, we did, you know the fire that's been on the news?" Pol continued to watch the screen

"I saw it on the news, was it you?"

"Yes it was," pol turned and looked at her he searched her deep brown eyes with his. She saw the sadness and pain in his eyes. "Twelve people died, Fleur."

"I know." She stroked his face with the back of her left hand.

"I shot and killed two of them." Pol spoke quietly.

"They wanted to rape and abuse that little girl." Fleur spoke.

"He had a gun and I shot him twice". Pol continued as if Fleur had not spoken.

"The bullet shot through and hit another bloke, it split his gut. I could smell it, his stomach was ripped". Pol's voice shrank, he struggled to contain his emotions. "The fire was an accident. I think Styx killed more of them as we went. He isn't stable"

"Well when this is over don't have anything to do with him" Fleur said.

"When this is over I might have to go to prison for fucking twenty years". Pol said.

"Good looking boy like you will be popular in there." Fleur got up to walk to the door and as she did she gave Pol a wink. "Best get ready for work, home boy," and blew him a kiss.

Pol climbed in the shower and got himself together.

Pol was only in the station for a few minutes when his boss came into his office with two mugs of coffee. "Morning Sergeant"

"Morning Inspector, how are you this morning?"

"I am well thanks, Pol. Are you alright? You have been really quiet this week"

"Yeah, I am a bit tired, Phil". What did the inspector know or want?

"Seen that job on the news, about that business meeting?" The Inspector asked.

"Yeah, for sure. Since that we have lost a couple of our prominent players. Kharon Khan and Tariq have disappeared." Pol continued.

"I wonder if they were there. South Yorks are telling us that lots of the people in the fire were shit bags of the highest order".

"Who knows, Guv', it is difficult to know. No one has been reported missing from this side". Pol continued the chat.

"No and I suspect that they won't ever be reported. Hey Pol, have you fitted a new light to your bike?" Pol had not fitted a new light to his bike, it was a weird thing for Phil to say.

"Do you want to come out and have a look?" Pol said.

"Yeah for sure, can do" the inspector winked and nodded.

Pol was unsure of where he stood with his boss. He didn't know where he stood at all. The sand shifted under his feet all of the time. Hicks seemed to have support in what he was doing in Rotherham. There was the information that Black had given him about the corruption ring. Pol could only trust Fleur. The two men walked into the car park and the mutual distrust was clear to both men.

"Phil, what is it?"

"The mayor, Ranjit Quereshi is missing."

"Right, when was he last seen?" Pol's stomach lurched.

"He saw the Superintendent on Tuesday. He was alright then". The Inspector said.

"Ok, maybe he has gone away on business?" Pol asked.

"Yeah, maybe. But his family contacted us. He didn't go home last night."

"Is he reported as a misper? Is he just out shagging somewhere?" Pol asked.

"No he is not a misper, we don't know where he is. We need to find out where he is."

"Yeah, ok, I will get some guys on it." Pol said.

"No Pol, this must be only you. You must report only to me on this. It is confidential."

"For fuck sake Phil! It's all fucking shit." Pol turned on the Inspector.

"What's up Pol?" The Phil had been taken aback.

"Secrets this... report only to me that... I don't know what to do, who to trust." Pol was on the edge.

"Look Pol, the deal is simple, those people that died in the fire were all villains and all associates of our lawfully elected town mayor".

"Phil, let's go out for a coffee, plain clothes, no radios. Man to man"

"Ok Pol,"

Both men returned to their offices and took off their uniforms. Mobile phones and radios were left locked in desk drawers.

They went to Frankie and Benny's diner. They sat down at a table and ordered a coffee each.

"Phil, we have known each other a long time. Do you trust me? Put aside what people may have told you recently. Do you trust me? It is a simple question."

"Yes Pol, I trust you implicitly. I would take you to war".

"Ok, Phil, I am going to talk to you about stuff now that you can never repeat. If it ever came out the damage to the force would be crushing". Pol's stomach fluttered with nerves.

"Ok, go on" Phil encouraged Pol to speak.

It was over an hour later they emerged from the diner. They returned to the station together.

As they drew into the station Phil turned to Pol. "You know, you can trust me, I won't say anything".

Pol looked over at his mate. "I know, you can trust me too."

Pol put on his kit and headed to the Mayor's house. When he stopped the patrol car outside of the mayors house he text Hicks.

Sms conversation:

Pol: Have you got him

Hicks: Yes

Pol: Meet

Hicks: Ok. Normal place 6 tonight.

Pol had a sinking feeling, the weight on his shoulders seemed to increase and drive down on him harder and heavier. He took a deep breath, cleared the messages from his phone and went to the house to go through the pretence of investigating a missing person.

Two days earlier the world as Ranjit Quereshi knew it had fallen down around him. He was used to a comfortable life of civic receptions and free lunches. He was held in high esteem by many and treated with sycophantic deference within the town. He had left the police station where the Chief Superintendent had served him a coffee and biscuits. Slowly he had walked down Corporation Road to the car park. He basked in the attention that he received. People passed him in the street. "Hello, Councillor" … "Good afternoon Mr Mayor" he heard all of the greetings and replied with an arrogant assurance. Business acumen had made him what he was. Given him the resources to buy the Audi. The foundations of his business, the suffering and the exploitation, the drugs and the whores, the squalor and the rivers of tears of loss meant nothing to Quereshi. To him business was business. After all his community was not hurt by the ripples of his business interests.

The Audi A8 was a sleek black car, wide, low, powerful, black. The windows were tinted black. The powerful engine was quiet and refined when driving around the town. The car moved with the effortless quiet grace of a big cat. The narrow streets and alleys were a challenge to manoeuvre the car through, but Ranjit knew that. He didn't care for him it was all about showing what he had achieved and the prohibitive price label of the A8 had guaranteed its exclusivity.

There had been an option of a keyless opening but Ranjit had not gone with that option. He liked the Audi key. He liked to be able to put it on a table and make it clear that he owned the big Audi outside.

As he walked towards his car he pulled the key from his pocket and unlocked the car. A drunk sat on the ground near the car. There was a puddle of fluid on the ground around the drunk and his grey trousers were wet. He pissed himself. Ranjit could not see the face of the drunk because of the hood of his top. He could guess this was just another homeless white trash waster. Ranjit reached and opened the door of the car and the drunk staggered to his feet. As the drunk got to his feet he lurched and fell against the Audi.

Quereshi stepped around the open door and towards the drunk. "Get off my car, this is worth more than your life". He spat at the drunk. Before he turned to move away the drunk was transformed. The drunk's weight transferred onto the balls of his feet. His left arm shot out and slid under Quereshi's right arm with the forearm hard against the older man's elbow. Quereshi looked down to see the latex glove on the drunk's left hand and in the right hand of the drunk he saw a flat black object. He recognised it as the blade of a knife, sharpened on both sides this was a dagger.

"Get in your car and move over to the passenger seat". Hicks spoke for the first time.

"Do you know who I am?" Quereshi asked.

"Of course I do, that is why I am here". Hicks replied in his matter of fact tone.

Hicks applied pressure to Quereshi's elbow and pushed against the joint. The sharp pain scalded up his arm.

"Ok, I am going."

The old man sat in the driver's seat and then shuffled over into the passenger side of the car.

Hicks slid into the car beside him and shut the door.

As Hicks sat in the car he pulled his hood down. He turned to face Quereshi.

"Do you know my face?" He asked Quereshi.

"I have seen you in the town, I have seen you out jogging." The mayor looked at Hicks.

"Yeah that's right. Now pass me your phone". Quereshi did as he was asked. "I saw you on Saturday, ok hold your hands out like a Christian prays", again the older man complied immediately. Hicks used a plasticuff and bound him tightly at the wrist. "Do you know why I am here?" Hicks asked Quereshi.

"Do you want money?" Quereshi asked.

"It's funny, that's what Tariq said, just before he died. No your money won't help you."

"What do you want?" Quereshi asked.

"It's a funny thing. How this all has come to be. Now we have to pay our dues and payback is a motherfucker"

The keys to the Audi were still grasped in Quereshi's hand. Hicks reached forward and took them from his fingertips.

As Hicks drove out of town and towards his lock up in

Santon he spoke to Quereshi. "This is a nice car, I bet it is pretty thirsty though".

"Yes, I think it only does about twenty to the gallon. But that doesn't really bother me much".

"Oh listen to your arrogance, you can't help yourself even now when your life is sliding away". Hicks shook his head. "I wonder if you can learn some sort of humility before this is over"

Hicks took the Audi straight into the lock up. He closed the door behind him.

"Ok, old man, we are here. This is the end of your journey". Hicks laughed at his own joke.

"I am an important person, you know? The police will be looking for me. They will want to know where I am. They will come looking and they will find you".

"Yeah for sure, let's just wait and see shall we? I don't think they will be so bothered, they know that you are a child abusing bastard and they know that you are in the drugs supply company. They won't mind if you disappear. To them it will be worth it. It will be for the greater good." Hicks climbed out of the Audi and walked to the passenger side opened the door and grabbed the small, slim, old man by the shoulder. He pulled the old man to his feet.

"This is a very nice suit, old man. I bet it makes you irresistible to women. Especially the younger ones". Hicks stood in front of Quereshi and lifted his right hand. Quereshi shied away, he thought that Hicks was about to hit him. "It's ok, why would I hit you?"

Hicks stroked the creases out of the tailored suit and straightened it out.

Quereshi looked around himself. He stood on plastic sheeting, the walls were lined with plastic sheeting. A single wooden chair stood in the centre of the plastic sheet under the harsh, bright white, two meters in front of the chair was a tripod and a small video camera. "What is this all about?" Quereshi said to Hicks.

"We are going to spend a couple of days together and during our little man break together we are going to chat about a few things. When we chat we will video it so that the world can see you for what you are."

"I will not tell you a thing".

"Well that's funny, because that is what Tariq said, anyway, please take a seat." Hicks motioned for Quereshi to take a seat in the single wooden chair. As the old man sat down in the wooden chair. Hicks turned his back on his captive and made his way to the large plastic box. He returned with a reel of silver duct tape and walked back across the sheeting.

"I don't want you to go for a stroll, do I?" Hicks taped Quereshi's legs to the chair. Hicks took hold of Quereshi's arms he pulled them straight down and taped his wrists onto the back legs of the chair.

Hicks left Quereshi taped to the chair. He left the light on. Quereshi sat on the chair and waited. He watched the door of the lock up and waited for Hicks to come back. He had no concept of what the time was. There was no natural light in the garage. There was no reference for him. The fear had started to creep into him. The more he had time to dwell upon his fate the more the shadow of fear spread its wings. Quereshi waited on the chair. He needed to urinate. He had sat and held it. As the unknown passage of time continued to run the need grew higher and higher and Quereshi became desperate. Finally there was no choice for Quereshi, he let his bladder go. The urine ran from him and pooled on the seat. The urine stained his trousers dark. He was a proud man and he felt ashamed as he sat in a pool of his own urine.

It was Wednesday morning before the door opened in to the unit and Hicks came back into the lock up. As he walked into the unit the smell of urine hit him. "Smells in here, Ranjit." Quereshi did not reply to Hicks. "Like some old vagrant has been here." Hicks continued. He walked up to the chair and to the old man. "Did you get caught short?"

"What time is it?" Quereshi asked.

"I bet you must be getting peckish now, well that's ok, I have bought you a snack". Ranjit was hungry and thirsty now.

"Yes I am and a little bit thirsty"

"Ok, that's cool, I have bought us a bit of a snack, after all we are in this together. Well you are in it anyway. In the piss puddle". Hicks reached into his bag and pulled out a pop bottle.

"Here you go, Ranjit. Have a drink" Hicks unscrewed the lid of the large plastic bottle and offered it up to Quereshi's lips.

Quereshi drank deeply. The black currant juice was stronger than he would normally make it but it quenched his thirst.

"Here, have some nuts," Quereshi opened his mouth and Hicks poured in salted peanuts. Quereshi chewed and swallowed the nuts and more were offered to him, which he also ate. "They are a little bit salty, have some more drink." Hicks placed the bottle back to Quereshi's lips and again he drank deeply.

"Right I will see you a little later, maybe today or maybe tomorrow." Hicks picked up the peanuts and bottle of juice and placed them back in the carrier bag.

Hicks turned the chair away from the door. Quereshi would no longer be able to see the door. Now he would only see the concrete of the wall.

"Are you going to talk to me about things?" Quereshi spoke to Hicks, he wanted some sort of contact. Hicks smiled to himself.

"We can talk another time. But what I want you to do is to think about what you have done. I want you to think about what you have done to those girls, to my niece Rhianna and all of the others."

"I didn't know she was your niece, I wouldn't have done it". Quereshi begged.

Hicks turned his back and walked away from Quereshi.

The blackcurrant squash that Hicks had given to Quereshi was heavily laced with salt. Hicks had made the squash so strong to disguise the taste of the brine.

Quereshi sat in his chair and stared at the wall in front of him. As the minutes and hours passed by the salt in Quereshi had worked upon his system. He had initially become very thirsty and this had turned to desperation. He dozed as he sat on the chair, the dehydration took control of his mind. The dreams came lurid and powerfully to him. He had not dreamed for many years and now the dreams were flooding over him in bright lurid torrent of awareness. He dreamed of a girl, he didn't know her name, he had never known her name. She was dead now. He would never know that her name was Jasmine. He dreamed of jasmine dancing. In his dream she started as the girl he had seen in the film, dressed as a white whore with make-up and wearing the underclothes of a whore. She danced like one of the women on a western pop video. As he looked at her she changed. Her face melted and morphed and moved and changed into the face of her mother. It was the face of his mother when she was a young woman, when Quereshi was just a little boy. In the dream he cried and he called for his mother, called for her like a child calling for his mother. She had been dead for many years and now he could see her drifting in and out of the dream dancing girl's body and face. The transformation was complete and the dancing girl had become his mother, she listened to his call and turned to him. When she got close to him she bent down to him, he was looking up to her from his small boy's perspective. Her beautiful face was only inches from his beaming with the happiness and pride of a mother. He looked at her eyes, but there was something wrong with them. He looked closely into her eyes. They were the eyes of the dancing girl. They were the eyes of the nameless lost girl, Jasmine. She spoke. "Ranjit, wake up now. Ranjit, you have been sleeping" as she spoke he could see something in her mouth. When she said his name the second time he was entrapped by the movement in her mouth. He saw it move and two long hinged legs appeared from the corner of her mouth. As she completed her sentence a huge dark spider pulled itself free from her mouth. Quereshi awoke.

"Time to wake up, Ranjit." It was Hick's voice that spoke to him. His mother had slid away into his subconscious.

Ranjit Quereshi awoke from his slumber and was overwhelmed by pain in his kidneys and the desperation of thirst. Hs eyes slowly adjusted back to the bright white light.

"Let's have a chat now shall we?" Hicks said.

"Yes, yes a nice chat would be nice yes." The confusion of Quereshi was clear. He was more confused than Hicks had hoped.

"Would you like a drink of water, Ranjit?" Hicks asked.

"That would be good, please. Please can I have a drink?"

Hicks produced a small plastic bottle of mineral water. He slowly unscrewed it in front of Quereshi. He placed the bottle to the old man's lips and poured t into his mouth. The water flushed into Quereshi's system and he drank deeply from the bottle, he did not let any drop from his lips.

Steve Wash

Hicks stood back and waited. The water hit Quereshi's
stomach. The cramps overwhelmed him and he cried out
with pain. He leaned forward in the chair. The sudden
rehydration shocked his system and the pain he suffered
was intense. The shudders and the pain left Quereshi and
sank forward in the chair breathing deeply.

"Ok, let's have a chat then." Hicks turned on the camcorder
and zoomed in on Quereshi. Fortunately the camera did not
record smell the old man. He was soiled and wet with urine.

"Who are you?" Hicks asked.

"I am Ranjit Quereshi, the mayor".

"What did you do last weekend?" Hicks asked.

"What?" Ranjit asked confused.

"In Rotherham, Ranjit?" Said Hicks.

"I went there because I did a deal where I got a white girl for
my friends."

"What do you mean?"

"I got her for my friends to have sex with."

Over the next two hours Ranjit Quereshi spoke at length
about his business. Quereshi told Hicks about the
exploitation of many girls, how it was videoed and how he
sold the videos across the country. He spoke about his drug
business. Every word he said was recorded by Hicks. When
he had finished Hicks gave him two more bottles of water.
Quickly his body was rehydrated and he became fully lucid

again.

"What happens now?" Quereshi asked.

"Well you have just admitted all sorts of things on tape. I don't think you will be safe. Think of the shame on your family."

Hicks turned and walked from the unit. The memory card from the camera in his pocket.

The old man wept, his head on his chest.

Pol walked up to his meeting point, Hicks was waiting for him. They walked together away from the pool and in to the town.

"I have Quereshi" Hicks spoke quietly.

"What have you done?" Pol asked.

"I needed insurance and I wanted it to stop, there can't be another Jasmine or Rhianna. It must stop". Hicks was intense and focussed. Pol watched the animation in his hands and in his face. Hicks was living a mission. He was caught in the operation and seemed unable to get out of it.

"I have uploaded it in a generic server shell script."

"In a fucking what?" Pol had never heard of this.

"I have to log in every week or an email is sent to the chief constable, the BBC, Sky news and several other agencies. That video tells the world about what has been happening in this town. Ranjit is the star and the show."

They walked on quietly and Hicks took Pol into an alley way behind the pensioners' flats on Thompson Street. There was a Vauxhall Astra parked in the alley with the tell-tale Enterprise car hire sticker on the bumper. Pol knew this was the car.

"Stu, where are Di and Rhianna?"

"They are safe now, I have an old buddy in the Highlands, I met him when I was in Arbroath."

The men drove out of town and towards Santon. Hicks had not taken Pol to the unit before.

When the door to the unit opened the smell hit Pol. He saw the old man taped to the chair.

"Jesus Christ, Sticks, what the fuck are you doing?"

"This is ok, I am stopping this fucker doing his sick thing. This is about looking after the poor kids". Hicks said easily.

"Fucking what? This shit wants sorting out."

"We are going to sort this out now." Hicks said.

They walked past the Audi and onto the plastic sheet. Pol instantly understood that the plastic sheet was to overcome any forensic examination. The wooden chair could be burned. But Quereshi had seen both of the men and would recognise them again. There was no effort to conceal the identities of either Pol or Hicks. All three of them understood that this meant that Ranjit Quereshi was never going home.

"Ok, Ranjit. How will we sort this out?"

"I have been thinking about this whilst I have been here today." Quereshi had regained his composure.

"My family can never know, I cannot go on."

"No that's right, you can't". Hicks agreed.

"I will tell my wife I have gone to do business in Pakistan. But I can't be found."

Hicks reached into his pocket and pulled out the black bladed dagger. He cut through the tape on Quereshi's wrists. He rubbed his wrists and stretched out his fingers.

"Thank you"

"I will give you your phone, but you know the deal. Do what you have to do and then give me your phone back."

Pol stood back and watched the drama unfold. The two men had formed a sort of allegiance. Pol knew all about the Stockholm syndrome, but he had never seen it before. He didn't realise that they would both share the identity of a joint destination. Even though they both knew that the destination is the death of Ranjit, one of the 'team'. Ranjit took the phone from Hicks and wrote the text to his wife. Without any further direction he passed the phone to his captor, his partner in this final endeavour, Hicks read through it and pressed the send button on the phone.

"Ok, let's go. Time is getting short now. We have to get out there?"

"Will it hurt?" Quereshi asked.

"No, I will make sure it doesn't"

Hicks removed the bonds from Quereshi's ankles and assisted the old man to his feet. After nearly forty eight hours tied to a chair he was unsteady on his feet.

"What day is it?" Quereshi asked.

"It is Thursday evening." Pol replied.

Greater Good

"I didn't know." Quereshi replied.

The three men got into the Astra and left the compound. They sat quietly and eventually when the men approached the village of South Ferriby, some ten minutes later, the first person to speak was Ranjit. "It was just business."

Pol looked over at Hicks, he could see his anger welling up. Hicks was silent.

"I was only satisfying a demand." Quereshi continued.

"It's time to be quiet now." Pol said to him.

"But if I didn't satisfy that demand, someone would." Quereshi continued.

"Not long now Ranjit." Hicks said to him.

Hicks drove down through Barton and to the old disused wharf on the Humber.

The Humber is a huge river, the estuary is a mile across at Barton-Upon-Humber. The brown silt laden estuary was subject to savage tides and currents. They made the river very dangerous to navigate and the ships queued up to file up the estuary to reach the industrial ports of the Trent.

Standing at the side of the estuary on the old concrete wharf the three men looked at the brown swirling tidal ebb.

Quereshi looked across at the city of Hull, the traffic on the other side of the river was just visible. He was alone in his thoughts. He wasn't ready to go. He had made no peace with himself and his realisation had come too late for him.

The hum of the traffic on the bridge was a constant droning. There was no distinction between the cars.

Whilst Quereshi watched the traffic going past Hicks put his hand in his trouser pockets and pulled out his black bladed knife. With fluid speed of movement he stepped forward and squatted behind the old man. His right hand flashed across behind the Quereshi's feet. The blade had swept through both of Quereshi's Achilles tendons. The cut was so sharp and so quick that Quereshi's first awareness was as he toppled over. There was no pain from the deep slices and very little blood. As Ranjit toppled forward Hicks placed his hand in the small of the old man's back and pushed him forward into the powerfully ebbing tide. The current took the old man and as he dropped into the water he was pulled straight under the surface and away from sight and away from the light.

"Why the cut, Styx?"

"Try swimming with floppy feet".

Chapter 17

"What the fuck is going on?"

"We didn't expect this to happen." Mr Green spoke quietly, he looked in to the dark depths of the espresso.

"It has turned into a fucking blood bath, your so called asset is a fucking liability". Mr White was calm, his eyes showed the extreme anger that he felt.

"I want them neutralising." White continued.

"Can I come in on that?" It was the first time Mr Black had spoken during the meeting.

"Yes, please tell me something I want to hear." Mr White focussed his inescapable fury on the junior agent in the meeting.

"I am sorry, Mr White, I have nothing positive I can give you. I need to show you a video that I have been given by Hicks. He gave it to me when we cleaned up Quereshi's car."

Black placed his lap top on the table. No one spoke as he opened the lap top and started to open the programs. Green was pleased that the ice cold, hard glare of White was falling upon someone else.

The video was the confessions of Ranjit Quereshi. The post script by Hicks explained how the video was lodged on various servers on the net and should he fail to log in to the server then the video would arrive in influential inboxes around the globe.

"Fuck. Can we find the video online?" White asked Black.

"It will be very difficult, we have people on it, but this guy Hicks is pretty smart. We are on it." Black replied.

"How long?" White demanded.

"Difficult to say, an hour, a month or a year." Black replied.

White leaned back in his chair. He puffed out his cheeks as exhaled. "Ok, the important thing is to get him off the streets and get rid of him somewhere far away and dangerous. I will talk to the agency and we can send him abroad."

"Ok, as soon as we hear from the agency I will see him. I will stay in the area." Agreed Black.

"Yeah, I will email you as soon as I know, probably before the end of the day. I want him gone in two days".

"The more difficult one is the police sergeant". Green observed.

"Yeah, what do you know about him?" White asked.

Green continued, "He is waiting for an operation on his ankle. We could get that done this week for him and then get him pensioned out of the police as soon as possible afterwards?"

White looked interested "Ok, that sounds promising. Can we do it?"

"Yes but I will need to have the spend on the private health care authorised by the department."

"Yes, that is no problem. I will authorise that now. Will he stay in the area?" White was far calmer now.

"I doubt it, he holidays in North Wales and he is from that area, I think he will go there."

"Ok, I want you both to keep me posted."

Fleur picked up the post from the doormat, as she did every other morning. Pol was at work he was on days again this week. He left the house at seven, just after delivering her a mug of tea and a kiss to keep her going through the day. She had done her chores and sat at the table enjoying a coffee and checking the mail. She quiet liked Monday morning. She loved Pol but also liked to be able to crack on in the house on her own. A bank statement, a few pieces of junk mail and a letter from Sheffield hospital addressed to Pol.

Sms conversation

Fleur: Hey sexy. Letter from hospital shall I open it? Xxx

Pol: Yes please xxxx

Fleur: Ankle op day after tomorrow it's a cancellation xxxx

Pol: Fuck

Pol sat in his office chair. He had been waiting for the operation for months. Now he had it with two days' notice. He walked up stairs and spoke to his boss.

"Hey Phil,"

"Morning Pol, how are you doing?"

"Yeah, I am ok" they looked at each other with the tired acknowledgement of their shared secrets.

"Boss, I am having my ankle op in two days".

"Hell's bells. That's quick."

"Yeah it is a cancellation" Pol placed a mug of tea in front of the Inspector.

"Well I guess that you will be off for a while then?" The Inspector felt a sympathetic relief for Pol and even a spark of envy at his friend being away from the world of hypocrisy.

Neither of them knew that it had already been decided that Pol would not be returning he would be pensioned out of the force.

At the same time the conversation was happening between Pol Winchester and Phil Robinson another conversation was occurring between. Mr Black and Stuart Hicks.

Hicks had been handed an envelope by Black. He had examined the contents.

"So you want me to go back to Guatemala?"

"Yes, the drugs trafficking has really taken off again in the last twelve months. We want you to go in there and get embedded. Report intelligence to us." Black replied.

"Your wife and the girl, her niece, will be moved to a house on the edge of Dartmoor, near Oakhampton." Black continued.

"I have been to Oakhampton, back in the day." Hicks paused. "What sort of money?"

"We will put fifty grand in your account if you agree today, then in a fortnight when you leave, another fifty grand. Then subsequently another twenty grand a month."

"How long?"

"Maybe two years, then you can retire, we will ensure there is a sufficient lump sum in your account so you can be comfortable".

"Ok, I am in". Hicks stood and shook Black's hand.

Black smiled "Good, now we no longer meet your new handler's details are in the papers".

Black knew that as soon as the electronic security experts had tracked down the video of Quereshi on the internet then Hicks would be neutralised.

Stu Hicks and Pol Winchester's paths had crossed and now had diverged again. Neither man knew but they would cross one more time.

Made in the USA
Charleston, SC
19 April 2016